The
Eagle
Stirs Her
Nest

The Eagle Wings Series

The
Eagle
Stirs Her
Nest

Linda Rae Rao

Fleming H. Revell
A Division of Baker Book House
Grand Rapids, Michigan 49516

Published by Fleming H. Revell
a division of Baker Book House Company
P.O. Box 6287, Grand Rapids, MI 49516-6287

Printed in the United States of America

Library of Congress Cataloging-in-Publication Data

Rao, Linda Rae, 1943–
    The eagle stirs her nest / Linda Rae Rao.
        p.   cm.— (Eagle wings series)
    ISBN 0-8007-5607-X
    1. Texas—History—Republic, 1836–1846—Fiction. 2. Frontier and pioneer life—Texas—Fiction. 3. Texas Rangers—History—19th century. I. Title. II. Series: Rao, Linda Rae, 1943–   Eagle wings series.
    PS3568.A5957E24   1997
    813'.54—dc21   97-8774

For current information about all releases from Baker Book House, visit our web site:
                        http://www.bakerbooks.com

To my dear nephews, Scott and Chris Griscom,
two fine young native Texans

Acknowledgments

Special thanks must go to Anna Wilson Fishel, not only for her editorial expertise, but her prayers and encouragement during the development of this book. She has truly been a blessing. The efforts of each of the staff members at Revell responsible for production of this volume are also appreciated so much.

Having been a long-time resident of Texas, I wanted the historical details for the setting of this story to be as accurate as possible. In addition to the normal avenues of research, I want to thank our dear friend Faye Roten of the Burnet and Marble Falls area for sharing her extensive collection of material about the frontier years of Texas, as well as her personal knowledge of this beautiful area of the state.

Thanks also to Greg "Doc" Bradburn for taking time out of his hectic schedule of teaching/mentoring the student athletic trainers at Willis High School to help in this research.

As always, without the loving support of my husband, children, and other family members, it would be impossible to devote the time and energy necessary to write at all. I'm so thankful for them.

Prologue

Boston Harbor basked in the brilliant spring sunlight of late April. As he stepped down from the carriage, Gibson Dunmar thought the clang of harbor buoys and screech of wheeling gulls seemed more noticeable than usual. Then he realized it was the sullen quiet that hung heavily in the salt air. Instead of the bustling activity that had enlivened this busy seaport just months before, Dunmar could see clusters of unemployed dock workers and sailors standing about. Some murmured among themselves, others wandered about aimlessly. Many just leaned against the brick walls of boarded-up businesses and stared blankly. In their faces he could see the frustration and hopelessness that had set in over the past few months since the financial calamity everyone now called The Crash of 1837.

In his early forties, Gibson Dunmar was of stocky build with hazel eyes and sandy blonde hair touched lightly with grey at the temples. The slight wrinkles at the corners of his mouth and eyes were evidence of a pleasant disposition; however, his square-jawed face was sober now. It had been months since a smile had exercised those creases. He too felt careworn and weary, an all too common feeling these days.

Dunmar climbed the steps to one of the few buildings along the street that remained open. The sign on the door read Macklin, Macklin, and Kendall Shipping, Ltd. He pushed the heavy door open and could see that this once flourishing shipping company had been forced to cut back the size of its staff considerably.

The jingle of a small bell over the door brought a lad of about fourteen from one of the offices. A broad smile of recognition brightened. "Uncle Gib," the boy greeted, his dark eyes shining with admiration.

The uncle took his nephew's extended hand in a firm grip and clapped him on the shoulder. "Chad, my boy, 'tis only a month since last I set eyes on ya," he declared in a deep Scottish brogue, "and you've grown another four inches taller. What's my sister feedin' ya, lad?"

At first Chadwick Macklin blushed but then was pleasantly surprised to realize he was now almost as tall as his uncle.

"If it was only his mother, it'd be one thing," came a deep voice from behind them.

James Macklin, Chad's father, stood in the doorway of his office. His six-foot-tall frame seemed much thinner than the last time Dunmar had visited a month earlier. His broad shoulders drooped slightly and his dark hair seemed more generously streaked with grey. The elder Macklin smiled, but the Scot could see that his dark eyes were filled with that same weariness Dunmar had seen in so many others.

"What? Ya mean his sisters continue to spoil him to death?" Dunmar grinned as he tousled the boy's dark hair.

James smiled sympathetically at his son. "Having three older sisters coddling a fella can get a bit tiresome at times, heh, Chad?"

"I sympathize with ya, lad." Uncle Gib smiled. "I remember what it was like growin' up with your mother and your Aunt Sophie both bein' older'n me. Could be mortally tryin' sometimes."

10

Pleasant greetings aside, the three stood for a long awkward moment. The pendulum of the old clock on the wall steadily ticked away the seconds as if measuring the silence. From the desk in the corner of the office came the scratching of the clerk's quill as he prepared a ship's manifest. Down the hall that led to the warehouse, they could hear the sounds of heavy crates being moved about. The sound of a dull thud accompanied by muffled oaths demanding greater care with the cargo broke the strained silence.

"Come in and sit down, Gib," James invited.

"Thanks, James, but I've just come from your house and said my good-byes to Hannah and the girls."

Chad looked down at the wooden plank floor as he tried to swallow the lump in his throat. He'd known this day had been coming, but he'd been hoping for some miracle that would change his uncle's mind.

"Is it Texas, then?" James asked soberly as he stepped away from his office doorway to stand beside his brother-in-law.

"Aye, it is." Dunmar nodded. "It's been a year now since they won their independence from Mexico. The place is a new land of promise. It'll be a chance like our parents had, James, to help build a new republic."

James nodded in understanding and glanced at his son staring miserably at the floor. Dunmar followed his brother-in-law's glance. A slight breeze stirred through an open window carrying the distant clanging of the buoys as he studied his nephew a moment.

Clearing his throat, he addressed the lad. "You listen to your father and your Uncle Alex now. They're two of the smart ones who kept their heads about 'em when everyone else was gobblin' up those British investment loans. And who knows," Dunmar continued, "maybe someday ya'll sail one of your dad's fine ships right into Galveston Bay and come see how I'm makin' out down there!"

The lad forced a smile. He knew his Uncle Gib had thoroughly discussed the matter with his father and his Uncle

Alex, the Macklin twins, who had tried to talk him into joining their company in the wake of the country's financial disaster.

Gibson Dunmar's decision had caused some to question the Scot's sanity. Yet many understood. He'd certainly suffered enough to disturb anyone's sensibility. Not only had the man lost a once thriving stock brokerage in the financial crisis, he had also recently endured the devastating loss of his wife to influenza. Without a doubt, Chad's uncle needed to find something to make his life worth living again, a challenge so big it would require all of his mental and physical resources to meet it. To Dunmar, the new Republic of Texas sounded like the perfect answer.

1

Although still early morning, the sun-washed air of the Texas summer was already oppressively hot. A few hand-held fans and the swishing tails of horses and oxen coaxed what little movement of air there was.

"Let this date of June 18, 1841, be marked down in our history books as the day the Republic of Texas launched forth on its first expedition for expansion!" President Mirabeau Lamar's words were nearly drowned out by the cheering of the crowd surrounding his small wooden platform.

Sarah Preston, a pretty sixteen-year-old with wavy light-brown hair, stood at the edge of the crowd. Shading her blue-green eyes from the blistering sun, she stepped forward to hear better. She was having a hard time joining in the excitement of the crowd. She wished she could share the enthusiasm of her twelve-year-old brother, Luke, who was jumping up and down beside her, whooping and hollering with the rest. But she couldn't. All she could think about was their father, Thomas Preston, who was setting off on a long journey across hundreds of miles of desolate country inhabited by Comanche and Apache Indians into territory still controlled by Mexico.

In spite of the noise, Sarah's thoughts turned to the earlier comments made by one of her father's friends. "A fool's errand," he had grumbled. "Our astute President Lamar hasn't the foggiest clue that Mexico isn't about to let the good citizens of Santa Fe join our republic. He's sending these men into the very jaws of death for a far-fetched notion that he hopes will divert attention from his carelessness with the Republic's treasury."

Her father had later explained that this man was a Sam Houston supporter and always critical of Lamar. He assured her that there was little to worry about, especially since the expedition would have a large military escort. Thomas Preston's excitement had been contagious.

"This one journey could open up a wonderful opportunity," he had explained to his two children. "We can regain all we lost back home in Virginia when my bank collapsed four years ago. The people of Santa Fe want us to come. There's a great potential for the business there. They just need the outside encouragement to help them declare their independence from Mexico and merge with Texas."

The excitement Sarah had shared then was now swallowed up in a terrible sinking feeling as President Lamar stepped down and the young Texan heard the first drum rolls. In a moment, a fife, bugle, and two clarinets joined the drum in a jaunty march heading down the main street of Austin, and the whole caravan began to move. Riding in the lead were the official commissioners representing the government of the Republic along with the commander of the two-hundred-seventy-man military escort. Merchant supply wagons heavily loaded with goods to be sold in Santa Fe followed.

This last detachment to leave Austin would travel twenty miles along the old military road to join the main body of the expedition now camped on Brushy Creek. Gathering the necessities had taken longer than expected, and they were leaving a month later than planned. Now they faced a trail that had been baking in the hot Texas sun. The grass was already withering and the water holes were drying up. Still, excitement and optimism surrounded the entire expedition.

Sarah quickly moved to the right and stood on her tiptoes to search for her father. Before long, she spotted him waving from the wagon of their neighbor, John Brookes. Brookes had sold his farm and talked Preston into investing nearly every penny from his fall corn crop and hogs into this wagonload of pots, pans, and farming tools. Brookes believed that the profit from this one load would enable them to open two dry goods stores, one in Austin, the other fifty miles northwest in the small settlement of Burnet.

As the dust began to obscure the sight of her father, Sarah fought back hot tears, and she glanced at her mother. Mariah Preston was waving the white embroidered hanky her husband had given her. When she felt her daughter's hand on her arm, she quickly brushed away Sarah's tears. "Everything's going to be all right, dear," she declared, nearly convincing herself.

"Of course it is," Sarah agreed, trying to sound cheerful for her mother's sake. "Look at Luke. He's still trying to convince Father to take him along, I think."

Mrs. Preston watched her son, who had run up alongside the wagon. She chuckled. "If your father would let him, I think he'd walk all the way to Santa Fe rather than have to stay behind with us womenfolk."

As the two women watched the caravan stretch out on the trail toward its rendezvous point on Brushy Creek, a slender man with a droopy black mustache approached them. Touching the wide brim of his tall-crowned hat, he greeted them with a polite smile. "Howdy, Mrs. Preston, Miss Preston."

"Hello, Captain Anderson," Mariah replied.

"Will you and the young'uns be stayin' in town tonight?"

"No, we're heading back home soon. We're riding along with the Hammersmiths."

The captain combed the ends of his mustache with his fingers. "Good," he said. "As I told your husband, Mrs. Pres-

15

ton, I'll be sending my Rangers by to check in on y'all from time to time. If we can do anythin' for ya, just give a holler."

"Thank you, Captain, we will," Mariah said.

Touching the brim of his hat again, the man walked over to speak with a group of people standing in the shade of one of the trees along the street. Many folks continued milling there talking long after the last wagon disappeared in a trail of dust.

After a short while, the three Prestons joined Mr. and Mrs. Hammersmith for the return trip to the farm. Randolph and Martha Hammersmith were the Prestons' closest neighbors. Their son, Dolph, was part of the Santa Fe Expedition. Randolph Sr. had fought alongside Sam Houston at the Battle of San Jacinto in 1836 and was a very strong, proud man. Randolph Jr. was one of the soldiers providing the military escort for the expedition. Sarah would miss him too. The eighteen-year-old was a tall, handsome young man with blonde hair and blue eyes. Rather shy, he was very serious-minded and polite. While they weren't exactly courting, Dolph had come right out and told Sarah he intended to ask her father for permission to come for social visits when he returned.

The Hammersmith farm lay thirteen miles up the Colorado River on the Austin-to-Burnet road. The Preston place was another two miles farther. The two families traveled steadily along the narrow, dusty trail heading to the village of Burnet. As the wagon plodded along, Sarah studied the landscape around her. How different it was from their home in the gently rolling, green hills of Virginia.

One of the first things she had learned when they had arrived in 1838 was that Texas was a land of contrast and variety. To reach their new home, the family had traveled through the salt grass marshes of the coast and then on through the dense pine forests where lush vegetation flourished in a mild but humid climate. Traveling farther west, they had crossed a broad rolling plain of thick prairie grasses dotted by small hardwood forests. The farther they had trav-

16

eled, the drier the air. Finally, they had reached their destination in the hill country that lay between the coastal prairies and the vast stretches of dry western plateaus and high plains.

Today their trail led northwest from Austin toward the Preston farm, winding through rocky hills dotted with cedar brakes, sycamore, hickory, and several varieties of oak. Patches of blooming prickly pear cactus and low mesquite trees appeared over long stretches of thin, rocky soil. Yet, in typical Texas contrast, the landscape also offered broad meadows of bright wild flowers and waist-high prairie grass hinting of rich black soil just waiting for a farmer's plow.

As the wagon bounced along, Sarah thought about their comfortable white-framed, two-story home back in Virginia with its wide porch and surrounding flower gardens. She still missed it. The transition to a small log cabin with its rough wooden plank floor had been difficult to say the least. However, over the past three years, the cabin had grown from the one main room to a fair-sized structure consisting of two bedrooms, one for Sarah and one for her parents, with a sleeping loft for Luke. A wide breezeway called a *dogtrot* connected the bedrooms with the kitchen. A covered front and back porch had been added to run the length of the house and, during the long summer, much of the family activity took place there where they might take advantage of a cool breeze.

Even though the Prestons' Virginia home had been a quarter mile out of Culpepper, their nearest neighbor had been just down the lane. In fact, the neighbor's rooftop had been visible from the Prestons' front porch. The only neighbors visible from their porch now were the animals. White-tailed deer grazed beneath large live oak trees where squirrels scampered along the massive, dark limbs. An occasional coyote would lope across the meadow toward the river or howl in the night. For the Prestons' daughter, this adjustment to the solitude of their new home had been the most difficult change to manage.

That night, the party camped along the banks of Canyon Creek, a branch of the Colorado River. The mood of both families was very subdued, leaving no one feeling like small talk. By late afternoon the next day, they had reached the wagon track turning off to the Hammersmiths' farm. The Hammersmiths turned onto the trail to their farmhouse and bid them good-bye.

The shadows grew longer as the sun slipped closer to the hills along the horizon. The Prestons had two miles left to go, but they could still make it home before dark.

Sarah noticed that her brother had picked up his short musket and laid it across his knees. She felt certain the serious expression on his freckled face meant he was doing exactly what Thomas Preston had told him to do just before they had left their cabin. "Son, you're the man of the house now while I'm gone," their father had instructed. "Keep an eye on everything."

Luke carefully studied the shadows cast by trees and rocks. Sarah was reminded how, as a six-year-old back in Virginia, he had imagined himself a fearless Indian fighter. Today he had that same determined look, only now there was the possibility they really might see Indians!

As they rode the final stretch home, Sarah wondered if her mother was feeling the same anxiety they all had felt when first settling here three years ago. An outbreak of Indian trouble with the Comanches before the Prestons had arrived to claim their new home had put everyone on edge. For the first month, one of the four of them had stood guard with a musket while the others worked. Even Sarah and her mother had been taught how to shoot the muzzle loader. Even though they'd been the ones to stand guard when Mr. Hammersmith and Dolph had come over to help raise the cabin, they had not had to put the muskets to use for anything other than hunting—yet.

Part of the reason for this was a strange Indian legend. The Indians believed that the ghosts of Coronado's men lurked in the hills surrounding the Prestons' valley. Three hundred years before, the Spanish soldiers had been victims of an Indian attack, and the Indians believed their ghosts were waiting to wreak vengeance on any Indians who dared to venture into the valley. Thomas Preston was not depending on some legend to protect his family in their isolated location, however, so he insisted that they keep a constant vigil.

Slowly but surely, over the past three years, Sarah had become accustomed to her new home. But with the absence of her father now, some of the old apprehension was returning. The reality of their vulnerability was hard to ignore, especially since the Indians were not the only danger they faced. Just two days before, Sarah had heard the blood-chilling scream of a cougar from the ridge above the old hog pen. Her father and Luke had found a faint trail that had quickly disappeared over a shelf of limestone swept clean by the wind. Before he left, Thomas Preston had assured his family that the big cat was more afraid of them than they were of it. "The rattlesnakes and scorpions are more of a danger than that cougar," her father had explained.

By now shadows were beginning to deepen beneath the ancient oaks that stood like massive sentinels keeping watch in the meadow beyond the north side of the cabin. As the wagon rolled into the farmyard between the house and barn, the western sky was ablaze with color. The threesome was greeted by the barking of Pepper, a black and white shepherd/coyote mix, named for the sprinkling of black dots across his white face.

Hector Medina, Pepper's master and their one and only hired hand, appeared from the corral and waved a hello. Small in stature, his silver hair framed a dark bronze face so wrinkled and weathered that, at first glance, he appeared to be a hundred years old. Looking closer, the bright sparkle in his black eyes indicated such a lively spirit within, it was difficult to guess his true age.

19

"Buenos tardes, Prestons," he called out with a wave of his straw hat.

"Good afternoon, Mr. Medina," Mariah Preston returned as she reined in the team. "No problems while we were away, I hope."

"No, Señora, but—"

"But what?" Mrs. Preston echoed as she climbed down from the wagon seat.

"Smoke, Señora. This morning, along the cliffs on the other side of the river," he answered pointing to the north-west.

"Friendly Tonkawa or Comanche campfire?" she asked uneasily as she handed him the reins.

The man shrugged his shoulders and waved off toward the river that lay only a hundred yards to the southwest of the cabin.

"I never see them, Señora, but I think they move on west. No sign they cross over. But we will keep sharp eyes."

"Yes, very sharp. Better put the horses in the barn instead of the corral tonight. No sense leaving tempting bait out if they are Comanche."

Medina agreed as Luke helped him unhitch the waiting team.

Later Sarah was returning to the house after drawing a bucket of water from the spring. Stepping up onto the back porch, she walked to the west end to look out at the river. The flaming colors in the sky, so brilliant moments before, were quickly fading to a warm lavender pink as the summer green of the hills was dissolving into a deep blue silhouette. Sarah set down her bucket and stood there listening to a mocking-bird sing its evening song. The girl searched the cliffs upriver toward the northwest for any sign of the smoke Hector Medina had seen that morning. She prayed fervently that if the Indians out there were Comanche, they would move on to the southwest and steer clear of the expedition's trail. For some inexplicable reason, Sarah feared more for her father's safety than for their own. She told herself that with the military escort, he was protected much better than they were here. Yet it didn't seem to help. She knew he was traveling well over a thousand miles across terrain that only the Comanche and Apache Indians knew well, into territory held by Mexican soldiers still resentful over the defeat at San Jacinto and Texas Independence. Anything could happen. Were they really being sent into the "jaws of death" as that friend had warned, just for some political whim or material gain?

"Sarah, dear." The sound of her mother's voice calling from the kitchen door startled Sarah out of her anxious thoughts. "If you'll bring the water in, I'll get dinner started."

As she picked up the heavy bucket, the girl took in a deep breath of the warm evening air. She knew she must shake this feeling of dread.

2

"What does a Texas Ranger actually do, Uncle Gib?" Chad Macklin asked as he and his uncle slogged through the ankle-deep mud across the main street in Houston.

The young man resembled his father, with dark brown eyes, dark hair, and strong, handsome features. The seventeen-year-old had also reached a height of six-foot-two, nearly five inches taller than his uncle.

"Well, lad, I s'pose ya'd say the main purpose of the Texas Rangers is to protect the good citizens of the Republic from attack by Indians, Mexican soldiers, and outlaws."

"Indians? You mean President Lamar hasn't kicked all of them out of Texas?" Chad asked, shifting his duffle bag to a better position on his shoulder. With each step the mud sucked at his leather boots making them feel like ten-pound weights.

They made their way around a wagon bogged down in the muck. The load of workers on the way to the new hotel being built at the end of the street noisily resisted the driver's demands to get out of the wagon and push. It was hard for Dunmar to hear Chad over the din they raised. Once past the noisy crew, he glanced over at his nephew. The scowl on Chad's face as he repeated his question made Dunmar shake his head.

"I know what you're talkin' about, lad. There are others, not many but a few, who're unhappy about the way the Cherokees and the rest have been pushed out of Texas. Sam Houston's one. Cherokee Chief Bowles was his good friend. But it's not the Cherokees or the Delawares or Shawnees or Caddos or any of those eastern bands I'm referrin' to. The Comanches are the ones causin' the biggest problems. Especially since the Council House Fight last year in San Antonio."

"What was that?" Chad asked as he skirted an ominously deep looking puddle of muddy water.

Joining his nephew on the other side of the puddle, Uncle Gib hesitated before explaining. "It seems a group of Comanche chiefs gathered to meet with Texas officials to discuss terms of a treaty. It ended up in a fight with thirty-five of the Comanches—mostly chiefs—dead."

Chad made no reply as they finally reached their destination and stopped in front of the livery stable door. Stepping through the open double doors onto dry, solid ground, they stamped most of the thick mud from their boots. After the two men had paused a moment to watch the other people navigating the sloppy street, Dunmar said, "I was very sorry to hear about your Uncle Ram. I never cared for President Jackson myself, and after what he did to the Cherokee people in Georgia when he blatantly disregarded Justice Marshall's Supreme Court ruling, I think even less of him. But he does have a lot of support for his views."

"Yes, he does," Chad agreed grimly.

Dunmar turned from the street scene. "How's your Aunt Marianne doin', by the way?"

Chad fought back the anger that still boiled within when he thought about his Uncle Ram's recent death. "Not well," he replied, following his uncle down the wide aisle between horse stalls.

"What was Ram doing down in Georgia anyway?" Dunmar asked. "Why wasn't he still at the mission at Mercy Ridge?"

23

Stopping in front of a stall where a fine palomino stood, Chad held out his hand then began to stroke the animal's face. "When news came that the Cherokee eviction from Georgia was going to take place in spite of Marshall's ruling, Uncle Ram went down there to help Aunt Marianne's sister and brother-in-law. He couldn't do anything to stop the confiscation of the family plantation or house. We were told he lost his temper and got in a fight with one of the Georgia Guard and was thrown into the stockade. He died there. We're not sure if it was injuries from the fight or scarlet fever that actually killed him."

"'Tis a terrible disgrace, that whole business," Dunmar sighed gloomily, his Scottish brogue as thick as ever.

After a long moment he shook his greying head and motioned for the boy to follow him farther along the stalls. "We do have a bit of a different situation here with the Comanches though. They're feistier than your Cherokee and Delaware cousins. They've shown no inclination to settle down as farmers or let anyone else in what they claim as their territory." He stopped in front of a stall with two saddled horses.

Chad dropped his duffle bag beside the stall door. "It doesn't seem to matter one way or the other, does it," he remarked angrily.

Without a reply, Chad's uncle pointed to the smaller of the two horses. Standing a fraction less than fifteen hands high, the line-back dun was a creamy grey with dark stockings. His dark mane and tail were coarse, almost bristly. The head was shorter and less refined than the thoroughbreds Chad was accustomed to.

"Here's your horse, lad. His name's Digby." At first Chad thought his uncle was kidding when Uncle Gib pulled back the door. "He's ornery as the day is long, knows every trick in the book, but bein' a mustang, he's swift and strong enough to run all day with little effort. Once ya let him know who's boss, he'll do fine. Just keep on your guard with 'im and you'll have no problem."

Curious, Chad studied the mustang with a wary eye. "Where'd he get a name like Digby?"

Dunmar crossed his arms across his broad chest. "When I was a lad my father sent me to Edinburgh for school. The headmaster there was a mean ol' curmudgeon. He'd walk around the classroom calm as can be and, outta the blue, whack the back of a lad's head with a ruler just to make sure he was payin' attention. His name was Matthias Digby. This fella here sorta reminds me of him. You'd better pay attention or he'll find a way to make you wish you had."

Chad put his hand out to stroke the mustang's nose, but the horse laid back his ears and bared his teeth in warning.

"So is this the way it's going to be?" Chad addressed the animal. Digby snorted. "Well, as long as you're wearin' the saddle, fella, I'm the one in charge. I suppose it'd be too much to expect you to just accept that right off?"

The mustang snorted again and stamped an impatient hoof. Chad gave a wry side-glance at his uncle who was leading a tall bay gelding out of the stall. "That's a fine horse, Uncle Gib. Appears to be calm and well behaved."

"That he is, lad." Dunmar grinned broadly. "Chester here's a fine fella, although not quite as excitin' as ol' Digby there." Pointing to the outfitted saddle on the mustang's back, he continued, "You're all set with the standard gear we Rangers must have."

Uncle Gib indicated each item as he spoke. "There's a Mexican blanket and a gum coat rolled up behind the saddle. A rifle's in the scabbard, a pistol and knife in the saddlebag. That pistol's one of the new six-shooter Colts. I think you'll be surprised by it. Your ammunition's in that wallet there on the side. I'm countin' on your good aim to provide us with some decent game for supper on the trail."

Chad was pleased with the compliment. At seventeen, he had already begun to show this skill on hunts with his father and uncles in Virginia and Kentucky. "I don't think I'll be needing to use your knife though, Uncle Gib. Grandfather Macklin gave me his."

"Well now, that's a handsome gift for a young lad," the Ranger responded as Chad pulled the knife from the scabbard in his boot. "Could that be the knife your grandfather, Andrew Macklin, carried during the Revolutionary War?"

"The same," Chad replied, holding the carved handle out for inspection.

"You've a proud name, lad. Your grandfather must think you'll continue the honorable tradition."

"I intend to do my best," the young man pledged as he returned the knife to his boot.

Gibson picked up Chad's duffle bag and laid it across the back of his bay's saddle. "Chester better carry this for now, just in case."

Wondering what Dunmar meant, Chad watched his uncle lead the big horse past him and toward the doorway of the livery. Calmly, he reached for Digby's reins. "We wouldn't want to change your name to Crowbait, would we?" he warned as he eyed the bared teeth.

Perhaps the calm in this young stranger's voice made Digby curious, for the ears twitched forward and the lip-curling stopped. Chad had been around enough horses on his Uncle Robert's thoroughbred farm in Virginia to know this was only the beginning of the testing of who was going to be boss. Sick and tired of being coddled by three older sisters and wanting to experience some real challenges to test his mettle, the boy had a feeling he'd just encountered one challenge that, if not handled carefully, could very well end up breaking his neck.

The two men and their horses stopped in the doorway to look out at the muddy street. Off to their right, the workmen had now climbed down from their wagon and were pushing it out of the deep muddy ruts. Several passersby on the boardwalk across the street paused to watch and call out rowdy words of encouragement.

As they watched the men clear the way, Chad was struck by the reality of actually being in Texas. The voyage from Boston to Galveston to visit Uncle Gib had been pleasant, the mid-summer weather causing Chad's ship no problems. In previous years, he had sailed with his father to such places as the West Indies and England and Spain, but somehow the sea did not hold the fascination for him that it did for his father. Although the young man suspected that his father already knew that his son's dreams did not lie in carrying on the Macklin name in the shipping firm, Chad had been reluctant to admit it. He knew he was the one most likely to someday take the helm, yet he felt almost trapped in a too neatly planned future.

When his cousin, Jeremy Page, had come from the family farm in Kentucky, Chad saw his chance. Jeremy was the son of Chad's Uncle Stephan and Aunt Christiana Macklin Page. He had come to Boston to try his hand at the shipping business. The two cousins discovered they shared a common desire to experience worlds not conquered by their fathers. Seeing how well Jeremy fit in at Macklin, Macklin, and Kendall, Ltd., Chad dared to express his desire to visit the frontier of Texas.

For nearly three years, the boy had been fascinated by the letters from Uncle Gibson about his adventures as a Texas Ranger. Now, here he was a young man at last, preparing to make the two-hundred-mile ride west across open prairie and rolling hills to Austin, the remote capital of the new Republic. His blood fairly raced with excitement.

Anxious to begin their journey, Chad was glad when his uncle nodded toward the wagonload of workmen. "Well, there they go on their way. Let's be on ours."

Chad eagerly turned to Digby and placed a foot in the left stirrup ready to swing up into the saddle. However, the mustang hopped sideways away from him, catching him off guard and sending him splashing down into the muddy street. Wet and dirty, Chad picked himself up, not sure if he was more put out by the cantankerous mustang, his own lapse of caution, or his bruised pride. After all, the horse had followed his leading, so he hadn't expected any more trouble.

Wiping wet mud from his face and looking down at his trousers soaked with muddy water, the New Englander was glad he hadn't yet changed into the new buckskins made by his Aunt Marianne. Chad scowled at the horse that was standing stock still inside the livery door staring at him to see what was going to happen next. The group of townspeople who had moments earlier been watching the workers push their wagon out of the mud were now snickering at him. Realizing how foolish he must appear, the young man resolved that this would be the last time Digby was allowed to embarrass him so.

"If you and Digby are goin' to play games all day, we'll never get off," Dunmar chided with a grin as he jammed a muddy boot into the stirrup and stepped up into his saddle.

Chad pulled his feet free of the gummy mud and stomped toward his horse. The mustang's ears twitched back and forth as he watched his rider approach. The animal stood perfectly still, the very picture of good ground manners, waiting for his master.

The young man picked up the reins, the ends of which were now well coated with mud. "If you're expecting a beating like some people might think you deserve, you can rest easy," he assured the animal through gritted teeth. Digby's shoulder muscles tensed and his ears laid back. "But you're not going to beat me either. I'm going to ride you and that's that."

The mustang's ears came forward, yet his body stayed tense as Chad stepped up into the stirrup. Before Chad could swing his leg over, however, Digby abruptly started walking off. Chad had expected this and settled into the saddle, his right foot quickly finding the other stirrup, ready to urge the horse forward. The young man was not going to be caught off guard again. Digby seemed to sense this and responded obediently to his rider's signals.

The two men stopped at a small inn on the edge of town to get cleaned up and have some breakfast before starting out. Although the sign over the door hailed the place as *Houston's Palace,* the dining room was only large enough for three small tables. Two keys hanging on hooks behind the desk just inside the front door indicated only two rooms on the second floor. A crudely painted sign that said *Bath 25 cents* hung over the back door. Chad discovered the bath house was a lean-to shed with a large wooden tub concealed by a curtain and a rain barrel filled with water heated by the sun. Regardless of the primitive conditions, Chad was refreshed by the bath and joined his uncle in the dining room dressed in a cotton shirt, comfortable buckskins, fringed knee-high moccasins, and his new buckskin jacket.

"Ya even look like your Grandfather Macklin now," Dunmar remarked as the boy sat down.

The proprietor of the inn set down plates of ham and eggs in front of the two men. "The lad looks like he belongs here more than you do, Ranger Dunmar," the man drawled good naturedly. "Always wearin' that dark suit and white shirt—"

"I've been wearin' suits like this ever since I started wearin' long pants as a lad in Scotland," the Ranger broke in. "Why should I throw out a perfectly good wardrobe just because I no longer sit behind a desk?" Dunmar picked up his fork.

Chad soon discovered that although the Palace was rustic with rough-hewn wooden floors and furniture, everything from the crisp checkered cloths on the tables to the Mexican pottery plates was surprisingly clean. The eggs, scrambled with chopped green chili peppers and onions, were deliciously spicy and accompanied by thick slices of ham and corn bread.

After their hearty breakfast, the two travelers bid the innkeeper good-bye and headed down the road out of town.

They passed other travelers in wagons and on foot, most coming into town to sell their wares of handwoven blankets, pottery, straw brooms, and the like. Drawing close to a narrow bridge over a muddy creek bed, Dunmar surprised his nephew by ordering him to stop and turn Digby off the side of the road.

The boy stopped, but before he was able to move off to the side, the mustang began nervously side-dancing and tossing his head. Chad reined him close, but the horse snorted and turned in a circle fighting the bit in his mouth. As the young man concentrated on bringing the agitated animal under control, he heard his uncle calling out in Spanish to a man leading a horse across the bridge. Dunmar reined his bay in between Digby and the man on foot who quickly hurried by.

"What's wrong, Uncle Gib?"

"Just hold him, lad," warned Dunmar. "Don't let him near that fellow."

Digby squealed, shook his head, and began crow-hopping toward the creek. Chad held on tight. He'd had one mud bath already; he wasn't about to take another one in this creek. Suddenly, the horse's wild gyrations stopped, his nostrils flaring and his sides heaving. Prepared for more bucking, Chad leaned forward slightly and gently patted the horse's sweaty neck, speaking in a low, calm voice. In a moment, the animal shook his mane and made a low grumbly noise in his throat as if to say he was all right now.

Dunmar rode up next to him and grinned. "Ya handled that well."

"Thanks," the nephew replied. "Now, do you mind telling me what that was all about?"

"I bought Digby from a horse trader over in Goliad," Uncle Gib explained as he led the way across the bridge. "He'd been badly mistreated and was nearly starved to death. I honestly didn't think he'd last the week. Figured I was wastin' the money. But there was somethin' in the animal's eyes that

30

made me do it anyway. As ya can see, he recovered very well, but every time he sees a Mexican man who reminds him of that trader, he goes crazy like that and tries to go after him."

Once across the bridge, Chad drew up next to his uncle again. "Are there any other little bits of information I ought to know about him?"

The Ranger shook his head, then smiled broadly. "One thing."

"What's that?" Chad asked warily.

"Whenever ya cross a stream, don't let him stop because he likes to paw the water and splash it up on himself and you too."

With this last bit of advice, Dunmar spurred the bay into a lope, and the two adventurers headed west toward Austin and the challenges the new Republic of Texas had in store for them.

Dear Family,

I hope this letter finds you well and happy. Arrived in Galveston today, September 16, 1841, after a smooth voyage. I was brought by ferry to Houston. The weather is clear and very hot. Uncle Gibson is looking well and sends his love. We have made camp for the night on the prairie about twenty-five miles northwest of Houston on our way to Austin. This prairie seems to roll on forever just like the sea, with an island of trees here and there. I made a new acquaintance today. His name is Digby. He's one of those mustangs we've heard about. Tell Uncle Robert that even after all of the temperamental thoroughbreds he's trained, this animal would test his patience more than he could imagine.

There's too much about this place to tell in a letter. I'll try to keep track of everything in my journal and tell you when I get back home.

Give everyone my love, Chad

3

A gust of wind sent a rustling wave through the cornfield where Sarah and Luke elbowed their way along the rows plucking ripened ears. Sweeping up from the Colorado River, the fall breeze was a welcome breath of cool air on the hot September morning. Their cornfield grew in dark, rich soil deposited by the slow but relentless river current about four feet above the wide waterway on a limestone shelf.

There had been little rain this summer, so Thomas Preston and Hector had built a bucket lift that swung out over the water's edge four feet below. With this they were able to irrigate the thirsty corn by drawing water up from the river and pouring it along the shallow ditches running between the rows. It was a laborious job, but a bountiful crop had been the reward Sarah and Luke were now harvesting.

When the bags hanging from straps over their shoulders were full of corn, the twosome climbed the steep, rocky trail up to a bluff fifteen feet above the cornfield. On top, the land stretched northward in a fan-shaped valley between two ridges of high hills. Clusters of oak, sycamore, and pecan trees created a narrow band of woods that ran the length of the western hills and across the narrow northern end of the fan. This band of trees stood like a gate separating the valley from a wide rolling plain and more hills beyond.

The Preston farm encompassed a fourth of this small valley, over three hundred acres. For now, it was more than enough to support the few head of cattle they had purchased from the sale of the last pieces of the Preston family silver.

Reaching the top of the bluff, Luke slipped the heavy bag's strap off his shoulder and set it down. Using a grimy shirt sleeve, he wiped the perspiration from his brow. "Sarah, do you think they've reached Santa Fe yet?"

Sarah untied the strings of her blue bonnet and removed it to let the stiffening breeze blow through her damp, wavy hair. "Maybe. Father said he thought it'd take all of July and most of August to make the journey. September's nearly over."

"Do you think I've been doing a good job lookin' after things?"

Sarah looked over at her little brother and knew he was leading up to something. "Yes," she answered warily.

"But there's nothin' really to show it," Luke replied, scuffing the toe of his brown boot in the dust. "Except maybe a full bin of corn. And you've done half of that!"

"Well, don't worry; Mother and I will tell Father what a good job you've been doing." His sister smiled and tied her dust-covered sunbonnet back in place.

"Look at those clouds movin' in over the hills, Luke. Maybe we're finally going to get some rain. Let's get back so we don't get caught."

"But, Sarah." Luke couldn't let the subject drop so easily. "Don't you think it'd be great if there was something that I could show Father?" Avoiding his sister's studying gaze, he continued, "He might think you and Mama are just takin' up for me. But if there was something, something *special* that would prove I've been doin' a man's job."

"What are you working up to, Luke Preston? You've got something on your mind. What is it?"

The boy hoisted the full bag of corn onto his shoulder and fell in step as they headed for the barn.

"Well," he paused a moment, "I heard that old cougar callin' again early this mornin'. If you could help me convince Mama to let me go hunt down that old cat before it gets a calf or one of our hogs, Mr. Medina could help me dress out the skin and it'd be all ready by the time Father gets back. Then there'd be real proof that I kept my promise."

Sarah smiled at her younger brother. His freckled face was dirty and streaked with perspiration; his blue eyes implored her earnestly. She had rarely been able to resist such pleading from the time he was a round-faced toddler, but this time the request was out of the question.

She gently replied, "You know Mother has told you to forget about hunting that cougar. It's too dangerous. Father would have a fit too if he thought you were even thinking about it. So we'll just have to think of something else."

"But, Sarah—" he protested again, stopping on the stone path.

"No, and that's final," she declared over her shoulder, walking on without waiting for him. "Even Mr. Medina says it's too dangerous to go up into those hills."

"He's more afraid of fallin' in a hole up there than he is of that cat," Luke argued with a stubborn frown.

"That's something you should think about too, Luke," she advised. Stopping, she turned to face him. "That, plus bears and whatever else might be lurking about. It's just too dangerous. Those hills are honeycombed with caves and holes hidden by bushes and grass. If you fell into one of those, no one would ever be able to find you. So just forget about it. You can't talk me into helping you convince Mother about this because she's absolutely right."

The boy kicked at a loose stone then walked toward her. "I'm not blind," he grumbled. "I'd be real careful and watch every step. I can do it. I know I can. Mr. Medina says I'm a better shot than he is now. Maybe I could get a bear too."

"There's no use arguing about it," Sarah said flatly as she started walking toward the barn again. "Come on, let's take care of this corn and then you can go see if Mr. Medina needs help finishing that hog pen before it rains."

That evening at the dinner table, Luke broached the subject of the cougar hunt once more but was quickly silenced by his mother. Seeing her son's disappointment, Mrs. Preston held up a morsel of catfish on her fork and smiled.

"You're doing a very good job taking care of us, dear. Look what a wonderful dinner you caught for us this afternoon."

"Listen to your mama, hijo." Hector's leathery face wrinkled into a scowl. "There may be more danger up in those hills than wild animals."

"Have you seen any more signs of Indians?" Mrs. Preston wondered as she passed a pan of steaming corn bread.

"Nothing since that hunting party across the river last week. But, someone else." The man's Spanish accent was heavy.

All eyes focused on the farmhand. Mrs. Preston quickly asked, "Who? Hunters? More settlers?"

"Not settlers," he answered, shaking his silver head. "Maybe hunters. Saw smoke from a campfire this morning."

"How can you be sure they're not Indians?" Sarah tried to subdue a rising fear.

"This afternoon I found something over in the creek that comes down from the springs." The man pulled part of a small cotton bag out of his pocket. It clearly showed the letters *COF* on it.

"It was caught on a twig floating in the creek." Medina handed the material to Mrs. Preston. "You can see it wasn't in the water long. I would say Anglos, maybe hunters of one thing or another. Either way, it would be wise to stay clear until they have moved on."

"You seem to be hinting at something out of the ordinary, Mr. Medina." The woman fingered the material, inspecting it carefully. "It does look like the bags for coffee beans we buy at the mercantile in Austin."

"There have been others, Señora. They are hunters of the treasure." Medina lowered his voice dramatically. Out of the corner of his eye, the man could see Luke watching him closely.

"Treasure?" the boy whispered as if he had never heard the fascinating story before.

Mrs. Preston laughed. "Luke, I'm sure Mr. Medina is tired of telling that legend."

"No, no, Señora," the man said solemnly as he crossed himself to pledge his truthfulness. "It is not just legend. Since I was a small boy, I have heard many stories about the conquistadors hiding gold stolen from the Indians in these caves. Always there are men who claim to have found ancient maps drawn on parchment leading to such treasures. I have seen one myself." Hector's black eyes widened with delight. "Even the Comanches fear the spirits of Coronado's men. They believe they hide in these hills."

"What makes you think these strangers are treasure hunters rather than hunting for game or just passing through?" Mariah asked.

Medina shrugged his shoulders. "There is no way to know, Señora, without going to their camp, which I would not advise. To this country come many families, but also many come hiding from the law. Many very bad men."

Mrs. Preston paid closer attention to this explanation, for her husband had warned that they needed to be wary of strangers. The vast expanse of Texas was a perfect haven for outlaws who could slip easily across the Louisiana border, avoiding prosecution in the United States.

"Whatever they are here for," Mr. Medina's warning broke in on her thoughts, "it is best to stay close until they move on."

"There you are, Luke, another very good reason to forget about hunting that cougar," Mrs. Preston gently reminded her son. "You're doing a fine job here. We'll tell your father how well you've taken on the responsibility he left to you."

Luke ducked his head and poked his fork at a bit of fish on his plate. "Yes, ma'am."

The conversation changed to work plans for the next day. Sarah was glad the cougar hunt idea had finally been put aside.

"Mr. Medina, the children and I are going to carry a sweet potato pie and some prickly pear preserves over to Mrs. Hammersmith tomorrow. It's her birthday. Sarah and I thought a visit and a pie might cheer her up with Dolph away.

"Perhaps it'd be a good idea for you to stay close to the house, just in case anyone happens this way."

"Si, Señora," Medina answered as he pushed back his chair and stood up. "There are several things that need attention at the barn."

"We'll leave at daylight and be back by early afternoon."

4

Gibson Dunmar glanced at his lanky nephew, who had found a comfortable perch on a large exposed root at the base of an ancient live oak tree. He had wondered how the boy would fare in this rugged environment after the civilized and pampered atmosphere of his well-to-do Boston home. The man had been pleased to discover that Chad was adapting with little difficulty. In fact, he appeared to be enjoying the experience.

"Is today September twenty-ninth or thirtieth, Uncle Gib?" Chad asked as he pulled a leather-bound book out of his saddlebag.

"Been a few days since ya wrote in your journal, eh?" the stocky Ranger replied as he picked up the tin coffeepot. "Let's see, must be September 29. We left Houston on the sixteenth and arrived in Austin on the twenty-seventh. Spent yesterday gettin' gear ready for this job and waitin' 'til it cooled off a bit. So, today would be the twenty-ninth."

Chad watched the man add chocolate-brown ground coffee beans to the fire-blackened coffeepot before setting it at the edge of the campfire. The young man then began to make an entry in the journal he had been keeping.

September 29, 1841. We are camped about twenty-five miles northwest of Austin today. The countryside is much different here than along the coast. The air is very dry. The rolling hills are sometimes rocky, sometimes covered with trees and thick grass.

The new capital of Texas has a long way to go before it looks like the capital of anything. Sam Houston was just elected president, but he won't take office until December. Seems Mr. Houston isn't happy that former President Lamar moved the capital from Houston to Austin when he took office. The new president thinks it ought to be moved back closer to the more populated areas of Texas. Right now, Austin has just one main street called Congress and thirty or forty wood-framed buildings set on the edge of town. It's sparsely settled territory. The biggest building in the capital is the president's house, which is a two-story, wood-framed place painted white.

Uncle Gib received his orders yesterday to track down two men suspected of theft and murder. Before leaving Austin, we talked to a man who had witnessed the murder. The victim was an old prospector who had bragged about a parchment map he claimed was going to lead him to a gold treasure. A carpenter working on the roof of a new building at the edge of town saw two men stop the prospector at gunpoint as he was leaving Austin. The old man refused to give up the map without a struggle and was shot. The murderers escaped with the map and the victim's burro. They rode off on a pinto and a black horse with a white face. One of the outlaws was recognized as a troublemaker from Louisiana by the name of Clifton Pruitt. The other was unknown but wore a red plaid vest.

Captain David Anderson is in command of the Austin Division of Rangers. They're shorthanded, so he seemed happy for me to go along on this assignment. I think Uncle Gib's worried about what Mother would say if she knew. I'm glad she and the girls don't know. If they could only understand that this adventure of surviving in this untamed land is so exciting it almost makes me dizzy. To me, it's worth any danger that may come my way.

> We were supposed to have a Delaware scout with us to help track these men, but he's with a Ranger company chasing after a Comanche raiding party that stole ten horses in Austin. The scout's name is Senihele, which means Sparrow Hawk in English.

Chad paused in his writing. "Uncle Gib, I heard Captain Anderson say you've worked with Senihele before."

Dunmar was busy paring pieces from a fist-sized slab of bacon into a skillet of beans. "Met him shortly after I arrived in Texas and joined the Rangers." The older man wrapped up the remaining bacon and returned it to the saddlebag of provisions.

"The Delaware scouts have proven to be the best the Rangers have had, and Senihele is the best of the ones I've worked with. Put him on the trail of Comanches and he's the most determined tracker you've ever seen. I s'pose it's because of his brother."

"His brother?" Chad wondered.

"Aye, he was a scout too. I never met him though." Dunmar began stirring the bubbling mixture in the skillet. "He and Senihele were workin' under Captain Jack Hays over in San Antonio before I came to Texas. It was before Captain Jack got his hands on the Colt six-shooter, and goin' up against the Comanches was mostly a losin' battle.

"The two brothers were ridin' with a small company of men chasin' after a band of Penateka Comanches who'd taken several hostages during a raid along the Guadalupe River."

The light was fading quickly, so Chad closed his journal and laid it aside, then leaned closer. Dunmar settled back for a moment to let the mixture in the skillet simmer.

"Did they catch up to the raiders?" Chad wanted to hear the rest of the story.

"Aye, that they did." His uncle nodded sadly. "There were fifteen in the Ranger company chasin' close to thirty Comanches. Unfortunately the Rangers caught up with them at the same time the raiders were joined by their main war party of nearly a hundred and fifty warriors."

Dunmar sat staring out across the gently rolling hills they'd ridden through that day. Finally, he shrugged.

"We Rangers have a reputation for not hesitating to go up against an enemy that outnumbers us, especially now that we have the six-shooter—it's tilted the whole balance in this running battle with the Comanches in our favor. But they didn't have it back then and the company was nearly wiped out. Senihele saw his brother die at the hands of a brutal warrior known as Antelope Runner. When Senihele tried to go to his brother's aid, Antelope Runner nearly took his scalp. The lad still has a bad scar to prove it. If a large force of militiamen following the Rangers hadn't caught up when they did, no doubt both brothers would've died that day."

"No wonder he's relentless on the trail," Chad remarked.

"Aye, that's why I was a bit surprised the captain assigned him to come along with us on this manhunt." Dunmar pulled out their tin cups and plates. "But he's a good man, and I'm sure you'll find him interestin' to talk to."

"I wish I had practiced with Grandfather Macklin to learn more words in Lenape."

"Senihele has no trouble with English," his uncle assured him as he gave a few last stirs to the mixture in the skillet.

Leaning back against the broad tree trunk, Chad breathed deeply. The aroma of hot coffee bubbling on the fire and beans and bacon simmering in the skillet mingled in the air with the spicy sage and cedar growing nearby. One lone star had appeared in the pale sky just above the western horizon, and a trio of killdeer piped their clear songs as they skimmed low over the edge of the small rock pond a few yards away. It was a screne, restful scene after a hard day on the trail.

Looking back over the past few days, Chad had been impressed with his uncle's stamina. Even more impressive was the elder Ranger's tracking prowess. Gibson proved to have a surprising talent for reading signs along a trail. Chad wondered if discovering this hidden ability had been one of the things that made his uncle consider making the drastic change in his life of striking out into a new frontier. It wouldn't be the first time he had done such a thing.

Chad's mother had told him how after their father's death, her younger brother had left their home in Edinburgh, Scotland, to emigrate to America. Although only fifteen, he had worked out his passage on a ship carrying supplies to British garrisons in Canada. Once there, he worked at various jobs, sending most of the money home to his mother and two sisters. Two years after arriving in Canada, he had worked his way to Boston. Two days after arriving in town, he was on his way to begin a new job unloading brick wagons at the site of a new bank building when he happened upon a man being beaten and robbed. Without a second thought, he jumped into the middle of the scuffle and was able to drive the attackers off, saving the man's life and wallet. In the process, however, his own arm was broken, making it impossible for him to begin his new job.

Out of gratitude for the young Scot's heroism, the gentleman offered him a reward. Gibson refused the reward but asked if the man could direct him to someplace he could get a job that he could manage with a broken arm. The gentleman happened to be the owner of the new bank that was being built. When he learned that Gibson had been educated in Edinburgh, he offered him a job as a clerk in the bank. Over the next five years, Gibson worked hard, proving to have the right combination of good business sense and a flair for taking a calculated risk in the world of investments. By the age of twenty, he had been able to bring his mother and sisters to Boston and provide a comfortable home for them. By twenty-five, he had married Elaine Pembrook, daughter of one of the bank's biggest investors. Her death brought an end to a long, happy chapter in his life.

Chad hoped he would be able to reclaim some of that happiness here in Texas.

Since coming to Texas, Dunmar had used many of the things he had learned from Chad's Uncle Stephan on hunting trips to Kentucky and Virginia. The rest he'd picked up from the Indian scouts and fellow Rangers. He had discovered that survival depended on learning the lessons well and using them expertly.

Earlier that day Dunmar had not been misled when the trail of two horses and a burro seemed to disappear in a shallow creek. He had unerringly turned upstream and showed Chad moss-covered stones that had been turned up, where the moss had been scraped off in places by the shod hooves of the outlaws' animals. Following this scant trace, they had soon come to a place along the bank where hoofprints of two horses and a burro left the water. They had found the remains of a campfire someone had tried to conceal by scattering charcoal and throwing dirt and grass over it. Chad had been further fascinated when the Ranger could tell by the degree the grass and wildflowers were wilted and by the slight smell of smoke that lingered when they uncovered the scattered coals that the outlaws were only a few hours ahead.

Dunmar broke in on Chad's thoughts. "Come and get it, lad. One of my trail specialties, beans and bacon."

Chad's brown eyes twinkled with pleasure. "Smells pretty good."

"I guess a body can't do too much damage to beans and bacon," Dunmar reasoned as he handed a tin plate full of food to the boy. "It's been some time now that I've given much thought to food, other than as a necessity. It's strange; your Aunt Elaine always made sure the cook prepared my favorite foods. Now I've almost forgotten what they were."

Chad caught the glimmer of a faraway look in his uncle's eyes. He quickly cleared his throat. "If we weren't trying to keep so quiet following those bandits, we might have had some of those fat quail we flushed out this afternoon."

Nodding in agreement, the Ranger squatted nearby with a plate in his hands. "If all goes well tomorrow, we'll go fishin' in the river and have catfish and corn bread for dinner tomorrow night. That's my other specialty."

Chad nodded and scooped up a spoonful of beans. "How soon do you think we'll catch up to these two men?"

"With their trail turnin' south again," Dunmar reasoned, "it's a good possibility they're headed for the caves in the next valley. If that's true, we should find 'em tomorrow."

Swallowing another bite, Chad changed the subject. "I'd sure like to meet this Senihele, but I don't know why the Captain thought you needed a scout to help trail these men. You're doin' just fine."

His nephew's comment brought a smile to Dunmar's face and his heart warmed with pride. Although he and Elaine had never had children, he had always had a special rapport with his nephew. Through his forty years, Dunmar had observed that as boys grow to manhood, conflicts can arise between father and son, especially as a young man tries to establish his independence. At such times, a good uncle can provide a stabilizing influence. He was thankful he had been allowed to be in such a position with Chad. It almost compensated for not having a son of his own.

Chad opened one eye as he pulled the colorful Mexican blanket up over his shoulder in the cool damp of dawn. Something had awakened him. Glancing about in the soft grey light he could just make out Digby restlessly snorting and stamping and tugging at his tether. Rising up slightly, the young man cautiously scanned the scene. The mustang was obviously bothered by something.

He saw his uncle rise from where he'd been adding kindling to the coals of the campfire. Rubbing the sleep from his eyes, Chad watched Dunmar walk toward the horses. "Steady, Digby," he heard him say, "it's only a young jackrabbit." Suddenly the man cried out in pain and fell to one knee

44

clasping his right shin bone. Chad sprang up and rushed toward his uncle.

The man gasped, "Careful, lad, it's a rattlesnake! He must've been after that rabbit, for he gave no warnin'."

As the young man reached Dunmar's side, the reptile slithered away into a clump of tall grass and rocks. Chad's first thought was to go after it and destroy it, but its thick diamond-patterned body and the size of the rattle disappearing into the brush told Chad it was a very large snake. Killing it would require more than the sticks nearby and it would be long gone by the time he got a weapon.

The experienced Ranger quickly pulled a knife from the scabbard on his belt and immediately cut his right pant leg. "Got me just above the boot, lad," he gulped.

Chad knelt beside the injured man, took the knife, and finished ripping open the pant leg. Dunmar jerked off his belt and wrapped it around his leg just below the knee as a tourniquet. The man then sank back onto the dew-covered grass with a groan.

"Look at this!" Chad exclaimed. "One of the fangs broke off against the top of your boot."

"Careful with it, lad." The wounded man's voice was already weakening.

Carefully Chad cut the broken fang from the hole in the fabric of the pant leg. It had not pierced through the leather boot.

"I can see one small puncture mark just above the top edge of the leather."

It took a moment tugging at the boot to get it off. Instantly Chad realized the area was already beginning to swell.

"Quick, lad, make a cut across the fang mark so it can bleed freely."

When Chad hesitated, his uncle nodded for him to continue. Taking a deep breath, the young man made a small cut across the one puncture mark. Dunmar moaned in pain as he clutched a handful of grass and earth. The boy then bent down and began sucking the venom and blood from the wound. After spitting several times, Chad heard his uncle.

"Find the small bottle of brandy in one of my packs and rinse your mouth. Then pour some of the alcohol over the wound."

Chad did as he was told. The stinging alcohol in the wound caused Dunmar to grimace in pain again. He clutched his nephew's arm. "By breaking one fang, he couldn't get me with all his venom, but I fear I'm goin' to be awfully sick very shortly."

Already worried by the deathly pallor of his uncle's face, Chad's eyes widened with concern when Dunmar began to shiver with violent chills. The young man grabbed his blanket and lifted his uncle enough to wrap it around the man's shoulders. "I've got to get you back to Austin and to the doctor there."

"To be honest with ya, lad, I don't think I can make it that far. The Prestons' farm isn't far from here, over close to the river. That's the family that the captain told us to look in on, remember?"

Quickly Chad gathered their things, saddled the horses, and helped his uncle into the saddle on the bay. Swinging up on Digby, he urged the mustang into a quick walk and led the bay. It wasn't long before the sun was cresting above the eastern hills and the cool of the early morning had evaporated. Chad removed his hat and wiped the perspiration from his forehead as he watched his uncle gamely trying to fight off the effects of the spreading poison.

At last, the two riders came across a wagon road. They hadn't gone far when Chad saw a horse-drawn wagon with three people heading their way.

Chad waved and called anxiously, "Ma'am, do you by any chance know the Prestons?"

Mariah Preston shielded her eyes from the bright morning sun slanting above the eastern horizon. As the two men drew nearer, she could tell the man slumped over in his saddle was in trouble.

"Yes, young man, I'm Mariah Preston," she answered, reining the team to a stop. "What's the matter with your friend?"

"It's my Uncle Gibson Dunmar," the boy rushed to say. "He's been bitten by a rattlesnake."

"Oh dear," the woman gasped. "Sarah, quick spread that quilt out in the back of the wagon. Luke, let's help get him into the wagon before he falls off that horse."

By this time, Chad had already dismounted and was leading the bay to the back of the wagon. His uncle had little strength left. Together, Chad and Luke lifted his stocky form up into the wagon, and Mrs. Preston and Sarah settled him on the quilt.

The stricken Ranger felt as if his whole body was on fire as he struggled to remain conscious, but he slipped further into a murky haze. Then he felt a gentle hand on his brow. Forcing his eyes to open, Dunmar blinked to see the face of a woman with cool green eyes and light brown hair pulled back neatly beneath a pale yellow bonnet. The image swam in front of him, and with great effort he tried to reach up to touch her face. "Elaine?" he whispered thickly.

A soothing, soft voice replied, "Rest easy now, Gibson Dunmar." Within seconds, the haze darkened around him and he slipped into unconsciousness.

"Sarah, turn the team around," her mother ordered. "We must hurry back to the cabin. Luke, hand me the canteen and the cloth covering that basket."

Chad watched as the girl and boy quickly obeyed their mother. After gathering up the bay's reins, he mounted Digby and cantered beside the wagon, all the while anxiously watching Mrs. Preston bathe his uncle's face with the cloth and canteen water.

It seemed to take forever to travel the mile back to the farm. At last the wagon slid to a halt in front of the cabin.

Hector Medina came running from the barn before the dust had settled to see what had brought the Prestons back in such a hurry.

With Luke and Medina on one side and Chad on the other, they carefully lifted the victim with the quilt and lowered him from the wagon. Then they carried him toward the cabin, following Mrs. Preston and Sarah.

"We'll put him in the single bed in Sarah's room," Mariah directed.

Within a few minutes the stricken man had been settled on Sarah's bed and the Preston women were hurrying about preparing to care for his wound.

Dunmar's leg was discolored like a dark ugly bruise and badly swollen from his ankle up to his knee. As soon as water was heated in the bedroom fireplace, Mariah cleansed the wound. Chad watched her mix a yellow powder from a small crockery jar together with an ointment that smelled like castoreum, making a strong-smelling paste. She carefully applied the poultice and then covered it lightly with a clean white linen cloth.

"He's going to be all right, isn't he?" Chad finally dared to ask.

As Mrs. Preston squeezed the excess cool water from a cloth and placed it across his uncle's forehead, she said, "It's between him and the good Lord now. I've done all that I know to do." She turned around and looked up into the young man's anxious face. "He's survived this far. That's a good sign. He looks strong. Getting struck by only one fang reduced the amount of venom he might've gotten. We'll just have to wait it out now and pray."

Turning to her daughter, Mrs. Preston continued, "Sarah, why don't you take young Mr. . . . ."

"Oh, sorry, ma'am. I'm Chad Macklin. I can't tell you how grateful we are for your help."

"Think nothing of it, Mr. Macklin. Out here we all must rely on each other in times of need. Now, Sarah, take young

Mr. Macklin out to the kitchen and see if he would like some breakfast."

"Thank you, ma'am, but I'm not hungry." Chad realized he still had his hat on and quickly pulled it off.

"Come now, you must keep up your strength," Mrs. Preston admonished. "It won't do your uncle any good if you fall ill. Go along with Sarah now and at least have a cup of coffee and a muffin."

Although Chad felt like his stomach was tied into knots, he followed Sarah out of the small bedroom and across the open dogtrot porch that connected the two separate sections of the cabin. Instead of entering the kitchen, however, young Macklin turned to walk along the back porch that looked toward the river. Suddenly overwhelmed by the possibility of his uncle's death, he knew he needed fresh air more than he needed food.

Sarah watched the handsome stranger as he took hold of the corner post at the edge of the porch. Wanting to help in some way, she went into the kitchen to retrieve a cup of hot coffee for him.

Returning to his side, she offered him the cup. "Here, at least drink this. It might help."

"Thanks." He took the coffee cup and leaned back against the wooden post. Everything that could be done for his uncle had been done, yet he kept thinking there must be something more. Knowing there really was nothing else to do left him with a sense of helplessness. The feeling made him angry.

Sarah empathized with his distress and wished she could think of something to say that might help.

The tall young man closed his brown eyes a moment and shook his head. "It all happened so fast. One minute he was standin' there; everything was just fine." He heaved a big sigh.

A gentle morning breeze riffled through the branches of a nearby sycamore tree and a crow cawed as it circled the cornfield by the river.

Sarah finally spoke up. "Just be thankful you were there to help him. He might not've had a chance if he'd been alone. We just have to pray his recovery will be quick."

Chad studied the young woman for a moment. She was slender with wavy brown hair. Her dark green dress brought out the green in her eyes. There was genuine concern reflected in those lovely eyes and he found it comforting. He took another drink of the hot liquid as he turned to look out over the countryside along the river.

"Are you sure you don't want something to eat?" Sarah didn't want to say much for fear of saying the wrong thing.

"I'm sure. Thanks," the young man replied. "Thanks for the coffee . . . Sarah, is it?"

She nodded and, backing toward the bedroom, added, "I'll go see if Mother needs anything else."

Suddenly, a horse's shrill whinny and angry shouts in Spanish exploded from the yard out in front of the cabin.

"Digby!" Chad declared with sudden dread.

The two young people rushed to the front porch to discover the mustang with ears laid flat, wild-eyed and teeth bared, chasing Hector Medina as if he were trying to take a bite out of the man. Just in the nick of time, the Mexican dived under the corral fence. Digby slid to a screeching halt, then reared up, striking out at the top rail.

Chad whistled shrilly, leaped from the porch steps, and ran after the frenzied animal. "Digby!" he shouted. "Stop!"

In frightened amazement, Sarah watched the young man catch the flying reins and bring the animal under control. The horse settled quickly, and although he still pawed the ground a few times, the incident was over.

Hurrying over to the fence, Sarah asked, "Mr. Medina, are you all right?"

"Si, Señorita, I think I am still in one piece." Medina removed his hat and wiped the perspiration from his face. "Señor, I swear to you I did nothing to him to cause his anger."

50

"I'm very sorry," Chad apologized. "Are you sure you're all right?" Holding the reins tightly, he stroked the horse's neck to calm him down.

Hector replaced his hat and stared at the mustang, who snorted a couple of times. "Si, I am all right."

"What on earth set him off like that?" Sarah demanded breathlessly.

Chad continued to stroke the mustang's neck gently. "Uncle Gib rescued him from a Mexican horse trader over at Goliad. Apparently he'd been treated very cruelly, because ever since, anyone who reminds him of that trader sets him off, especially if they try to touch him."

Sarah studied the creature who was still watching the farmhand warily. "Why do you have such an unpredictable animal? What if he suddenly decides you look like this horse trader?"

"Oh, he's a smart one," Chad grinned wryly. "He knows me now, and we've sort of come to an understanding. He behaves himself as long as I always stay ready for anything he might try."

"That doesn't sound like a very good arrangement." Sarah frowned and shook her head. "Always having to be on guard, never able to enjoy riding."

Chad tightened the lead, gave a slight tug, and the mustang calmly walked beside him toward the barn. "My Uncle Robert raises thoroughbreds back in Virginia. He says that even the mildest mannered horse can occasionally be spooked. Lots of times it's the horse whose good humor and steadiness you take for granted that can end up hurting you." Chad lightly scratched the side of Digby's jaw. "The fact is, there's just something about him. The challenge to outwit each other has been kinda fun."

Sarah raised a skeptical eyebrow and turned to address Luke, who was watching from the barn door. "Luke, I think Mr. Macklin had better take care of his own horse while he's here."

5

For three long days and nights Chad, Sarah, and Mariah took three-hour shifts by Dunmar's bedside. The third night, Sarah had taken the nine-to-midnight watch. The next morning after a few hours of sleep, she started across the dogtrot to the kitchen when she noticed her brother standing out by the gate of the cedar rail fence across the front yard. He was kicking rocks. She walked outside to see what was wrong.

As she reached the fence, the first rays of sunlight streamed from the crest of the eastern hills, flooding the meadow stretching before her with warm light. She noticed Chad and Mr. Medina riding away from the cabin toward the north. Pepper, the dog, trotted after them.

"Where are they going?" she asked as she shaded her eyes from the brightness.

"Mr. Medina's showing Chad where he found that piece of a coffee bag in the creek and where he thinks it might have come from."

"Why?" she asked.

"Ya know, Chad told us his uncle's a Texas Ranger and they're after two men who killed a fella over by Austin and stole his burro and all his gear. Chad said they even stole a treasure map, an old map on parchment paper, just like Mr. Medina was talking about the other day."

"Treasure map? For goodness sake, Luke, don't be ridiculous. For the last time, there is no treasure."

The girl scoffed at the idea as the two riders disappeared into the grove of pecan trees stretching along the dry creek bed at the foot of the hills to the east.

Luke climbed up on the lower rung of the fence and looked at his sister. "Mr. Medina says his great-grandmother's grandfather was given a map by an old Indian. It came from the relative of a scout for Coronado and it shows this part of the country. He told me that a pack train of twenty mules was ambushed by Waco Indians and that Coronado's party barely escaped. The pack mules were carrying gold that was stolen from Indians around Santa Fe. The Spanish soldiers hid the gold and tried to ride the mules, but most of them were killed. One man drew a map of the cave they hid the gold in. I bet it was the very map that Mr. Medina's ancestor had!"

"That's pretty far-fetched, Luke," Sarah said with a grin.

"Not too far-fetched," Luke replied confidently, scratching his freckled nose. "Mr. Medina even saw it once when he was a little boy. Besides, two men killed another man just to get their hands on that map."

Realizing it was useless trying to convince her brother that he could be wrong, Sarah climbed up on the fence rail beside him. The riders were out of sight. "How long are they going to be gone? Chad sat up with his uncle after I did. I'd think he'd be wanting to sleep."

"He said they'd be back for breakfast. His uncle was trying to get up to go out looking for those two murderin' hombres." Luke gave his sister a side-glance to see her reaction to his choice of words. Both she and his mother insisted that living on the frontier was not an excuse to be careless with one's speech. When she didn't notice, he hopped down from the fence and crossed his arms to rest on the top rail.

"The only way Chad could quiet him down was to promise him he'd go scout out their trail and see where they might be camping. Mama wouldn't let me go along. I don't know why. I'm not a little kid anymore."

"I know you're not, dear." Mrs. Preston's voice came from behind them. Placing her arm around his shoulders, she added, "You heard what Chad said."

Luke looked up at his mother. "Yes, ma'am," he mumbled.

"What'd he say?" Sarah asked.

Luke answered, "He said he thought it'd be best for one of the menfolk to stay here and watch out for you two. Since Mama had already told me I couldn't go, I didn't tell him that you two are almost as good a shot as me and you can watch out after yourselves."

"Almost?" Sarah teased and stepped down from the fence beside him.

Sarah's teasing didn't make Luke feel any better; he made a face at her.

"All right, you two, that's enough," their mother ordered. "Now, Luke, you go fetch some fresh water, and Sarah, you see about gatherin' the eggs. I don't want to leave Mr. Dunmar alone for too long. He was resting quietly a moment ago, but I don't want him to try to get up."

A few minutes later, Mrs. Preston returned to the sleeping quarters side of the cabin. Entering Sarah's bedroom, she was dismayed to see her patient sitting on the side of the bed attempting to stand up.

"Mr. Dunmar, what do you think you're doing?" She rushed to the bedside. "You must lie quietly or your leg will swell even more. Now, get back in bed this minute." With gentle hands, she helped him lie back against the plump feather pillows.

"Where's my nephew?" the man sputtered weakly. "I had a dream he was going after the two murderers."

"I think your fever may be down a little," she stated quietly after placing her hand on his forehead. "But you must lay still or it will only get worse."

"What about Chad?" he insisted.

After three days of fever and delirium, there was at last a clearness in his eyes. Mariah was relieved at this first encouraging sign. She smiled patiently. "Your nephew and Mr. Medina, our hired hand, have gone to scout their trail."

"No!" Dunmar groaned and caught her hand as she began to fluff his pillows. "He can't. He's just a lad. Those men are killers."

"Calm yourself, Mr. Dunmar." She patted his hand gently and placed it on his chest, then pulled up the patchwork quilt. "They're only going to the creek. Mr. Medina found a piece of a coffee bag that could have come from the camp of those men. They're only going to check for a trail leading up to the caves and they're coming right back. I'm sure your nephew has more sense than to try to apprehend those men with only Mr. Medina's help." She stepped back. "Besides, you've been here three days. Those men have probably cleared out by now."

"Yes, yes," Dunmar sighed and relaxed slightly. "Chad's a smart lad. He wouldn't do anythin' foolish."

Mariah picked up an earthenware pitcher on the nearby washstand and poured a glass of water. After helping Dunmar prop up just enough to take a sip, she checked the dressing on his leg.

"Are you really a Ranger?" she asked as she removed the old bandage.

"Yes, why?" he said grimacing at the ever-present pain in his swollen leg.

"Just curious," she replied absently as she unrolled a clean linen bandage and began to wrap it around the affected area.

"You mean because I'm older than most of them?" Despite the thick feeling in his head, Dunmar grew quickly irritated with this conversation.

Perplexed at having voiced her curiosity, Mariah nevertheless replied, "One might wonder what a man your age is doing in such a dangerous job."

"I could ask why a woman like you is out here in the wilderness with your children while your husband's off on a fool's errand?"

This reply struck a nerve. "I beg your pardon?" She met his angry gaze directly.

"Captain Anderson asked me to look in on you while we were up this way. Told me your husband was with the Santa Fe Expedition, a fool's errand if there ever was one."

Mariah gathered up the old dressing and her scissors then stepped back from the bed. She declared icily, "I'm sure a gentleman from Boston would not presume to say such a thing if he weren't so ill. Forgive me; it was rude of me to ask something that is certainly no one's business but yours. If you'll excuse me, I'll go start breakfast." Striding quickly out of the room, she commanded, "Stay quiet there and don't try to get up again."

The Ranger watched the woman disappear through the door with an impatient swish of her dark grey skirt. He closed his eyes. He didn't feel like doing anything but lying quietly anyway.

Dunmar pulled the quilt up over his shoulders. He regretted snapping back at the woman so sharply. He realized he had no right to say such a thing to her about her husband, especially when she had been so kind. He didn't want to admit it, but he had been trying to ignore the fact that the majority of the Rangers were half his age. The past two years had been physically demanding, and he had pushed himself just to prove he could do the job as well as the younger men. Pursuing marauding Comanches and protecting settlers from the unscrupulous and sometimes deadly dregs of society that sought refuge in the wide open territory of the new republic required an almost reckless courage and selfless determination.

At first, it had been the perfect antidote for his grief over the loss of Elaine. He had taken chances that even the younger men had marvelled at. He really hadn't cared what might happen to him. As time passed, he had discovered he was very good at his new career. Regardless of the many dangers, he found this wild, beautiful country fascinating.

Sometimes it almost seemed like someone else's life when he thought about his past. He and Elaine had lived a very comfortable existence in a fine home. They had been married three years when her father persuaded Gibson to go into partnership in a stock brokerage house. When he wasn't sitting behind a desk in a fancy office dealing with large monetary investments, he would be discussing work with fellow businessmen at one of the elite men's clubs in Boston. The spiral downward came when British interests began offering loans with terms too good to resist. When sure-fire investments suddenly misfired, the national economic dominoes began to tumble, resulting in The Crash of '37. The memory of that dark time settled on him, adding to his mental and physical discomfort. However, it had been losing his wife to influenza that had been the crushing blow.

Dunmar had felt her nearness while struggling through the dismal murkiness the last three days. As he lay silently, now clearly aware of his surroundings, he realized that it must have been Mrs. Preston's presence he had sensed. Perhaps that was why he had been so sharp with her. He couldn't imagine asking any woman to suffer the hardships out here. Even less understandable was how a man could leave her and her children to fend for themselves while chasing some foolish scheme.

The patient moved slightly. A shot of pain in his leg sent a wave of nausea flooding over him. He clutched the quilt covering him until the feeling subsided. Thoughts of his nephew returned. Dunmar only hoped the lad would confine his scouting efforts to simply locating the trail. He would not rest easy until Chad returned. The lad had a good head on his shoulders, but the uncle quietly prayed that his nephew wouldn't choose this opportunity to show everyone that he could handle any situation regardless of the danger.

Mariah stood at the plank table in the kitchen and pressed her hands against the smooth, worn surface to make them stop trembling. She took a deep breath to shake off the effects of her emotional reaction to Gibson Dunmar's criticism of her husband. Why should she be so upset by the ranting of someone so ill he might say anything? Thomas was a good man. He had been a good husband to her and a good father to their children. If she had begged him to stay, she had no doubt that he would never have gone on the expedition. Yet, he'd been so excited that the venture would restore their wealth, she had been unable to express her fears about the danger he faced or about their being left to fend for themselves. Knowing that this was his chance to restore his sense of worth was more important to her than the fortune he was seeking to reclaim.

The woman forced herself to begin preparing breakfast, but as she stirred the coarse batter of corn meal, egg, and buttermilk, her thoughts were drawn back to that day nearly eighteen years ago. Standing beside her father's bed, she had clutched his big rough hand and listened with an aching heart as he revealed the plans for her future.

Uriah Sutton had been a big burly man, strong as the oxen that pulled his plow. With enormous strength of will, tireless energy, and a deep love for the land, he had carved an impressive farm holding out of the fertile Shenandoah Valley of Virginia. Sutton was a widower and his only child, Mariah, had worked beside him, learning how to care for the land and be rewarded by its bounty.

Then one brisk winter morning in November, the year Mariah was sixteen, a hunting accident left Uriah Sutton paralyzed from the waist down and hovering at death's door. The person responsible for the carelessly aimed weapon was Thomas Preston, son of the wealthiest family in the county.

A contrite Thomas, standing with hand on heart pledged, "Mr. Sutton, on my oath as a gentleman, tell me whatever it is that I can do to help make up for this terrible thing I've done."

It was then that Uriah Sutton took his daughter's hand and placed it in young Preston's. "Today, you've made my daughter an orphan. Now, make her your wife and care well for her, for she has no one else."

She could still remember the look in Thomas's eyes, shock and surprise at first, then polite resignation. So it was that the next day they were married, two strangers. It caused quite a stir in the senior Preston's house; however, Thomas was true to his word. Ironically, the tough old Sutton survived for twelve more years, managing his vast farm from a cot carried to the fields each day by his workmen. Six months after the wedding, Mariah had overheard the rather cruel complaint of her mother-in-law that, after Sutton had played such a trick on Thomas by making him marry Mariah, he ought to have had the decency to go ahead and die. But Thomas was a kind man of integrity who quickly ended such comments, and he had never given the slightest indication that he was not happy with his situation.

It took some time, however, for the independent Mariah to accept it in her heart. She loathed the idea that she should be the pitiful object of someone's charity. As time passed, however, a friendship deepened between them, and their lives were blessed by Sarah and Luke. It was a comfortable, pleasant existence until The Crash of '37. Then everything changed.

A bang against the kitchen door startled Mariah from her thoughts. Luke backed against the door to open it as he lugged two heavy buckets of water into the kitchen.

"How long till breakfast? I'm starved," he announced breathlessly.

An hour after sun-up, Sarah was coming from milking their cow kept in the small pasture next to the barn when she saw Chad and Medina riding up. A wave of relief washed over her. Mr. Medina was more than just a hired hand; he had become a very good friend. Sarah was glad this young tenderfoot, Macklin, had not gotten them into a dangerous situation.

"How's my uncle?" Chad called to her as he dismounted at the hitching rail.

"He woke up a while ago and wasn't delirious anymore," the girl replied, walking up to the rail. "He has been very worried about you though. Did you find anything?"

Chad nodded. "We found their trail and one cold campsite," he said, tying Digby's reins. "Mr. Medina thinks they're probably at the other end of the valley near the caves. He said it'd take until noon or longer to find 'em, so we came on back. I wanted to wait 'til I knew my uncle was going to be all right before going off."

She set the heavy pail down for a moment, then picked it up with the other hand. "You don't mean you're really considering going after them yourself?"

He looked at her. "I don't know why not."

"I can tell you why not," she declared, moving toward the gate. "You're not a Ranger." She walked a few paces, then turned and exclaimed, "Why, you haven't even been in Texas long enough to know your way around! It's a ridiculous notion."

The young woman pushed through the gate and marched up the path to the porch steps fearing the influence this stranger's reckless attitude could have on Luke. Some of the milk sloshed out of the pail onto her skirt. Annoyed, she held the bucket away from her and stomped up the steps.

Macklin watched her, then with a long stride reached the porch and sprinted up the steps. "Well, there's no one else to do it, is there?" he argued. Throwing his hand in the air toward the north end of the valley, he added, "They could get away before Uncle Gib feels up to going after them."

Stopping outside the kitchen, she looked at him. "Your uncle won't let you go after them by yourself," she said confidently.

He pushed open the kitchen door for her. "But they're probably the murderers." Chad followed her inside. "If they are, they need to be stopped and taken back to Austin for a trial."

Sarah hefted the pail up onto the plank table next to a stone crock covered with a piece of cheese cloth. "I think half the men in Texas have committed murder or stolen something." She began to strain the milk through the cloth into the crock. "Getting yourself killed isn't going to help a bit."

"What kind of attitude is that?" he asked indignantly as he held the cheese cloth in place and steadied the crock. "What about enforcing the laws of the Republic? Like Uncle Gib says, the only way this country's ever going to be safe is if the desperados aren't allowed to control it."

"I hardly think he expects you to take part in enforcing anything," the girl said with a wry smile before setting the empty milk pail aside. "Sit down and I'll fix your breakfast."

She sounded like his sisters, Chad thought. He refused to sit down. "No thanks. I'll go see how Uncle Gib's doing."

Watching him leave the room, she found herself irritated and perplexed. Although she knew it would be dangerous for Chad to do as he planned, she couldn't help but feel a small measure of admiration for his courage, foolhardy or not. As she wiped the milk drops off the table, Sarah regretted speaking to him like he was her brother. After all, she thought, they hardly knew each other. She had no right to be giving him such advice, even though she believed that what she had said was true.

As Chad left the kitchen, he met Mrs. Preston walking across the dogtrot toward him.

"You're back," she said, her brow furrowed with concern. "Your uncle wanted to see you the moment you returned."

"How's he doing?" Chad pulled off his hat and slapped it against his pant leg to shake off the dust.

When Mrs. Preston didn't answer immediately, he was filled with dread. "What is it? What's wrong?"

"Chad, I think it'd be wise for you to ride to Austin and bring the doctor."

"Is he getting worse?"

"I can't be sure. Apparently you were able to draw out most of the venom or he'd be dead by now. But there's still the problem of his leg. What little venom that remains could cause the wound to turn gangrenous. If that happens, we need the doctor to—"

Macklin stared at her in disbelief. "To what?" He swallowed hard and closed his eyes to block out the unwelcome vision.

"Chad, is that you?" His uncle's faint voice broke in on the grim thought.

With a nod, Chad went inside. He walked to the bed and grasped his uncle's hand. "Uncle Gib, how're you feelin'?"

The patient was still deathly pale, but he managed to return a slight grin. "To tell the truth, lad," he said weakly, "I've felt a sight better. Mrs. Preston tells me you were out scoutin' a trail. Find anythin'?"

Chad nodded and explained what they had discovered.

Dunmar closed his eyes. "I must ask a favor of ya, lad."

"Anything, Uncle Gib. What is it?"

"I need ya to ride back to Austin and tell the captain so he can send another Ranger out here to find those two men."

Dunmar reached up and clutched Chad's plaid shirt-sleeve. "Don't worry 'bout bringin' a doctor. All he'll want to do is take my leg off. If Mrs. Preston's medicine doesn't work, at least I'll leave this world with both legs."

"But Uncle Gib . . ." Chad started.

"No buts about it, lad. That's the way it's to be." Another wave of pain and nausea forced the Ranger to wait a moment before continuing. "Now, give me your word of honor that even if I become delirious, you won't let 'em take my leg off."

The words stuck in Chad's throat. He couldn't speak.

"Please, lad. Word of honor. If the good Lord sees fit to save this ol' man, that's fine, but if He takes me home, that's okay too, for I'll be with my Elaine. Promise me."

Chad looked into his uncle's hazel eyes and his own vision blurred. At last, he nodded his promise and turned to go. Mrs. Preston stood just outside the door. Chad squared his shoulders, walked out of the room, and stopped in front of the woman. "You heard?"

"Yes, I heard," she replied icily.

"I gave my word," Chad declared in a low resolute voice.

He left the cabin and headed directly for the barn, where he'd left their packs and weapons. He gathered up an extra canteen, a small canvas feed bag with oats for Digby, his uncle's saddle wallet with provisions of coffee beans, some sweetened parched corn, and a leather packet of salt. For the Colt pistol in his own saddlebag, he grabbed some extra ammunition. Back at the hitching rail, he was stuffing these items in Digby's saddlebag as Mr. Medina stepped down the porch steps carrying a small brown burlap bag. The man walked to where his own pinto stood tied to the hitching rail, keeping a wary eye on Digby as he passed by Chad.

"I go to Austin to invite an old friend of the Prestons to visit. Señora Preston ask me to take your message to the Rangers so you can stay close in case your uncle becomes worse."

Hector tied the bag onto the pinto's saddle. Anticipating Macklin's next question, he nodded. "It has been a long time since their doctor friend was here for a visit."

Chad was now used to the rhythmic flow of the man's Spanish accent. His meaning was clear. "Doctor?"

"Si. Señora said she made no promises. Now, you want me to take a message for you or no?"

Chad was relieved and nodded a quick yes.

"Just a minute." The boy pulled his journal out of the saddlebag and tore out a blank sheet, then hastily wrote a message to the captain.

Hector placed the folded note in his wrinkled shirt pocket and swung up into the saddle. Leaning forward, he peered intently at the young man. "Keep your weapons loaded and with you at all times. Do not sleep too soundly. Listen to Señora Preston, sabe mucho. She is very wise. Adios, muchacho."

Chad watched the small figure ride away at a lope, the warning still ringing in his ears. His steady gaze followed the tree-lined horizons to the west and east, then along the cliffs above the river to the southwest.

He had yet to see his first Comanche, but he had heard plenty about them. Then he saw it. A pencil-thin line of smoke was rising from the ridge at the north end of the valley. The hair on the back of his neck prickled. With a strange certainty, he sensed it was a signal of more trouble ahead.

6

Around noon Chad was chopping wood when Mrs. Preston called him in for a bite of lunch. He was starving. His shirt was soaked from the exertion of swinging the axe. The third day of October was hot. He was not used to such temperatures, especially at this time of year. In Boston, the colorful trees would soon be bare and the autumn days were more than likely brisk from the northeastern winds.

As young Macklin approached the porch, he caught sight of Sarah pouring water into a tin basin on a low washstand outside the kitchen door. When she saw him step up onto the porch, he sensed the coolness in her attitude toward him. He had noticed it more with each passing day and wondered why. He was certain he had made it clear that he was capable of doing chores himself and didn't need her to be waiting on him.

"Soap's here on the side of the washstand. We're eating lunch out on the back porch today where there's a little breeze."

Chad thanked her and eagerly splashed the cool water on his face and neck. Lathering up the lye soap, he winced when he realized how many raw blisters he had on his hands. He hadn't laid his hand to an axe handle since helping his Uncle

Stephan rebuild an old split-rail fence last summer. But he didn't care. He felt better about sitting down to eat the Prestons' food if he helped with the chores.

Lunch consisted of corn bread dripping with honey and milk kept cool in a crockery jug submerged in the rock spring along the bluff above the nearby river. After his third cup of the fresh sweet milk, he apologized for making a pig of himself. Mrs. Preston smiled and assured him that it pleased her to see a young man with a healthy appetite. With that, he gladly accepted a refill of milk and another piece of corn bread.

"I'm doing the last of the laundry, Chad," Sarah said as they were finishing. "If you have a spare shirt that needs cleaning, I'll add it with your uncle's to this last washpot."

Glancing down at the shirt he was wearing, Chad knew by the time he finished with the rest of the chores today, he would be needing a clean shirt and his spare shirt was already dirty. He decided it wouldn't hurt to accept her offer of help this one time.

"Thanks, I do have a shirt that could use a washing. I'll go get it out of my pack." He turned to Luke, who was scraping his plate for the last morsel of corn bread. "Then we'll go finish that hog pen like I promised, Luke," he added.

The boy quickly agreed, glad to have an excuse to get away from his duties of stirring the laundry and hauling wood. As the man of the house for the time being, Luke felt he should be working at the men's chores, not helping with laundry.

He enjoyed having another boy around, even though Macklin was older. Over the last three days, Chad had shared some interesting stories about his life in Boston, his aunt and uncle in Kentucky, and the places he'd traveled on his father's ships.

"Go ahead," his mother told him. "I'll help Sarah finish up the laundry. We'll need that pen to fatten the hogs for slaughter."

While Luke helped clear the table on the porch, Chad excused himself to go in to check on his uncle. The nephew was glad to see that Dunmar was resting quietly, and so he went on out to the barn to retrieve his dirty shirt. Pulling the shirt out of his duffle bag, he decided to keep the Colt pistol handy along with his rifle, which he had kept close by while chopping wood earlier. He slipped the holster on his belt and shoved the pistol into it. He also put some extra cartridges inside the ammunition pouch. He was taking the earnest warning in Hector Medina's voice seriously.

After delivering the shirt to Sarah, Chad picked up the rifle where he'd left it before lunch and walked to the corral to find Luke feeding chunks of carrots to Digby. Pepper sat watching curiously, his red tongue hanging out the side of his mouth as he panted in the heat.

"I thought Sarah told you to stay away from him," Chad grinned as the eager mustang stretched his neck over the fence to reach another crunchy carrot.

"Ah, she worries too much. She's always bossin' me around," Luke grumbled. "Like I was some little kid without any sense."

Chad chuckled and clapped the boy on the shoulder. "I know the feeling too well."

"You do?"

The boy held up empty hands to the mustang's nose. Digby nudged his velvety upper lip against the boy's hand to make sure nothing was hidden, then he snorted.

Chad patted the mustang's neck. "Yes, I have three older sisters, and all of them worry as much as Sarah does. It can get under a fella's skin, especially when they're always tellin' a body what he should and shouldn't do."

"Three!" Luke's blue eyes widened. He tried to imagine three Sarahs standing on the porch telling him what he ought to be doing. "How'd ya ever keep your wits about ya?"

Chuckling again, Chad took the shovel leaning against the corral post and handed it to Luke. "Oh, they mean well, but every once in a while I had to let them know I was able to think something through myself, without advice from them."

He picked up the axe leaning there and, with the rifle in his other hand, headed with Luke toward their work site, Pepper tagging along.

"Did it do any good?" Luke wondered, falling in step.

"Nah. I usually had to do something on my own to prove that I could, like sail a skiff across the harbor by myself or—"

"Track a wild animal?" Luke interrupted as he tried to match the older boy's longer stride.

Chad remembered his first solo hunt on a visit with his Uncle Stephan and Aunt Christiana in Kentucky. "Yeah. Of course, it's not quite as bad as it was, now that the two older ones are engaged and have someone else to worry about."

"You mean I'll have to wait 'til Sarah gets married before she stops worryin' about me and bossin' me around?" The boy wailed and threw a stick for Pepper to chase. The dog raced off after it.

"Probably, but that shouldn't be too long." Chad grinned, watching Pepper sniffing the ground for the stick. "Sarah's a pretty girl, and if she was in town, I'm sure there'd be lots of fellas wanting to court her."

Luke mulled over the idea of Sarah getting married. "What would you think about courtin' her?"

Pepper came charging back with the stick in his mouth. After wrestling it away from him, Luke sailed it away again. The dog followed it in hot pursuit.

Chad felt his ears grow red at Luke's suggestion, and he cleared his throat as he raised the rifle to carry it across his shoulder. "For one thing I don't think she likes me very much. It doesn't seem to take much for me to stir up her temper. Like this mornin' after Mr. Medina left for Austin, I mentioned that I'd read a book about Coronado's search for the cities of gold and wasn't surprised there were rumors about treasure maps. She snapped back that she didn't want to hear another word about treasure maps."

"I'm sorry about that," Luke apologized. "That's partly my fault, I guess; but mainly, I think maybe she's worried about our father. She's usually as kind and polite as can be to folks. She's never snapped at Dolph Hammersmith."

"Dolph Hammersmith?"

"Yeah, he's eighteen already and a soldier. Went with our father on the expedition to Santa Fe. I think he kinda likes Sarah."

"Does Sarah like him?" Chad found the idea strangely aggravating.

Luke burst into laughter and pointed at Pepper. The animal had picked up the stick just as a squirrel went scurrying by. The surprised dog jumped back, then immediately dropped the stick and took off barking at the squirrel.

"Well, does she?"

The distracted boy glanced at his new friend walking next to him. "What?"

"Does Sarah like this Hammermill?" Chad tried to sound casual.

"Hammersmith," Luke corrected, kicking at a dirt clod. "Well, I guess so. He's awful serious though; doesn't laugh or smile like you do. I don't think Sarah would have as much fun with him as she would with you."

"Come on." Chad decided it was time to change the subject. "We'd better stop lollygaggin' about or your mother and sister will both be gettin' after us. Is that the hog pen over there?" He pointed at a stack of cedar posts under a spreading oak tree.

"Yep, that's it," Luke replied. "Mr. Medina and I spent last week cuttin' cedar. We have to keep the horses in close or the Comanches would have 'em before you could blink. But Mr. Medina says they don't like pigs or hogs. He must be right 'cause we haven't lost one of them yet."

Reaching the spot marked off for the hog pen, Chad could see that posts had already been set for one side of the enclosure. Three two-post sets were lined up six feet apart and sunk in foot-deep holes eight inches apart. This created three slots for a cedar rail to drop into.

"Have you ever seen a Comanche?" Chad was curious as he leaned his rifle and axe against the oak tree.

"Only from a distance," Luke said, placing his shovel beside the axe. "Last year we lost two cows and a horse, probably Comanches took 'em. Nobody around here has gotten by without losing at least one or two horses. They scalped a couple of men up the river three months ago. The men were cuttin' cedar posts to sell down in Austin. They were gettin' ready to make their last trip downriver when they were caught by a Comanche hunting party. Those Comanches are mean as the devil himself."

Chad picked up the piece of string tied to the corner post that Mr. Medina had used for a plumb line.

"You've only seen them from a distance, Luke. How do you know what they're like?"

The young Preston eyed Chad curiously. He'd never heard anyone question this fact before.

Stretching the string out, they began stepping off measurements for placement of the posts for the remaining three sides.

"If someone came in and killed all your animals and took your house away, I bet you'd be mad enough to fight back as hard as you could, wouldn't you?" Chad reasoned as he placed a rock to mark the center post and then the corner post.

"Well, sure," Luke replied as he went over to get the shovel.

"You'd probably fight back as fierce as all get out, and those folks you were fightin' would probably think you were pretty mean, too, don't you think?"

Luke handed the shovel to Chad. "I never thought about it like that," he said, scratching his head. "But they've done terrible things, even to women and little children."

"There've been plenty of Indian women and children who've been mistreated by whites too," Chad said, pushing the shovel blade into the red soil with his boot.

"You sound like you feel sorry for them," Luke murmured in disbelief.

"Uncle Gib says they're different here than back east, but I know a lot of the stories you hear about Indians aren't true."

"How do you know?" Luke asked, watching young Macklin dig the hole deeper.

"It happens. I'm about ready for one of those posts," Chad interjected as he lifted another shovelful of dirt, then continued. "For instance, my Grandfather Macklin is half Delaware Indian. During the Revolutionary War when he was fighting for General George Washington, the British accused him of scalping four British soldiers."

Luke's eyes widened. "Did he?"

"No." Chad stopped digging and leaned on the shovel. "Now, you see what I mean? There was a fight between him and two soldiers and he won, but he has never scalped anyone in his life."

Considering Chad's story, Luke nearly stumbled over the posts on the ground. "Gosh, that means that you . . . you're part Indian yourself."

Chad nodded soberly and pointed to one of the cedar posts.

Luke picked up one end of the rough-barked pole and dragged it to him. "I heard some Delaware Indians were scouting for the Rangers," Luke said thoughtfully. "They don't like the Comanches either."

Chad smiled at the boy's comment. "Well, I didn't say I agree with scalping and the things they've done. It's just that when you've grown up hearing the other side of the story, you see things differently. Take my Uncle Stephan. His folks were killed by the Creek Indians and he was taken captive when he was seven years old. He grew up in a Shawnee village and even though he returned to the white ways of liv-

71

ing, he still respects the Shawnee ways. He says Tecumseh was a better man than some of the white officers he fought under during the War of 1812."

Chad hefted the post into the hole and Luke steadied it while he shoveled dirt around it. While Chad worked, Luke mulled over his words. He liked the way Chad talked to him—as if he was more than just a kid without any sense. But he had to admit this was a different way of looking at things. He'd never heard anyone say even one good thing about the Indians before.

A warm breeze was blowing across the valley as Sarah hung the last wet shirt on the rope strung between the corner of the cabin and a nearby sapling. The clothes would be dry before long. The girl looked across the meadow to one of the large oaks where her little brother and young Macklin were setting posts for the hog pen. She had to admit that Chad Macklin had a nice smile and an appealing twinkle in his dark brown eyes. He might even be considered good looking, if it weren't for the fact that he had such a stubborn streak. Over the past three days, he seemed to resent any suggestions she offered about some task he was about to undertake or any offer of help to do the slightest thing. She'd been surprised earlier when he admitted he had a dirty shirt that needed washing. "As independent as a hog on ice," her Grandfather Sutton would have said. While an independent nature was necessary on the frontier, she knew too much of a good thing could also get someone into trouble. Chasing after outlaws alone was a prime example.

As Sarah picked up the empty laundry basket, she thought about Dolph Hammersmith. With his no-nonsense attitude, he seemed able to cope with the difficulties of frontier life very well. He was taller than Chad Macklin and handsome too. And even if he didn't have the same good-natured twinkle in his eyes as Chad Macklin, he was steady and dependable and didn't argue with her at the drop of a hat.

7

By horseback, the ride from the Preston farm to Austin could easily be made in one day. Riding steadily but allowing his pinto frequent rest periods, Hector Medina reached Austin just before dark.

The Mexican had just handed Chad's note to Captain Anderson when the door opened, and in walked an Indian dressed in a trade cloth shirt with breechcloth, buckskin leggings, and moccasins. He was nearly six feet tall. He had straight black hair, strong even features, and a long scar from the hairline at the middle of his forehead almost to the right eyebrow line.

"There you are, Sparrow Hawk," Captain Anderson called as Senihele, the Delaware scout, entered the Ranger's office. "Glad to see you got some rest last night." The Ranger held up a piece of paper and motioned toward the farmhand. "This here's Hector Medina. Works for the Prestons out along the river northwest of here. He's brought a message from Gib Dunmar. Looks like ol' Gib could use a hand out there. Tangled with a rattler, he did."

"Who won?" the Indian asked without changing his stoic expression.

The Ranger smoothed his mustache with his fingers. "Well, Dunmar's a bit under the weather. Don't know 'bout the snake, but knowin' Gib he probably has himself a new belt now. Anyway, since Webb took a rifle ball in the leg, he can't ride with you. With Jack Hays requesting half the company to come over to San Antonio for a while and the other half headin' back upriver, looks like you're the only one to spare right now."

Senihele nodded in agreement. He had worked with Gibson Dunmar before, and he did not mind doing so again. The man had more courage than sense sometimes, but he was a good shot and made a good cup of coffee. Senihele knew that Dunmar's sister was married to a man who had Delaware blood and that the son of that man was coming for a visit.

Almost as if the captain was reading the Indian's mind, he chimed in, "By the way, Gib's nephew, Chad Macklin, is with him. Medina here says he and the boy found a cold campsite they think was made by the two outlaws Gib's chasin'."

Senihele and Hector Medina made plans to leave for the Preston farm at first light the next morning. The Indian then left to get supper.

"Señora Preston sent me to get the doctor for Señor Dunmar, but I haven't been able to find him," Hector reminded the captain.

"I was just gonna say something about that when Sparrow Hawk came in." Captain Anderson frowned. "Doc's gone down to Houston; won't be back before the end of the month. But I'm sure ol' Gib's gonna make it just fine. After all that gent's been through, I doubt one little ol' snakebite is gonna stop him."

Mariah Preston moved silently past the young man dozing in the old rocking chair beside his uncle's bed. She placed her hand on the patient's forehead and was disappointed to find that his fever had come up again. The man murmured and turned his head restlessly. Taking a cloth from the basin on the bedside table, she gently bathed the man's face. In a moment his eyes flickered open.

"Do ya never sleep, woman?" His Scottish brogue was weak.

She put a quieting fingertip to her lips. "We've been taking turns," she whispered, motioning toward his sleeping nephew. "We wanted to be sure you didn't become delirious again and try to get up and go wandering about. Your nephew's been here since two this morning. It's about five o'clock now."

The sky outside the small window was beginning to pale as dawn approached. Dunmar's body still felt as though it were on fire, and his leg was in terrible pain. Mariah placed a teacup to his dry lips and helped him prop up enough to sip the cool liquid.

"This is willow bark tea. It should help bring the fever down."

The fluid eased his parched throat.

Suddenly Chad sat forward. "Uncle Gib?"

"Easy, lad. I'm all right," Dunmar managed as he lay back against the pillow.

"His fever's back up, but that's to be expected," Mrs. Preston said. "Here, keep this cool cloth on his forehead. I'll go fix some broth for his breakfast."

An hour later as the morning sunlight spilled over the crest of the eastern hills, the fever was down and Ranger Dunmar was resting peacefully.

Coffee was bubbling in the pot hanging in the fireplace when Sarah opened the kitchen door to see her mother preparing a breakfast of bacon, eggs, corn pone, and wild plum preserves. With an armful of wood for the cooking fire, Chad nodded a silent good morning to her as he placed it in the woodbox.

"Good morning, dear," her mother greeted her. "Please call your brother for breakfast. We need to get an early start shuckin' that corn this mornin'."

Sarah turned back out into the dogtrot between the sleeping quarters and kitchen and living area. She climbed the ladder to the sleeping loft above the two bedrooms. Luke was not in his bed. When she reported this to her mother, Mariah suggested that he may have decided to feed the horses early. Chad offered to go see.

"No sign of him in the barn," he reported when he returned. "Does he take early morning rides by himself?"

"No, of course not," Sarah replied.

Instant concern filled Mariah Preston's face. "Well, you two sit down before your food gets cold. I'll go call him in. He probably decided to go fishing." Mrs. Preston handed a wooden ladle to Sarah and walked outside. The girl hastily spooned some warm scrambled eggs and bacon onto a plate and handed it to Chad, then quickly followed her mother. Chad hungrily gulped down a couple of mouthfuls of eggs and grabbed a piece of bacon as he rushed out behind them. Mariah was already headed toward the bluff calling her son's name.

"Listen, Mother; that's Pepper barking," Sarah yelled from the porch step.

"Sounds like he's over by the hog pen." Chad was already bolting across the front yard and past two huge live oaks that shaded the broad grassy field.

Sarah was right behind him. They discovered the spotted animal tied to one of the posts. He wagged his tail eagerly when he saw them. It took a minute for Chad to calm the dog down enough to untie the knot in the rope.

Sarah walked around the pen calling her brother's name, but there was no response. She scanned the hills to the northeast and moaned out loud, "Oh, no . . . He didn't . . . He couldn't!"

"What?" Chad asked as the liberated dog dashed after a squirrel that had been teasing him.

"I can't believe he'd disobey Mother, but I bet that's what he's done."

"Done what?" the young man insisted.

The girl turned and ran back toward the cabin without answering. Chad followed. Her mother, who had just reached the gate after checking Luke's fishing spot, turned to follow her daughter as she bounded up the porch steps and into the main room. Sarah's heart sank. It was true. The musket and powder horn were gone from the hook over the mantel.

"What is it, Sarah?" Mrs. Preston asked as she stepped through the door.

Sarah tried to catch her breath as she went to her mother's side. "Remember Luke talking about that cougar?" The color drained from Mariah's face as the girl continued. "I think he's gone after it."

"Oh, dear Lord, no," Mariah choked, clutching at her heart.

"Cougar?" As he spoke, a sudden sinking feeling hit Chad's stomach. He recalled the conversation he and Luke had had the day before about tracking wild animals.

"But I told him—" Mariah's words hung helplessly in the still air.

Chad and Sarah exchanged worried glances.

Mrs. Preston turned and clutched Macklin's arm. "May I borrow one of your rifles, Chad?"

Instantly, Chad realized what she was thinking. "Well, ma'am, if you'll excuse me, I'll go. I'd feel much better about goin' after the boy m'self. You know much more about helping Uncle Gib than I do."

Mariah's first impulse was to say no, but she knew the young man was right. She also realized Chad would probably be able to track Luke more quickly than she could. The decision was made.

Wasting no time, Chad hurried out to the barn to saddle Digby. Sarah followed right behind him. He thought she was going to offer some advice on where to look for her brother. However, he was surprised when she reached for a bridle hanging on a wall peg just inside the barn door.

"What are you doing?" he asked, lowering his saddle onto Digby's blanketed back.

"I'm goin' with you," she replied as she slipped the bridle on their sorrel and led him out of his stall.

"No, I don't think . . ." he began, but the girl cast a withering look his way. Obviously, there was no reasoning with her. In a moment, as Chad pulled the cinch snug, Digby reached back as if to nip at him. In his aggravation with Sarah, Chad growled, "Don't start that now." The mustang snorted and stamped a hoof, narrowly missing Chad's foot.

Within ten minutes, the two young people were riding swiftly away from the farm along the same trail Chad had followed the day before. A few yards beyond the hog pen, deep impressions in the red dirt and disturbed clumps of grass showed where Luke had spurred his horse to a gallop once he was far enough away from the cabin not to be heard. His tracks continued along the familiar trail until they crossed a dry creek bed that meandered through a grove of pecan trees.

Until then, the two riders were able to lope easily along the clear trail. They could see where the boy had crossed the creek bed and started up the slight incline on the other side. But here the ground was becoming rockier and the trail practically disappeared. The early morning sunlight had not yet reached this part of the valley and the shadows seemed deeper.

The couple rode slowly, searching for signs of the boy's trail. Shortly, Sarah spotted a broken cedar bough hanging over a small game trail that emerged from a narrow draw sloping down from the hills. Chad noticed several disturbed stones and a partial hoof print. He acknowledged her find with a silent nod.

As his partner spurred her horse past him along this new direction, Chad was suddenly struck by the picture before him. It reminded him of an illustration of a beautiful lady seated on a prancing charger from a book by Sir Walter Scott.

There was an elegance about this girl in calico. Her slender hands moved the reins confidently. She rode with a natural grace as her long skirts fluttered in the slight breeze. Watching her study their surroundings, he knew luck had nothing to do with finding evidence of Luke's trail.

Chad couldn't imagine any of his sisters or their debutante friends doing what Sarah was doing. They would have been appalled at the thought of hopping on a horse and striking off into the rough countryside of wild animals and even wilder Indians. The two Preston women might look as soft as the women he knew back east, but they had an inner strength and confidence that reminded him of his Aunt Christiana, who had grown up in settled Virginia but had gone to live on the Kentucky frontier when she married.

Forcing his attention back to the trail, Chad pointed toward the overturned stones.

"Whatever was he thinking to try such a foolish thing?" Sarah fumed as she ducked under a tree limb.

"I'm afraid I might be partly responsible," Chad confessed as Digby started up the narrow draw.

"What?" She asked the question sharply, turning in the saddle to face him. "How?"

"We were talking yesterday about bossy older sisters who worry too much," he replied. "I just mentioned that sometimes I've had to show my older sisters I was capable of doing things too."

"Bossy!" She reined her sorrel to a stop. "How dare you? Look what you've done."

Chad pulled Digby to a halt. "How was I to know what Luke had in mind," he blurted out. "I had no idea he was thinking about something like hunting a mountain lion on his own. Besides, if you didn't fuss over him and boss him around so much, maybe he wouldn't feel like he had to go off and prove to you he's not some little kid anymore."

Sarah's face flushed with anger. Unable to think of a sufficient retort, she spurred her horse up the trail.

Chad instantly regretted his sharp words. While he believed what he said was true, he'd said more than he meant to. He was already feeling guilty that his casual comments the day before could have set her brother off on such a dangerous quest. If anything happened to the boy, he would feel responsible.

Lightly tapping Digby's flank with his heel, Chad directed the mustang to step out quickly and follow the other horse. "Wait!" he called after her.

Digby's shoes clattered over the rocky ground of the draw. When Chad caught up with the girl, Sarah was staring hard at the ground.

"Look here," she said curtly, pointing at a patch of soft red soil with grass sprigs trampled down and horseshoe marks going in both directions. "I think he turned around and headed back the way we came."

Chad jumped down and knelt beside the tracks. The print heading back the way they had just come was on top of the one going in the opposite direction.

"You're right," he said as he stood and brushed off his buckskins. "Sarah—"

Before he could apologize, the girl spun her sorrel around and spurred past him. "Are you coming?" Her words were hurled at him like a war lance.

"Hey, I'm not the only one at fault here, you know," he called after her in exasperation. Chad started to step up in the stirrup, but Digby sidestepped. "Whoa, you ornery bag of bones," he growled, swinging himself up into the saddle without the stirrup. The contrary animal trotted roughly after the sorrel.

When they reached the dry creek bank again, Sarah turned right to head north. She walked her horse slowly as she scanned the ground for more clues.

"How do you know he came this way? There are no signs at all," Chad asked as he pulled up beside her.

Her voice was calm but cool. "Because this is the way Mr. Medina told my father they'd be able to find the cougar they heard last year."

Chad trotted Digby farther up the slight incline to find three fresh hoof prints. "You're right. Here's the trail again."

The trail zigzagged up the hillside and down into another wooded draw to cross a dry spring bed with a variety of animal paw and hoof prints molded in dried mud. Clearly visible at times, the elusive trail sometimes disappeared for several yards. It demanded their total concentration.

As the horses entered another cedar brake, two white-tailed deer jumped up and dashed off into the brush. Digby stopped instantly and watched the fleeing creatures disappear with their white tails raised like bright flags flashing through the dark green of the cedar bushes.

The sudden white flashes spooked the Preston sorrel into a spin. Chad had been studying the tracks on the ground so closely that the unexpected movement startled him too. He was glad Digby didn't spook and was about to go to Sarah's aid when she quickly regained control. The determined set to her jaw and the anger still flashing in her eyes told him not to say a word. She was all right and apparently did not need or want his help.

The trail began to climb a steep hillside. Being in the front, Chad hurried Digby up the incline, scrambling across some loose caliche and finally reaching the crest. Sarah's older sorrel struggled to make the climb, reaching the ridge to stand beside Digby, winded from the exertion.

It was late morning already, and the sun broiled down on the top of the ridge. From the crest, Chad and Sarah could observe the valley and the Colorado flowing to the southeast. Looking to the valley's north end, they gazed past the gap to rolling hills and the vast plain beyond.

"Shall we rest the horses in the shade of that big tree over there?" Chad asked as he wiped the perspiration from his forehead with a shirtsleeve.

Their travel the past hour had cooled Sarah's anger and she nodded in agreement. She was glad for a chance to take a rest herself. Although still perturbed, her anxiety for Luke's safety had increased as they traveled farther from the ranch. Her growing fear that he could have fallen in a hidden hole or become the prey of the very animal he hunted overshadowed everything else.

The shade beneath the spreading canopy of the live oak provided a cool relief. The weary riders dismounted, loosened their saddle cinches, and allowed their horses to graze on the sparse grass growing beneath the tree.

Chad offered Sarah a drink from his canteen. She reluctantly accepted. Handing back the canteen, she scanned the surrounding hills.

"He must be headed for the caves," she sighed as she shielded her eyes from the bright sunlight beyond the shade.

Caves, Chad thought. *Uncle Gib said those killers might head toward the caves.* "Have you ever been to the caves?" he asked.

Brushing damp wisps of wavy hair from her forehead, she replied, "Luke and I came this far with Father and Mr. Medina once last fall looking for some cows that had strayed up this way. Luke found a large cave just below us, but Father wouldn't let us explore it." She pointed toward the north. "The caves of the gold legend are supposed to be off over there toward the gap."

Turning to face her, Chad asked, "You really think he might head for those caves?"

"He's been so fascinated by that gold legend, I wouldn't be surprised." Sarah sighed and sat down on a large rock next to the tree trunk. "Coming this far, he probably wouldn't be able to resist the chance to have a look at the caves himself."

Chad glanced up through the branches at the position of the sun in the sky then leaned back against the trunk beside her. "It's taken us about three hours to get this far," he said.

"How much longer to get down there to the caves, do you think?"

Surprised that he'd ask for her opinion, the girl estimated, "At least another hour, I'd think." Picking up a stick, she drew several lines in the dirt. "This ridge angles off farther east than we need to go. If I remember correctly, Mr. Medina said there's a long narrow canyon down there somewhere that curves around to the base of some limestone cliffs. The caves can be seen from the hillside just below the cliffs." She drew three circles to illustrate. "He said you can't see that end of the canyon until you're right at the opening because of the way the trees overlap at the entrance."

Chad studied her dirt map then searched the hills to the north and shook his head. He grinned. "You know, Luke's a brave kid to travel all this way by himself and not give up."

Sarah scratched through the lines in the dirt. "No one has ever doubted that Luke's brave. In fact, he's been daring enough to take a body's breath away sometimes. It's a wonder Mother isn't completely grey with some of the antics he's pulled."

"This isn't just an antic to show off, is it?" Chad reached down to pick up a twig and turned to look at her.

Sarah bit her lip as she searched the horizon. "No, he's trying to prove something to Father when he returns. But of course, it isn't necessary." A sharp edge returned to her voice as she stood to glare at him. "And Mother and I had him convinced of that until you came along."

Chad snapped the twig and threw it down. "How was I supposed to know he was thinking about doing something like this?" he responded defensively.

"Haven't you noticed he practically hangs on your every word?" Sarah complained. "He has since you first got here." The concern in Chad's dark eyes told her he was worried nearly as much as she was. Glancing away, the girl softened her voice. "You should be more careful."

Chad was no longer listening to her and didn't reply. Looking back at him, Sarah could see his attention was riveted on something in the distance. "What is it?" she asked.

"Look there, below that ridge of rocks just this side of the gap. Isn't that smoke?"

In a moment, Sarah saw it too. The sight gave her a sudden chill. "Even with his head start," she choked back the words, "I doubt he could've made it down there yet. Do you?"

"Not by taking the trail we've been following," Chad replied, his mouth in a thin line. "It has to be someone else."

A look of fear replaced the concern in Sarah's eyes. Luke was still somewhere ahead of them. Who else was out there?

8

The couple followed clear tracks from the ridge down into the canyon to a fresh spring where they stopped to drink cold sweet water bubbling from a crevice in the rocks. The horses sipped from a small stone basin that trapped the water just before it disappeared again into rocks and brush on the canyon floor. The trail then vanished. The prints in the soft earth by the spring were the last they found as they followed the canyon around its curving course. They were certain Luke couldn't have climbed up the steep sides rising above them.

It was well past noon when they emerged from the canyon and found themselves on a low rise just above the valley. A large cluster of sycamore trees shaded the canyon entrance, and the riders studied the hard-packed ground where sparse grass poked up through a covering of gravel-sized rocks.

"This was the only way he could have come," Sarah's voice was edged with despair. She was hot and tired and at the moment uncertain of which way they should turn. Suddenly a series of muffled pops disturbed the oppressively still air. "Did you hear that?" Sarah turned toward Chad.

"Gunshots!" Chad cocked his head trying to tell from which direction the noises had come.

"Luke?" Sarah gasped.

"I don't think so. Listen!" Chad raised his hand to hush her. Several more pops rang out. "That's more than one rifle, but none of them sound like that old musket Luke has."

Digby's ears were pivoting nervously. Chad knew the mustang was listening to other sounds he himself could not hear yet. Following Digby's lead, Chad stared toward the rocky cliffs now visible from the canyon entrance.

"It's coming from over there at the base of the cliffs," Chad said abruptly as he urged Digby forward toward the sound of the gunfire. "Wait here. I'll go see what it is."

Ignoring his direction, Sarah nudged her sorrel forward and followed him.

Quickly, he eased his rifle from the saddle scabbard as they progressed cautiously along the tree-lined slope. When they drew near a thick cedar brake that blocked their path, the gunfire grew louder. All of a sudden, yelping and whooping sounds pierced the air.

"Comanches!" Sarah reined in suddenly, her throat constricted with fear.

Quietly, Chad slid from the saddle and motioned for her to remain where she was. After looping Digby's reins around a tree limb, he began moving carefully up the incline toward the right edge of the dense cedar. As he checked the load in his rifle he was startled by a slight noise right beside him. Sarah had again disregarded his directions. His frown had little effect, for she continued to follow close behind.

The two of them reached the high point of the incline at the edge of the cedar to find themselves peering down into a small clearing at the base of the limestone cliffs. They crouched down to conceal themselves and could see two white men huddled behind the cover of several rocks in the clearing.

The men were firing their rifles at three Indians racing by on horseback in front of them, well within range. Every time one of the men rose up to fire, a horseman would release an arrow from his short bow. They realized that one of the men on the ground had already been struck twice in the leg.

Relieved to see that her brother was nowhere in sight, Sarah whispered close to Chad's ear. "I told you they were Comanches. What should we do?"

Before he could answer, one of the Indians wheeled too close to his intended victim and was knocked from his horse by a rifle ball. A second Comanche attempted to rescue the downed warrior, but his horse stumbled and the brave was sent flying over its shoulder. Scrambling to its feet, the horse galloped away toward the gap a few hundred yards to the north. With his two companions down, the third Comanche whipped around in retreat.

The wounded white man had slumped to the ground, but the other one was instantly on his feet walking toward the two Indians now on the ground. The one who had been shot lay still. The other had pulled himself to his knees and was shaking his head trying to clear his senses.

Chad watched in horror as the armed man walked up to the wounded Indian and promptly shot him again. Sarah gasped. The man then strutted over to the kneeling Indian, reloading his rifle as he went.

Without thinking, Chad leaped forward. Sarah grabbed his arm, but he pulled away.

"Stay here! I mean it," he ordered sternly.

This time, the girl listened.

By now, the armed man had raised his rifle to his shoulder and was pointing it at the Comanche's head.

"Hey!" Chad shouted as he scrambled down into the clearing.

Startled, both the armed man and the Indian whirled to look at him. Seeing another white man, the armed man grinned through stained teeth and turned his aim back on the kneeling Indian. "Be with ya in a minute, kid."

"Put the rifle down!" Chad's authoritative tone took the man off guard.

"What?" he asked, certain he hadn't heard correctly.

"I said put the rifle down," Chad ordered as he reached the level ground of the clearing.

"Yeah, just as soon as I finish this."

With that, the killer took aim once more. The Indian didn't flinch.

The sudden boom of Chad's rifle echoed off the cliffs. The armed man cried out in pain as his left leg buckled under him and his weapon dropped to the ground. The Indian stared in disbelief at the man who was now clutching his bleeding leg and swearing loudly. Dumbfounded, he looked up at Chad.

"You shot me!" the white man shouted in agony. "You're either the worst blasted shot in this wide world or you're the biggest fool ever there was!"

"You were going to murder him in cold blood," Chad declared. "I'm sorry, but I had to stop you."

"Well, you're the one to be sorry. You just saved his life so's he can come back and kill and maim and prob'ly take your scalp someday." Clutching his leg, he wailed, "And I hope he does."

The Indian, who had jumped up and retreated a few steps back, now watched the young stranger pick up the man's rifle.

Chad could see that the Indian brave was not much older than himself, stocky in build and several inches shorter than he. The Comanche wore no shirt, only a breechcloth and moccasins. His black hair was parted in the center, hanging in braids on either side of his face, except for a scalp lock that fell from the top of his head. The black feather stuck in this scalp lock had been broken by his fall.

For a moment, the two young men studied each other without saying a word. Finally, Chad motioned to him to leave. The Indian studied him warily and took another step backward, not able to comprehend a white man who would save the life of an Indian by shooting another white man. He moved back to his fellow warrior and bent down to hoist the body over his shoulder. Still watching Chad, the brave retreated a few more steps then turned and rushed away toward the gap.

Before long, the third Indian had reappeared, leading the horse that had stumbled. The mounted Comanche lifted his fallen companion across his horse while the other one swung back up on the second animal. In the blink of an eye, they were obscured by a cloud of dust as they galloped away through the gap.

Sarah darted to Chad's side. She was speechless. The man on the ground, however, was not. He harangued Chad in loud profanity.

"Hold your foul tongue!" Chad demanded. "Can't you see there's a lady present!"

Sarah was still so stunned by what she had just seen that she hardly heard most of the man's words. When Chad handed the rifle to her, she smiled. "You know he's probably right about having to fight that Comanche again some day."

Chad shrugged his shoulders. "Maybe," he replied. "Here, hold this on him while I check his wound."

The girl took the rifle then pointed it at the wounded man. "I hardly think he's going to run anywhere."

"Probably not, but he might try to use this." Chad pulled a pistol from the man's belt and held it up for Sarah to see, then turned to the wounded man. "Your name wouldn't happen to be Clifton Pruitt, would it?"

"Who's askin'?"

Chad motioned toward the three animals picketed by the cedar bushes and replied, "Someone who's been followin' those two horses and burro, a fella with a red plaid vest like your friend over there's wearing, and his partner who likes to shoot unarmed old men."

"That old codger wasn't unarmed. He had a bowie knife the size of—" The man stopped, realizing he'd given himself away. He could see the disgust growing in Chad's eyes. "Yeah," he boasted, "I'm Clifton Pruitt."

Chad ripped the man's pant leg and examined the bullet wound while Pruitt yowled in pain.

"You've crippled me," he accused with a moan.

"You'll be fit enough to face the judge," Chad told him grimly. "The rifle ball just grazed the shinbone. Your friend doesn't look quite as lucky. What's his name?"

"You a Ranger?" the man grumbled.

"My uncle is," Chad replied. "And we have a witness who saw you and your friend rob an old prospector, murder him, then take his burro and ride off on a pinto and a bald-faced black horse. In fact, what's this?" He pulled out a tattered piece of brown stained parchment slipping from between the buttons of the man's shirt front. "I don't suppose this could be the map you stole from him?"

"What if it is?" The wounded man grumbled trying to see his wound. "It's the old geezer's fault fer gettin' shot. All he hadda do was give us this map, but no, he hadda pull out that ol' pig-sticker and nearly cut my hand off." At this Pruitt pulled the cuff away from his wrist to reveal a red scratch. "Looky there."

Chad merely shook his head.

Pruitt clutched his knee in agony and whined. "Who'd ever thought the great Clifton Pruitt would be tracked down and shot by a kid."

"Great Clifton Pruitt," Chad mumbled with disdain as he stood to go check on the other man.

"That's right!" Pruitt retorted. "You just wait till my brother, Rayburn, hears what you done to me, lettin' that Injun go after he killed poor ol' Brandy Jacobs there."

Chad found Jacobs, the man with the red plaid vest, was not dead but more seriously wounded than was evident before. The man never regained consciousness, however, and died before Chad and Sarah could put together a litter to carry him back to the farm.

Pulling one of the shovels from the outlaw's pack, Chad directed the wounded man to dig a grave for his deceased partner. The man cursed under his breath but did as he was told. As he began to dig, a shout echoed across the clearing from the edge of the cedar brake.

"Sarah! Chad!"

Whirling around, Sarah was overjoyed at the sight of her younger brother riding toward them, leading Digby and the sorrel.

"Luke," she cried with joy.

"What's happenin' here? Don't you know all that shootin' ruined my hunt? I had that cougar in my sights when—" Suddenly the boy noticed the outlaw with a shovel and the body covered with a blanket next to him on the ground.

After explaining what had happened, Sarah started to scold her brother for leading them on such a wild chase. But remembering Chad's words, she held her tongue. To Luke's surprise, his sister restricted her reprimand. "You had Mother worried to death. I'd better get back and let her know you're all right. Thanks for bringing the horses around."

"I saw y'all down here first," Luke explained, "then Digby whinnied at me, so I figured I oughta bring 'em on down."

Sarah reached for her sorrel's reins and prepared to mount. With her back turned, she heard Chad tell Luke, "One of the best ways to prove you're growing up is to choose to do something that's not going to get you killed in the process or cause your sister and mother to fret too much." Clapping the boy on the shoulder, he lowered his voice and added, "Or get somebody else, like me, in trouble while you're at it."

Luke looked over at his sister, who had just stepped up into the saddle. "You were in trouble?"

Chad nodded. "Let's just say when Sarah found out that our little talk yesterday might have set you off on this adventure, I probably came closer to being scalped than either of these two outlaws did today."

Out of the corner of her eye, Sarah saw a teasing smile curve Chad's mouth. She refused to smile in return. "If we stay here much longer," she declared icily, "we may all come close to being scalped. Bringing that murderer along and riding straight down the valley, you two might make it home before dark. I'll hurry on by myself so Mother can stop her fretting." With that, the girl turned her horse toward the south end of the valley and galloped away.

While Pruitt finished burying Jacobs, Chad removed the saddle packs from the stolen burro and put them on Pruitt's horse. Luke helped, asking questions the entire time.

"What're ya gonna do with that map, Chad?"

Putting it in one of the packs, Chad replied, "It has to go to the judge with the rest of this stuff. It's all evidence that helps prove Pruitt is the one guilty of that robbery and murder."

"Can I take a look at it?" Luke begged. "Just one little peek?"

The young man handed it to him. "Be careful; it's pretty old and starting to fall apart at the edges."

Luke held his breath as he gazed at the old brown parchment with its faded drawing and Spanish words scribbled across it.

While the boy studied the map, Chad brought Pruitt over and made him climb onto the burro, then tied his hands behind his back.

"Hey, if he spooks," the outlaw objected strenuously, "I could fall off and break my neck."

"Behave yourself, and I'm sure he'll be good," the young Bostonian replied grimly.

As Chad walked over to Luke, the boy grinned up at him. The young Preston's eyes were shining with excitement. "I knew there was a map. I knew it!"

"You boys take good care of that map." Pruitt grinned menacingly. "'Cause when my brother comes, we're gonna get it back, and anyone what gets in our way of findin' that gold will be sorry."

The outlaw's threat made Luke look to Chad for his reaction to the intimidating words. He handed the map back to him.

"The longer I'm around you, Pruitt," Chad declared with contempt, "the more I doubt that anyone would ever want to admit that he *was* your brother."

Pruitt was temporarily silenced by this, and Luke burst out laughing.

Chad turned to the boy and said, "Come on, Luke, let's mount up. I don't know about you, but I'm gettin' hungry."

A wide smile of admiration lit the boy's face as he nodded, then climbed up on his horse. Macklin handed Luke the lead ropes of the outlaws' two horses, then he swung up onto Digby's back and led the burro south down through the valley with Luke riding proudly alongside.

9

The sun was dropping low against the western hills when Mariah spotted two riders approaching the ranch along the road from Austin. She recognized Hector Medina on his pinto and was surprised to see that the man with him was not the doctor but an Indian. She waited on the porch.

She had seen friendly Indians come into Austin to trade before, still she was always a bit wary of any of them. Since coming to Texas, she had heard about the depredations committed by hostiles. There'd been many negative things said about the Mexicans too. The threat of being taken over by Mexico again at any time made many Texans suspicious of the Mexicans remaining in the Republic. Yet, seeing Hector Medina with the Indian comforted Mariah somewhat. Their farmhand had not survived his long years in this rugged and dangerous land by being foolish or careless.

"Señora Preston, this is Senihele, Delaware scout for the Rangers," Medina began. "He's come to help Señor Dunmar find his bad men."

"How do you do, sir," Mariah responded politely.

The man's face revealed little, but he nodded in return. Mrs. Preston relaxed a bit after learning he was a scout for the Rangers. Turning to Medina, she asked, "Where's Dr. Wendell?"

"Lo siento, Señora. I'm sorry, but the doctor's in Houston. How's Señor Dunmar?"

"Still very ill, I'm afraid," she sighed. "We have another problem as well. Luke has gone after that cougar. Sarah and young Macklin are out looking for him. They've been away all day. I'm nearly beside myself with worry."

Medina shook his head wearily. "Senihele is a very good scout, Señora. He could help us find them without any trouble."

"Have a bite of supper first and let your horses rest," she replied. "If they're still not back, I'd be very grateful if you'd go after them."

The older man agreed. Mariah turned to the Indian. "Mr. Sen—"

"*Sĕ-nē-hĕ-lā,*" the scout pronounced. "Most Rangers call me Sonny. My name means Sparrow Hawk in English." While his facial expression did not change, the tone of his voice and his attitude put her at ease.

"Sparrow Hawk seems more suitable than Sonny," she remarked candidly. "And I won't be as likely to mispronounce it as I might your Delaware name. Would you like to speak with Mr. Dunmar a moment?"

The Delaware nodded.

As Mariah motioned for him to follow, she added, "Just make sure he doesn't get upset. He must keep as still as possible.

"Oh, Mr. Medina, there's chicken and dumplings in the stewpot if you'd like to help yourself to some supper."

Dunmar was just stirring from a restless sleep when Mariah entered the bedroom with Sparrow Hawk.

"Senihele, good to see you," he grinned weakly, lifting his heavy hand with great effort.

The Indian grasped it and sadly noticed the lack of strength in the Ranger's grip.

"Have ya met my nephew, Chad?" Dunmar asked, looking toward the door.

"No." The Indian noticed the Preston woman step forward.

"I think that's enough visiting for now," Mariah quickly interjected before anything else could be said. "I'm sure Mr. Sparrow Hawk is hungry after his ride from Austin, and you need to rest, Mr. Dunmar. I'll bring you some broth in just a minute."

Irritated by his helplessness, he snapped, "Mrs. Preston, stop fussing about. Please. We have a tracking job to discuss."

"The lady is right." Senihele's words were deliberate. "There'll be time for that later. It's been a long day in the saddle, and even longer since breakfast."

Sinking back against the pillows, the Ranger nodded without further argument.

As they left the bedroom and crossed the dogtrot to the kitchen, Mariah said, "Thank you for not saying anything about his nephew and the children. He's already tried to get up once. I can't tell if the poultice I've been putting on his leg is helping or not. I don't know what else to do."

Before Senihele could reply, the sound of approaching hoofbeats drew their attention to the front yard. It was Sarah, alone. Mariah's heartbeat doubled and she hurried out to the hitching rail. "Sarah?"

"He's all right, Mother." The girl quickly jumped down. "He and Chad will be along in a little bit. I hurried back to let you know we'd found him. And listen to this. Chad shot a white man to keep him from killing an injured Comanche!"

"What?" her mother exclaimed.

Sarah quickly explained what had happened while she looped the reins around the hitching rail. She turned to tell her mother more when Senihele stepped off the porch. The sudden appearance of the Indian startled her. It took a moment for her to realize he was not a Comanche like she had seen earlier that day.

"Sarah, dear, this is Sparrow Hawk, a Delaware scout for the Rangers. He's come to help Mr. Dunmar."

Mariah turned to the tall scout. "This is my daughter, Sarah. Sounds like your work's nearly done already."

"Hmm, yes, it does." Senihele's black eyes surveyed the valley. "But I think I'll ride out to meet them," he decided soberly.

The light had nearly faded from the sky by the time Chad, Luke, and Sparrow Hawk arrived back at the ranch. The outlaw, Pruitt, was still complaining about his leg and being hungry as well as the humiliation of being forced to ride such a lowly beast as the burro.

"I'm sure he hasn't been any happier about it than you have," Chad commented wryly as he and Sparrow Hawk escorted the limping man to the smokehouse, a sturdy log shed that would not be used again for a while and had no windows, making it a perfect holding cell.

"I need some food," the oafish Pruitt demanded. "And I need a drink. My leg is killin' me."

"We'll bring you something in a little bit," Chad said, ushering him into the darkened room. "Just settle yourself down on that stack of gunny sacks and be quiet."

After the prisoner was settled, Medina and Luke took care of the horses. Chad brushed, curried, and fed Digby. Just as he was about to remark on the horse's good behavior, the mustang lifted his hoof slightly and set it squarely on the toe of the young man's boot. With a mighty shove, Chad pushed the animal sideways. "I'll give you the benefit of the doubt that that was an accident," he declared as he restrained his reflex to give the horse a pop on the shoulder. "Although I doubt it was. But watch those feet!"

Digby laid his ears back and gave his master a quick glance before returning to his feed bucket.

That evening, dinner brought considerable debate on whether to tell Chad's uncle about Pruitt's capture. Mariah was afraid the news might agitate him, but Chad and Senihele felt that he ought to be told so he could stop worrying about the assignment. As a compromise, they decided to wait until morning. The discussion turned to the task of taking the outlaw back to Austin.

"Will you rest here tomorrow and then take Pruitt back to Austin the day after?" Chad asked the Delaware.

The Indian sipped his coffee and stared at Chad for a long moment.

Before he could reply, Sarah interjected, "You really do have a lot to learn about Texas, Chad."

"Don't be rude, Sarah," her mother reprimanded.

"What'd I say wrong?" Chad looked to Mrs. Preston for an answer.

"Well, it's just . . ." Mariah eyed Medina and Senihele. "You see, with the tension between the settlers and everyone else, someone might not understand an Indian escorting a white man tied up as a prisoner. Some Texans might get the wrong idea and shoot first and ask questions later."

Instantly Chad realized that he should have considered the possibility that anyone who was not aware that Senihele worked for the Rangers might assume that an innocent settler had been taken captive by a hostile Indian.

"I guess I'd better ride along then, to make sure no one gets the wrong idea." The young man cleared his throat in embarrassment.

Senihele nodded. *"Wanishi."*

"You're welcome," Chad returned.

Surprised, the Indian ventured, *"Ktalenixsi hach?"*

"Kexiti," Chad smiled. *"Lenape nemuxumes."*

"What are you saying?" Luke was watching the two men curiously.

Chad grinned. "He said thank you, then asked if I speak Delaware. I told him that I do a little because my grandfather is a Delaware Indian. I'm afraid it's been awhile since I've practiced though."

It was obvious that the boy was impressed with Chad's knowledge of an Indian language. Out of the corner of his eye, Chad could see Sarah watching him closely. He found himself wondering if she was impressed or still irritated because her little brother still seemed to be hanging on his every word. As angry as the girl had been with him that day, Chad decided she was probably more annoyed than anything else.

The Indian pushed back from the table. "Thank you for the meal, Mrs. Preston. It's been a long day." Turning toward Chad, he added, "We should leave early in the morning, Macklin."

Chad agreed to be ready to leave at daylight. The Delaware left to sleep in the barn, and Chad excused himself to go sit with his uncle.

As the two women cleared the dishes from the table, Sarah found herself deep in thought. Still perturbed that Luke seemed to hang on the young Bostonian's every word, she had to admit that she was just a little impressed by Chad's linguistic ability. *This day has been full of surprises,* she thought. *Many more such days and Chad Macklin had better learn Comanche. It's very likely today's encounter won't be the last.*

As he started to open the bedroom door to see his uncle, Chad was startled by a movement beside him. Medina stepped silently into the circle of light from the oil lamp Macklin carried. The hired man pulled his hat from his head and clutched it to his chest, saying, "Pardon, hijo. There was a map? Luke says there was a map."

Chad could see an intense light dancing in the man's black eyes. The old weathered face was filled with eager anticipation. Nodding, Chad replied, "Yeah, there's a map." At these words, he could hear the man suck in a deep breath between clinched teeth. "Would you like to see it?" he offered.

Medina nodded slowly, seeming unable to speak. He followed silently as Chad led him to the barn where he'd left the packs. Sparrow Hawk was just settling down on his blanket spread on the straw-covered floor nearby as Macklin retrieved the piece of parchment from the old prospector's pack. The young man held it out to the Mexican, who stared at the folded brown paper a long time before putting out his hand to take it.

Chad brought the lamp closer when the man finally took the map and began gingerly to open the brittle folds. His dark eyes darted about the opened page as he whispered in a rapid flow of Spanish. Finally, looking up at Chad, his eyes shining, he whispered dramatically, "It is the one." Refolding it with great care, he handed it back to Chad. "It is the one."

"What?" the young man asked.

As if in a daze, Medina walked past him still whispering to himself. Filled with curiosity, Chad turned to watch the man walk out of the barn with Pepper trotting behind him.

Sparrow Hawk had been watching this exchange. Chad glanced his way. "I wonder what that was all about?" The Indian shrugged his broad shoulders and lay down to sleep.

10

Sarah stood at the door before entering the room and watched Chad seated next to his uncle's bed reading aloud from a book. When Chad finished the sentence he was reading, he stopped and noticed her standing there.

"I'm sorry, I didn't mean to interrupt," Sarah whispered.

"It's all right." He stood up and glanced at his sleeping uncle as she entered the room. "I hadn't noticed he'd fallen asleep. I'll just have to read over what he missed later."

Catching a glimpse of the book cover, she whispered, "Is that James Fenimore Cooper you're reading?"

He nodded. "Yes, it's his newest book, *The Pathfinder*. My mother sent it to him." With a touch of irony in his voice, the young man smiled. "She thought it might give him some helpful ideas about surviving on the frontier."

Sarah returned the smile. She knew that many folks had discovered the real frontier was a far cry from the idyllic view easterners had of the frontier in Cooper's popular novels.

"My father must have read *The Prairie* and *The Pioneers* a dozen times back home in Virginia," Sarah replied wistfully. "I think he found Texas a bit more than he bargained for." The thought of her father made her blink back sudden tears that threatened.

Walking over to the bed, she quickly changed the subject. "Looks like your uncle's resting as comfortably as possible." She gently touched Dunmar's forehead. "His fever seems to be down a bit."

"Good." Chad sighed and stretched wearily.

"Go on and get some sleep," Sarah directed. "Mother and I will take turns sitting with him tonight. You have a long ride ahead of you tomorrow."

Shaking his head, he replied, "That's not necessary." He had noticed the tears well in her pretty eyes and remembered Luke's comment about how worried she was about their father.

"But you'll need to be especially alert to escort Pruitt all the way back to Austin," she reasoned as she turned to look up at him.

She had overcome the tears, and her tone once more reminded him of his sisters. "I'll be fine," he insisted.

Trying not to be irritated by his stubbornness, she firmly suggested, "It wouldn't be a very good idea to be nodding off in the saddle, now would it?"

"I think I can manage." Chad put the book down on the bedside table. "Besides, it's not like I'll be having to watch him all by myself," he returned. "Senihele will be riding along."

His continued reluctance to accept any help nudged her temper. "Tell me, Mr. Macklin," she challenged with her hands on her hips. "Is it just me or have you always been this stubborn and contrary?"

The sleeping patient moaned and stirred slightly. They both lowered their voices.

"Neither," he whispered sternly. His temper was beginning to rise. "I just don't need anyone coddlin' me. From what I've seen around here, you and your mother work every bit as hard as any man does. Why should you stay up half the night just because I've got a long ride tomorrow? Thank you, but I'll stay with him myself."

102

"As you wish," she replied curtly as she turned swiftly on her heel. "I was only trying to help."

As she walked next door to her parents' bedroom, Sarah wondered why she even bothered. The man was indeed very stubborn, and he foolishly resented any offer of help. She had been surprised, however, by his recognition of the demands she and her mother faced in keeping the household and farm in good order. Over the past three years, the hard work had become an accepted fact of survival.

The young Mr. Macklin seemed accustomed to the ladies of the house enjoying a much less strenuous life. As she reached for the bedroom door latch, Sarah looked down at her hands. She was sure the young ladies with whom he was acquainted didn't have calluses on their soft hands or sunburn from working out in the cornfield all day.

Raising her chin and squaring her shoulders, the girl stepped away from the door and walked to the edge of the porch to look out into the surrounding darkness. On the other hand, she was sure none of them could spin their own thread, skin a rabbit, or hit a wild turkey on the fly with the first shot. None of them could say they were helping carve a home out of a wilderness, let alone willing to face wild animals and Indians. Sarah was certain of this because before coming to Texas she had never done any of these things either.

The night sky was like a wide black velvet cape covered with sparkling diamond stars. Looking up into the vast expanse, Sarah prayed softly. "Forgive me, Lord. I know You won't abide a prideful heart, nor an ungrateful one. I'm thankful for Your watching over us and the blessings You've given us here. It's just that sometimes I do miss the way things used to be back home in Virginia."

Her father had been chagrined to see his wife and little girl reduced to back-breaking chores, such as scrubbing laundry and chopping weeds from the cornfield. The fact that they refused to complain about the difficulties only seemed to cause him deeper distress. How many times had he apologized for their situation and promised that one day soon, they would have a beautiful house even bigger than the one they'd left behind. They'd have twice the number of servants to wait on them hand and foot. This business venture to Santa Fe would be just the beginning, he had vowed.

Sarah continued praying for her father's safe return and tried to dismiss the haunting dread that had filled her heart since he waved good-bye that day. Instead of fading as memories do, the unsettling feeling seemed to sharpen as the days and weeks passed.

Inside the bedroom, Chad Macklin stood silently staring out the window into the darkness. Would he and Sarah ever be able to carry on a conversation without snapping at each other, he wondered. He also began puzzling over Hector Medina's strange behavior regarding the recovered map. Wishing he could discuss it with his uncle, he realized that the less said about the outlaws, the better for right now.

"What's this about a long ride tomorrow?"

Chad turned from the window to see his uncle awake. Taken by surprise, he chose his words carefully. "The strangest thing, Uncle Gib. Today Luke went out hunting against his mother's wishes, and Sarah and I went after him." He couldn't lie to his uncle, but he too was afraid the truth would agitate the man's condition. "While we were looking for him, we came across the two men we've been tracking."

Pulling the rocking chair closer to the bed, Chad sat down. "They'd been attacked by Comanches. One of them died. The other one, Pruitt, was slightly wounded. We caught him off guard."

The young man turned to reach for the book on the table to avoid his uncle's perceptive gaze. "Then Luke found us and we brought Pruitt back. He's locked up in the smokehouse right now. Senihele and I are taking him back to Austin tomorrow."

104

"Wait." Dunmar managed to reach over and put his hand on his nephew's shoulder. "Wait a minute. You caught this Pruitt off guard?"

"Yeh." Chad tried to change the course of the conversation. "At first I thought Senihele could take him back himself, but they reminded me tonight that some people might resent an Indian bringing in a white man."

Dunmar smiled grimly. "That's puttin' it mildly."

"You feeling any better?" Chad continued to steer away from any further discussion of Pruitt's capture. "Sarah said your fever was down a bit."

"I think I feel a little better." Dunmar thoughtfully rubbed the beard stubble on his chin and turned toward his nephew. "It sounded like you two youngsters were quarrelin', lad. What seems to be the problem?"

Chad shook his dark head and met his uncle's glance. "I don't know really. She acts like my sisters. I mean, I'm older than her, yet she keeps trying to tell me what to do. I believe she thinks I have less sense about things than Luke does."

"Well, lad," Dunmar said knowingly, "she comes by it honestly. Her mother isn't shy about making her opinions known either."

Chad went on. "But she can ride as well as Aunt Christiana, Uncle Gib, and track almost as well as you and Uncle Stephan."

"Is that so?" His uncle listened with interest.

"I've never seen a woman work as hard as she does. I tried helping her carry water from the spring yesterday afternoon and she nearly bit my head off. Mumbled something about no sense gettin' spoiled letting someone else do her chores. Then she gets mad at me because I won't accept her offer to stay up half the night watchin' after you."

"Well," Dunmar confessed, "I've never been one to be able to figure out what goes on in a woman's head. I do know there are all kinds of people who come to Texas, but only two kinds who end up stayin' for more than a year: the ones who die tryin' and the ones strong enough in mind and heart to survive. The Prestons have been here three years now, I'm told."

Dunmar's voice was growing weak, and Chad could see he was exerting more energy than he should. "Would you like some water?"

"Aye. Thanks, lad."

Chad propped him up to drink water from a small cup then helped him lie back against the pillow. "I didn't quite finish that chapter I was reading. Would you like me to continue?"

The older man, exhausted from their brief discussion, only nodded silently. Chad read aloud for a while until his uncle was again sleeping. Soon his own eyelids grew heavy.

The next thing he knew, Mrs. Preston was tapping him on the shoulder.

The fifteen-mile trip to Austin was uneventful. Pruitt proved to be a whining coward. Without a rifle and partner, he was little more than a bitterly complaining nuisance who tried to talk his way out of his predicament. He threatened that his brother, an important man in New Orleans, would send his army of gunmen to get revenge. He then fell to grumbling and cursing his wretched luck of falling in with bad companions who had led him into his present unhappy state.

Chad found no patience or sympathy in his heart for this bad example of society coming to the frontier. After many miles, however, the prisoner's grovelling finally subsided.

At last, Chad was able to carry on a conversation with Senihele. This was the first opportunity he had ever had to speak with a Delaware, other than his Grandfather Macklin. As a child, he had been fascinated by the fact that he had Delaware blood in him. Although his family tree was predominantly Scotch-Irish, he had inherited dark eyes and hair from the Delaware side of the family. His Grandmother

106

Macklin had often told him how much he looked like his Grandfather Macklin when they had first met during the Revolutionary War.

When Chad was a rambunctious young boy, his sisters had declared that he was truly a wild Indian needing to be civilized. Such comments always gave him great pleasure because he secretly longed to escape the stuffy confines of his fine Boston lifestyle and enjoy the kind of life his grandfather had lived growing up. Although most people he knew would try to hide the fact that they had Indian blood, Chad had always been drawn to that element of his heritage. Now, here he was face to face with someone whose past generations may have shared the same hunting grounds as his own ancestors. To come so far and find a man who spoke words of the language he had been taught by his grandfather was intriguing.

Upon reaching Canyon Creek, a narrow branch of the Colorado River crossed by the road to Austin, the three men stopped midstream to allow their horses to drink.

It was Senihele who broke the ice. "So, your grandfather taught you to speak Lenape?" The Indian watched the rippling current swirl past as his horse nosed the water.

"Yes, a little," Chad replied, watching Digby drink his fill. "He's been away from the Lenape people for a long time, but when I was six, I asked to learn how to speak it." Chad smiled as he thought about his grandfather. "Unfortunately, he lives in Virginia and I grew up in Boston, and we haven't been able to spend a lot of time together. That's why I only know a few words and phrases." Turning to look at Sparrow Hawk, he added, "You speak better English than a lot of Texans I've heard."

"Your grandfather taught you Lenape; mine taught me English," the Delaware explained. "He was a good friend of a Baptist missionary named Isaac McCoy. Grandfather insisted we all speak English as well as Delaware. He told us never to forget our past; but to survive in the future, we had to learn to live with the white conquerors and that meant speaking the same language."

As Chad tried to imagine the talks with Sparrow Hawk's grandfather, Digby started pawing at the water. Chad knew this was a prelude to the mustang's vigorous splashing of water up on his legs and underbelly. Not in the mood for a shower, the young man tapped the horse's flank and urged him across the stream with Pruitt's horse following.

Continuing along the trail, Chad and the scout carried on their conversation.

"My folks were young when their band moved to Missouri from up in Ohio," Senihele said. "That was about 1793. They settled just west of the White River and stayed there about fifteen years. White settlers began moving in again, and a group of our people moved on down just south of the Red River. I was born a couple of years later."

"How'd you come to join the Rangers?" Chad asked.

"Long story."

Chad was curious to hear it.

After a pause, Senihele began. "Five years ago—I was about your age, I guess—my older brother decided to head farther west to look for a new place to settle. He stumbled into a fight between a band of Texicans on their way to join General Houston and a small force of Mexican soldiers. He ended up siding with the Texicans. After the Battle of San Jacinto, he returned home for a few days and talked me into going to San Antonio as a scout for a new group being formed to protect the citizens of the new republic. I've been scoutin' for the Rangers since."

"Uncle Gib told me about that Comanche, Antelope Runner. Have you caught up with him yet?"

Senihele stared straight ahead, his face set like flint. His hand went absently to touch his forehead, tracing the scar left by his old enemy.

"Sorry, I . . ." Chad wished he could take back his question.

"The time will come," the Indian replied stonily. The determination in his voice made it clear that Sparrow Hawk would stay on the Comanche's trail no matter how long it took to avenge his brother's death.

"I'm hungry," Pruitt interrupted loudly. "You boys ain't gonna eat all the food that purty missus packed by yerselves, are ya?"

The outlaw had watched Mrs. Preston hand young Macklin a satchel and heard her tell him it held some corn muffins, hard-boiled eggs, and apple fritters for their lunch. When his earlier threats and pleas for sympathy had fallen on deaf ears, the man had turned his thoughts to the food satchel. The more he thought about it, the hungrier he became.

Chad resented Pruitt's interrupting Sparrow Hawk's story and shook his head in disgust.

"The old military road about a mile up ahead is shaded by some big oaks," Senihele suggested. "There's also grass for the horses."

"That sounds good," Chad agreed and turned in the saddle. "Pruitt, you'll just have to wait a while longer."

"You enjoy makin' me miserable, don't ya, boy," Pruitt complained. A sinister tone crept into his voice as he glared at Chad. "You just better hope I never get the chance to return the favor."

It was shortly after dark before they finally rode into Austin. Being the dinner hour, the broad main street was quiet. Senihele led the way to the crude wooden building behind the Ranger Headquarters. Made from rough logs, the crude jail was much like the smokehouse. It did, however, have iron bars on the single window and across the door.

Chad was not surprised when Pruitt complained about his quarters. "It won't take Rayburn's boys two minutes to break me outta this shack," he warned.

After locking Pruitt in, they left their horses and gear at the livery stable and reported to Captain Anderson's office. A note on the captain's door announced that he was dining at the Bullock Hotel just down the street.

"Dinner sounds pretty good to me too," Chad commented with a grin. "Why don't we go join him?"

The Delaware's dark brown eyes widened and he studied Macklin briefly with raised eyebrows before he shook his head. "You go ahead. I need to see about that loose shoe on my roan."

"I'm so hungry I could eat a bear," Chad warned cheerily. "I can't promise I'll wait 'til you get there."

Senihele smiled slightly. "Don't wait," he replied as he turned toward the livery.

A few minutes later, Chad entered the hotel dining room. Several kerosene lanterns lit the inside brightly. A faint odor of freshly cut lumber and paint mingled with tempting aromas wafting from the kitchen. The dining room had only a few vacant places here and there. Macklin spotted the Ranger captain sitting by himself and reading the *Austin City Gazette* in between bites of apple pie. The captain looked up as Chad approached.

"Well, son, I'm surprised to see you here." The man brushed pie crust crumbs from his black mustache. "Sit down. How's your uncle?"

"Hello, sir," Macklin returned, pulling out a chair. "Uncle Gib still isn't doing too well, but Mrs. Preston says these things take time to heal."

"That they do," the captain agreed; the leathery wrinkles around his eyes deepened as he smiled encouragingly. "Knowing ol' Gib, he'll be up and about before you know it. What brings you back to Austin so soon? The doc's still gone. Don't expect him back 'til end of the month."

A woman in a blue apron with carrot-red hair pinned up in a neat bun interrupted the conversation. Chad ordered a buffalo steak with sweet potatoes and corn bread, milk, and an extra large piece of apple pie.

"Senihele told me not to wait on him," the young man said after the woman left.

"Course he did," the captain replied as he wiped his mouth with a white cloth napkin. "Scouts eat back in the kitchen."

Immediately Chad realized that scouts were not allowed to eat in the dining room because they were Indians. He felt bad but went on to give his report. "Sir, Senihele and I brought in one of the men you sent Uncle Gib after."

"You caught one of those bushwhackers?" The captain leaned forward.

"Yeah, it's Clifton Pruitt. The other one was killed by Comanches. We took Pruitt on over to the jail just now. Here's the map Pruitt was carryin'." Macklin pulled the parchment out of the old prospector's saddlebag he had brought with him. "He admitted it was the one they took from that old fellow they killed."

"Good job, son! I'd say you more than earned your supper with this," Captain Anderson exclaimed, accepting the folded map. "I bet your uncle is mighty proud. Sure you wouldn't like to join up? We could sure use a few more young men like you."

"I've been considering it, sir," Chad confessed, "but I have to go back and wait until Uncle Gib can travel before I do. The Prestons have been very kind, but if I know my uncle, he can't impose on them much longer."

"The Prestons are fine folks." The captain took his last bite of pie. "Truth is, with Tom Preston away, it probably wouldn't hurt for Gib to rest up there awhile and keep an eye on things. I'm sure the Preston ladies would be glad to have another man around to help protect them."

Chad smiled thinking about the independent Preston women. He was then reminded of their hired hand, Hector Medina, and the man's strange reaction to the map he'd just given the captain.

The Ranger pushed back the empty dessert dish and reached for his coffee cup, moving the parchment paper out of the way.

"Captain, ya don't suppose," Chad pointed to the map, "that map could be the real thing?"

Anderson tapped the folded paper with a leathery brown finger as if testing its authenticity. He looked squarely at Macklin through hazel eyes that had witnessed more excitement, danger, and death in his twenty-eight years than most men ever see in a lifetime. Shaking his head, he drawled, "Don't really matter much whether it is or ain't. It's cost at least two lives that we know about 'cause someone thought it was. Way I see it, somethin' like this only means trouble."

The waitress placed Chad's meal in front of him, interrupting their conversation. After she walked away from the table, the Ranger captain finished his coffee and pulled a coin out of his vest pocket to lay on the table. "Better saunter on over to the jail and check on our new guest." The man stood and gathered up the map and prospector's saddlebag along with his hat and newspaper. "Just tell the clerk at the desk who you are, and he'll give you a room for the night. It's the least the Rangers can do for ya after catchin' Pruitt."

Chad thanked him then turned to his full plate. Although the buffalo meat was tough, the meal was tasty, and Chad began to feel human again.

As he sat finishing his food, Chad noticed the other people in the dining room. Several men in black suit coats with high starched collars sat nearby. He surmised these were probably office holders in the Texas government. Two of them were accompanied by their wives. Chad could hear them discussing the recent election of Sam Houston as president of the Republic. The sound of German accents came from a table where a finely dressed man and woman sat with two young boys. Chad knew they must be part of the settlement of German immigrants established between Austin and San Antonio. His uncle had called it New Braunfels. The rest of the guests appeared to be merchants and other members of the community.

Chad realized his long day on the trail had left him looking unkempt and dusty. He could use a bath and change of clothes; however, he hadn't brought anything except his buckskin jacket. The thought struck him that if his sisters and mother saw him now, they'd give him a good scolding.

As the scarce bit of sleep, the intense search for Luke, the capture of Pruitt, and the long ride to Austin began to catch up with him, the young man's appearance concerned him less and less. By the time he had finished eating, all he felt like doing was finding his room and sleeping for a week.

11

A good sound night's sleep left Chad refreshed and feeling as if he *had* slept a whole week. Stepping out onto the hotel porch, the young man squinted into the bright October morning sun. Having finished his breakfast, he decided to go to the Austin mercantile and purchase the supplies Mrs. Preston had requested. Then he'd try to find Senihele and tell him good-bye before heading back to the Prestons' farm.

Stepping off the walk into the dusty street, he started over to the mercantile when he noticed a young boy dashing down the wooden walk, dodging people in his way. The boy turned in to the hotel and in a minute came flying back outside chasing after Chad.

"Are you Chad Macklin?" the boy called across the road after him.

Surprised to hear his name, Chad turned around. "Yes," he answered.

"Captain Anderson wants to see you right now," the boy declared, gulping a deep breath. "You better git over there quick. Just wait 'til you see."

With that, the young messenger ran down the street, stopping every once in a while to report something to adults passing by. Macklin wondered what could be causing such a commotion and walked quickly down the block to the Ranger's office. A small crowd had gathered outside. The grave expressions on their faces warned Chad that whatever it was had people very upset.

Forging his way through the crowd, the young man entered the office. Several men crowded around a chair by the captain's desk. Senihele stood to one side. Beside him were three Indians, all shorter and of stockier build than the Delaware. Chad was curious what tribe they were from. The scout saw him and nodded, so Chad started to cross the room to speak to him, but the captain spotted him.

"There you are, Chad. Come over here."

Drawing closer, Macklin discovered a young man in the chair. His clothes were in tatters and hung over a tall, gaunt frame; his skin was blistered and peeling from long exposure in the sun; and his fair-colored hair was so caked with dirt, it looked almost black.

The captain stepped next to Chad. "This is Dolph Hammersmith, Chad," he explained. "He was one of the soldiers escorting the expedition goin' to Santa Fe."

"What happened?" Chad whispered as he noted the far-away look in Hammersmith's pale blue eyes. It was obvious he was suffering from more than just long exposure to the elements.

"Near as we can make out, the expedition ran short of water and rations," the captain explained. "They got lost and apparently fought off several Indian attacks. Dolph was knocked out during one attack. When he came to, everyone was gone. He started walking. These three Tonkawas found him about fifty miles west of here."

"What about Mr. Preston?" Chad wondered. "Does he know what happened to him?"

Without a word, the captain held out a small leather wallet used to carry rifle cartridges on a man's belt. "Take a look inside."

Chad found a small neatly folded piece of paper smudged with several dark red stains. The Ranger went on, "Go ahead, read it."

Opening the paper, Chad found scrawled letters reading "Last Will of Tom Preston." A sinking feeling swirled in the pit of his stomach.

"Preston was mortally wounded in a fight with some Apaches. Before he died, he asked Dolph to bring this back to his family. They buried him five days before the last attack Dolph knows about."

"Ahh, no," Chad sighed. Glancing at the paper in his hand, he shook his head sadly. "Someone's goin' to have to break the—" he stopped. Suddenly, by the look in the captain's eyes, it was clear he was turning the task over to the young Macklin.

Chad started to protest, "I couldn't. What can I say? All this time they've been looking for him to be coming back."

The captain clapped him on the shoulder firmly. "I'm sure you'll do just fine, son."

A commotion sounded at the door as a man and a woman pushed through the crowd. "That's Dolph's aunt and uncle," the captain explained to Chad as the crowd parted for the couple. At the sight of her nephew, the woman gasped and began sobbing loudly. Her husband quieted her down, and in a few minutes they carefully led the young man out the door.

"I told them you wouldn't mind going by and telling the Hammersmiths their boy is back," the captain informed Chad as the couple helped Dolph into their wagon. Chad agreed, and the wagon pulled away carrying the young soldier to the couple's home at the edge of town.

The bright October morning had suddenly turned gloomy. Chad refolded Preston's will and returned it to the leather wallet. A heavy weight settled on his broad young shoulders as he contemplated the message he would be carrying to the Prestons. He wished he hadn't come to Austin

116

after all; then someone else would have had to deliver the tragic news.

This would not improve Sarah's attitude toward him either, he was certain. And poor Luke. The boy had nearly gotten himself killed trying to accomplish something to make his father proud of him. Macklin wondered what Mrs. Preston would decide to do. They had put in a tremendous amount of work to make their farm what it was today. It was a shame to think of all that effort being wasted. Maybe they would go back to Virginia or perhaps move to Austin.

A short while later, Chad had finished making the purchases at the mercantile when he ran into Senihele at the livery.

"The captain is sending me to San Antonio to tell Captain Jack Hays about this thing in case Rangers are dispatched to help find the expedition, or what's left of it." The scout watched as Chad saddled Digby. "It's good you have a mustang. He'll carry you farther and quicker than most other horses can."

Leading his roan from its stall, Senihele offered his hand. *"Xu lapi knewel."*

Chad took his hand in a firm handshake. "Yes, I hope we'll see each other again someday."

"Hurry to the Prestons as fast as you can," the scout directed in clear English. "The Tonkawas told me about seeing a large Comanche village two days' ride northwest of here. They also came across signs of a good-sized hunting party heading this way. Keep a sharp eye out."

12

"Well, look at this," Mariah Preston exclaimed with a triumphant smile. "You've eaten all of your supper." The woman placed her hand on her patient's forehead and added, "No fever this evening. It would appear, Mr. Dunmar, that the worst is over. It'll take some time yet for that leg to heal, but it's looking a lot better. The Lord has answered our prayers. You'll be walking out of here in another week or so."

Dunmar was indeed feeling better. His appetite had returned, and the simple venison stew tasted better than any he'd ever had before. Watching Mrs. Preston picking up the tray with his empty bowl, he cleared his throat.

"Madam," he announced in his thick Gaelic accent, "I will forever be in your debt for savin' m'life and leg. A Scot does not like to be in debt to anyone. But ya have my word, if I can ever be of assistance to you and your family, all ya have to do is ask it."

"Your debt is not to me, Mr. Dunmar, but to the good Lord. I grew up helping my father on his farm in Virginia, and I've seen men die or lose a limb from bites that seemed less severe than this one. God is the one who decides who will recover and who will not."

"I suppose you're right, though I'll never understand why He'd spare this stubborn carcass and take a fine, gentle creature like my—" The Ranger fell silent, unwilling to continue. The question had been swimming in his subconscious for a long time. It slipped out almost before he realized it.

"Your wife, Elaine?" Mariah finished for him.

Taking a deep breath, he continued, "Even so, 'twas your carin' hands that have ministered to bring me back from death's door, and I thank you."

"You're welcome," she said as she headed out of the room and paused on the threshold. "Now, if you behave yourself and rest as you should, we'll see about moving you out to the porch for a little while tomorrow afternoon. Some fresh air and a little sunshine might be just the thing to help bring some color back to your face."

"Aye, I'm sure it would," Dunmar agreed heartily. "By the way, wasn't it just yesterday that Chad left for Austin? I've lost all track of time."

"Yes. I imagine he'll be back tomorrow evenin'. After the little bit of sleep he's been getting, he's probably spent today resting in Austin and will start back in the morning."

"No doubt," Dunmar agreed absently as he thought about his nephew. He had finally gotten the real story of Pruitt's capture from Sarah. While he had been a bit unnerved by their precarious situation, his heart had swelled with pride as he listened to the girl's account of the incident. His nephew had never been one to hang back from a challenge.

Perhaps inviting Chad to Texas had not been the best idea, however. Everywhere one turned in this new republic there were challenges and risks to face. He would never have been able to face his sister nor his nieces if anything had happened to Chad in confronting the outlaws or Indians. Now the lad was off doing the job Dunmar himself should be doing. With his clearing senses came a sharpened anxiety for his nephew.

Despite Mrs. Preston's conjecture, Dunmar felt sure that Chad would allow himself only one night's rest before making the return ride to the Preston farm. If that were the case, the lad should have arrived by late that afternoon, but the light had nearly faded from the sky and still there was no sign of him. Dunmar hoped that Mariah was right and the boy was still safe in Austin.

Lying on his bed, the patient tried not to think of all the dangers that could be encountered between the capital and the Preston farm. His turbulent thoughts were interrupted when Sarah knocked at the door.

"Mother says you're feeling much better, Mr. Dunmar. Would you like for me to continue reading from where we left off last night?"

"I'm sure you have better things to do than sit and read to a tired gentleman," he returned wearily.

"Perhaps," she replied with a saucy tilt to her chin. "But I can't think of what it might be at the moment." She picked up the book Chad had brought from Boston. "Besides, I'm enjoying this myself. Mr. Cooper was—is—my father's favorite author."

The Ranger noticed that the girl's slip of the tongue brought a slightly perplexed expression to her blue-green eyes.

She quickly opened the book to the marked pages and read the first two words only to stop. "How long do you think it should take the expedition to get back from Santa Fe?" She laid the book on her lap.

"That's kinda hard to say," Dunmar replied, meeting her questioning gaze.

"Surely they'll be returning any day now, don't you think?"

"Aye, it's possible, but then perhaps they've met with such great success, they've decided to stay awhile."

Sarah appreciated Dunmar's encouraging suggestion. She only wished she could believe it. The recurring feeling of cold dread she had felt that day watching her father wave to

120

them from the wagon headed for Santa Fe only swept over her stronger than ever.

She had to force her attention back to the book. Slowly but surely she was able to begin concentrating on the printed words and their meaning. Outside, darkness descended upon the land and a coyote yipped a woeful song somewhere in the distance.

Chad blinked, trying to clear the swimming vision before him. A small campfire burned brightly just a few feet away. Outside the circle of firelight the surrounding darkness closed in like a thick curtain. The young man thought he heard voices and was dreaming some eerie dream, yet the strange faces and shadows moving on the other side of the fire were very real.

His arms ached, and he couldn't feel his hands. When Chad realized he was lying on the ground, he moved slightly, only to discover his hands were bound securely in front of him, restricted by a rough limb that passed in front of the crook of his elbows and across his back. This crudely simple device effectively immobilized his hands and arms and was extremely uncomfortable. Suddenly the figures on the other side of the fire stood still.

A dull ache in Chad's head prevented his gathering his thoughts enough to explain what was happening. He heard voices again but couldn't understand what was being said. As his vision cleared, he realized that the faces across the fire from him were Indians! A knot doubled in his stomach. These were Comanches.

All at once, one flash of memory tumbled over in his mind, then another, until he suddenly remembered riding Digby along the wagon road from Austin. They had crossed Canyon Creek, and he had stopped to give the mustang a rest from the steady pace they had maintained since leaving the capital. He had sat down in the shade of a tree, allowing the horse to graze on a small patch of grass along the road.

121

The next thing he remembered was being surrounded by five Comanche braves on horseback. When one of them reached for Digby's reins, the feisty mustang sidestepped and the warrior slid off his own horse. Suddenly the mustang turned, flattened his ears, and with bared teeth, charged at the grounded brave.

By this time, Chad had jumped to his feet and was poised for a fight. Digby's actions had distracted the war party's attention and the one brave was already scurrying back up on his own horse. Instantly, Chad's horse reared up on his hind legs and thrashed at the Indian who had tried to grab him. The brave whipped an arrow out of the quiver slung on his back. Another Comanche charged toward the mustang to distract him while his companion readied his bow and arrow.

Almost before he knew what he was doing, Chad hurled himself at the brave preparing to shoot. He clutched the Indian's arm and yanked him backwards off the horse. The released arrow flew straight up into the air. The brave crashed to the ground like a stone and lay motionless, stunned by the fall.

The Indian pony that bolted out of the way knocked into a third brave rushing toward Chad with a war lance. Before the man could wheel around for a second try, another pony suddenly pushed between Macklin and the other braves.

Its rider held up his hands to stop the attack and looked down at Chad. In that moment, young Macklin was astonished to recognize the young Comanche whose life he'd saved. Then a sharp blow on the back of his head had blacked everything out.

Now Chad struggled to sit up. The pounding inside his head increased and the scene before him blurred until his dizziness subsided. His arms and back still ached from the crude hobble.

Four braves sat across the fire, silently staring at him. The aroma of something cooking drew Chad's attention to a long stick anchored in the dirt and leaning over the fire. A long, thick strip of meat was impaled on the sharp point of the stick. It reminded Chad of a narrow flag hanging from a pole with flames dancing beneath the lower end.

A movement to Chad's right brought his attention to that same young brave he had recognized earlier. Firelight glinted on the blade of the long knife the Indian toyed with in his hand. Chad swallowed hard as he returned the brave's steady gaze. The Comanche then turned and Chad breathed a quiet sigh of relief as he saw the brave use the knife to cut a small chunk from the strip of meat. To Chad's surprise, the brave turned back toward him and held out a chunk of the meat.

The meat was still raw, and although Chad was very hungry, he shook his head no. "Thanks anyway," he said softly.

The Comanche shoved the dark red chunk his way again then pointed toward a buffalo hide on the ground a few feet away. Chad took the meat in his teeth. He was glad it wasn't a very big piece, for it was barely warm. Trying not to choke, he managed to chew and swallow it. The others were eagerly cutting portions for themselves and voraciously devouring their meal with relish.

The young Comanche cut another piece of meat and crouched next to Chad. Chad raised his bound hands as much as his bonds permitted and tried to gesture that he'd had his fill. The brave shrugged his shoulders and quickly consumed the portion himself.

Chad wished he could understand the conversation going on, because he was sure they were talking, at least in part, about him. He shifted uncomfortably and tried to wiggle his fingers to restore the feeling in them.

Suddenly the gleam of a shiny knife blade flashed inches away from his chest. In one heart-stopping moment, the familiar Comanche grabbed Chad's left wrist and with a slash of the knife severed the rawhide straps binding his hands. Now Chad was able to move his arms enough to let the thick limb across his back drop behind him.

Slowly Chad began to rub his wrists. "Thanks. *Wanishi.*" He cautiously tried the Delaware word for thank you.

It worked. The word caught their attention. Chad wondered if they understood the Delaware language. Almost instantly a less comforting thought sprang to mind. The Delaware word might mean something entirely different in Comanche. Venturing further with, *"Ktalenixsi hach?"* he asked if they spoke Delaware.

The braves exchanged questioning looks. Finally the one sitting next to him replied, "Speak English?"

Chad was so surprised, it took a moment to say, "Yes."

The brave thumped his chest proudly. "I speak English."

"Thank goodness," Chad sighed as he pulled the strips of leather away from his wrists. He could feel the young brave's dark eyes staring at him and looked up to meet the studying gaze.

"You save Bobcat," the Comanche declared gruffly. "Why?"

Chad was a little surprised by the question. The answer should be obvious, he thought. He answered directly, "I couldn't stand by and watch a murder."

The two young men stared at each other for a moment longer, then Chad offered his hand. "My name's Chad Macklin. You're Bobcat?"

The Comanche glanced at his companions across the fire. They watched in stony silence as he hesitated then shook hands with the white man.

Chad guessed that Bobcat's curiosity about a white man who would shoot another white man to save a Comanche's life was what had saved his life. The memory of seeing the brave with the poised lance convinced Chad that he would probably be dead if not for Bobcat's intervention. Keeping this in mind, he wondered just what their intentions might be. He felt sure that his best chance for survival was to try to reach some sort of understanding with the young Comanche, for he evidently had influence with the others.

Macklin soon learned that the young Comanche's command of English was somewhat limited. He had learned the vocabulary of a ten-year-old boy who had been taken hostage three years before in a raid along the Guadalupe River. The boy had been adopted by Bobcat's family.

Using a combination of diagrams drawn in the dirt and sign language charades to amplify their English words, the two young men communicated long into the night. Chad learned that the band to which Bobcat and his friends belonged had been hunting buffalo in a broad valley several miles to the northwest. This small raiding party was out gathering as many horses as they could. Chad realized this gathering was in reality the stealing of horses from the settlers.

At one point, Chad asked about Digby. Bobcat indicated that the mustang had escaped. Macklin was relieved. As cantankerous as Digby could be, he was afraid if they caught the mustang, they would lose patience and kill him.

Bobcat began to ask questions about Chad and why he spoke Lenape. Learning about Macklin's grandfather being Delaware, the young Comanche seemed to accept the fact more easily that Chad had saved his life.

It was very late and the other braves were already curled up in their blankets and asleep by the time the conversation came around to the Prestons. Yes, Bobcat knew of the farm; he had seen it from the cliffs across the river. He admitted that his people avoided the Prestons' valley because of the stories passed down by the old ones. They had been warned that it was a place of death for any Indians venturing in there.

"But you and your friends went into the valley," Chad commented curiously.

"We follow two men, good horses, one burro. Watch from ridge." The Comanche stopped a moment, recalling how his friend, Bold Calf, had dared the other two to enter the valley. The horses would be worth more if they were taken from the place of the ancient Spaniards, Bold Calf had reasoned. They soon convinced themselves that since the white man's camp was not very far into the valley, they could strike as quick as lightning and be out through the gap again before the vengeful spirits even knew they were there. "We are wrong," Bobcat said grimly. "They kill Bold Calf. Your medicine is strong, Macklin. You say no and the spirits listen."

Chad began to deny he had any such power when one of the other braves raised up and grumbled something to Bobcat. The young brave replied gruffly but reached for his blanket and wrapped it around himself. Turning to Chad, he said, "Sleep now. You are safe. Sleep." With that the Indian lay back and closed his eyes.

For a long while, Chad sat there wide awake studying the situation. All five Comanches appeared to be sleeping. But on looking closer, Chad could see that two of them had their hands on their lances, and one had a war club lying next to his hand with another's bow and arrows at his side. Even Bobcat's dark hand rested on the handle of his scalping knife.

Despite the knife scabbard tucked away in Chad's knee-high moccasins, the young man felt certain if he made a move, he wouldn't get more than a few paces. Considering this, he finally tossed a couple of small rocks out of the way and lay down, glad his family couldn't see him now. What an entry this would make in his journal if he lived long enough to write it.

The fire was dying down, and Chad could see a million stars glittering in the blackness above him. He thought about other nights, like the ones spent on his father's ships in the middle of the ocean, nights sitting on the farmhouse porch in Kentucky with his Uncle Stephan and Aunt Christiana, and the nights in Texas camping out on the trail with his uncle. Never once could he have imagined being here like this, sharing a campfire with Comanche Indians. He could only wonder what daylight might bring. Sleep overcame him as he was praying for the strength and courage to face whatever it might be.

13

Dawn crept silently but gloriously over the crest of the eastern hills. The warm luminescence gently unveiled the valley shrouded in a powder grey mist. Sarah sat on the front porch steps, a blanket wrapped around her against the cool dawn air.

Strange, disturbing dreams made sleep too unpleasant to linger there. She couldn't remember what the dreams were about, only that she was glad when she had awakened.

Since Chad Macklin and Mr. Dunmar had entered their lives a week and a half ago, Sarah had been sharing her mother's bedroom. Unable to get back to sleep after awaking a third time, the young lady decided to sit on the porch and watch the sunrise so she wouldn't disturb her mother. She loved the break of day; it always seemed such a blessing after the blackness of the night, especially in Texas where one was never sure what might be lurking in the darkness.

Taking a deep breath of the dew-freshened air scented with sage and cedar, Sarah stretched lazily and looked down the trail leading toward the Hammersmiths' place and Austin. Chad should be returning today, she thought absently. While Sarah would never admit it to anyone, she had missed him. Since the day they had searched for Luke, her resentment of the fact that her brother looked up to him had diminished. She had been impressed by the way he had handled the situation with the outlaw and the Comanche. Apparently he didn't lack courage. But he might survive longer if he exercised a little better judgment.

Pulling the woolen blanket closer, Sarah wondered if she should tell Chad how reckless it was to go marching in between an armed outlaw and a wild Comanche. She couldn't guess what might have prevented the brave from jumping Macklin while he was reloading, unless he was as stunned as everyone else by Chad's actions.

Uncle Gibson had explained to her about Chad's Delaware ancestry and the bitterness over his Uncle Ram's death as a result of trying to help his Cherokee wife's relatives during the forced removal from Georgia. After hearing this, Sarah had been able to understand Chad's sympathetic views toward the Indians. She only hoped the young Macklin would not learn too late that the Comanche Indians were different than any other Native American tribe the white settlers had yet encountered.

Mr. Medina called them a warrior society. Sarah knew that by perfecting the skills of horsemanship they had become the rulers of the southern plains. They could strike like lightning, leaving death in their wake, and withdrawing before help could ever be mustered. Sarah also knew they intended to hold the vast plains and buffalo hunting grounds by whatever means possible, showing no mercy to man, woman, or child.

However, the Prestons' cabin had never been approached by Indians the way nearly every other homestead up and down the river had. Maybe there was something to Mr. Medina's story that the Indians were afraid the ghosts of Coronado's men did inhabit their valley and surrounding hills. She felt her father believed it; otherwise he never would have left them on their own for such a long time. She prayed he would return soon, having gained the success he so badly wanted; maybe then life would be like before his bank was lost.

128

"Sarah?"

Startled, she turned to see Luke hop down from the sleeping loft ladder.

"Shhh, you'll wake Mother," she cautioned. He came over to sit down beside her.

"Whatcha doin'?" he yawned.

"Watching the sunrise."

The boy stretched his arms behind his back. "You s'pose Chad'll be back today?"

"Probably," Sarah replied.

"You know, Sarah, you could be a little nicer to him," Luke said.

"What?" Her brother's suggestion caught her off guard.

"You're always snapping at him. I told him you're just worried about Father," Luke explained. "He thinks you're pretty, but the way you always argue with him makes him think you don't even like him, so he probably won't ever come courtin'."

"Courting?" She stared at the boy, astonished that he would bring up the subject. "Why in the world would I care if he came courting or not?" Her brother stared back with a big grin on his face, making her turn away. "Besides, he's only visiting Texas. He'll be goin' back to Boston someday, if he doesn't get himself killed first."

"Well, if he asked ya to marry him, you could go back to Boston with him," Luke teased.

The young woman jumped up and propped her hands on her hips, the blanket falling down at her feet. "Marry? What in the world possessed you to think of such a thing? And what makes you think I'd accept even if he asked? I couldn't care less about—"

"Whoa, Sarah." Her brother's grin widened. "If you don't care, why are you gettin' so upset?"

"Upset? I'm not upset. I'll show you upset. Mother'll be upset if you don't get down to the barn and gather those eggs before breakfast."

She turned toward the door. "And how do you know he thinks I'm pretty, anyway?"

"He told me so." Luke was enjoying himself immensely. He was seldom able to get the best of his sister, and when he did, it was a sweet victory.

"I don't believe a word of it, nor do I care." With that, the girl stormed into the house.

No one was stirring in the Indian camp as the first grey streaks of dawn appeared along the horizon. Chad, who had only catnapped through the night, was now lying on his side, his head pillowed on his arm. Looking across a broad clearing, he watched the dark shadows soften under the trees along Canyon Creek.

All of a sudden he spied a light-colored object in the gloom beneath the trees. He blinked his eyes and stared harder at a pale grey form. In a few moments, he knew it was Digby. There at the edge of a stand of sycamore trees stood the little mustang looking almost like a ghost. Chad could not suppress the smile that came to his lips as he watched the mustang stare at him across the clearing between the camp and the trees.

Suddenly a war whoop pierced the quiet grey dawn. Instantly, all five Comanches were on their feet, weapons in hand. Chad too was startled by the unnerving cry. The horse disappeared. The sound had apparently spooked him as well. A slight movement caught Chad's attention, and he could just make out the mustang's form in the denser shadows. Meanwhile, three riders thundered across the clearing about fifty yards down the creek from where Digby remained partially concealed in the trees.

Chad stood poised for action, but Bobcat and his companions relaxed as they recognized the approaching riders who wore breechcloths with fringed buckskin leggings and fringed moccasins just like theirs. As they reined to a sliding halt, Chad saw that the braves had red paint streaked on their faces and one of them wore a buffalo headdress. Their war shields of thick, tanned buffalo hide decorated with red paint and feathers attached to the rims made a spectacular sight.

Bobcat's party greeted the newcomers with exuberant shouts and shaking their weapons in the air. They almost forgot Chad's presence until the leader of the newcomers stopped short. Bobcat rapidly spoke something in Comanche to the leader. The group eyed Chad suspiciously.

Within two minutes, all of the braves were preparing to leave. Chad could hardly believe his eyes. As they whooped and hollered, the Indians wheeled their horses and rode away, leaving Chad standing there speechless and feeling a little like he had just been in the center of a whirlwind.

Macklin drew in a deep breath, thankful to be alive. Then one of the riders dropped back and trotted back toward him. It was Bobcat. Chad watched the young brave warily, not quite sure what to expect.

Bobcat jumped to the ground almost before his horse had stopped. He gestured with a rapid fire of Comanche words, and Chad frowned in frustration at being unable to understand.

The brave took a breath and with deliberate care chose English words. "We go join my father, war chief Stands Before Running Buffalo. Leads war party to destroy all whites along river."

"What?" Chad's heart sank.

Bobcat whipped his knife from the scabbard and slashed a line in the dirt, then drew a circle. "Prestons," he named the circle. Then pointing at the farthest end of the line he added, "Begin attacks upriver." He slashed across the circle. "Two days. Prestons hurry to Austin, now!"

"You'll give them time to get away to Austin?" Chad asked, his heart pounding.

Bobcat repeated, "Strike in two days."

"What about the ancient Spaniards?" Chad asked.

131

"No time to explain." Bobcat jammed his knife back in the scabbard. "Just take friends and leave."

Chad nodded.

The Comanche brave quickly offered his hand and the two young men grasped each other's wrist in a brotherly shake, then the Indian took a running leap, sprang to his horse's back, and galloped away to follow the lingering dust cloud of the other warriors.

Chad watched him leaving for only a moment, then started across the clearing. Before he had taken five steps, Digby emerged from the trees and trotted briskly to meet him. Chad held out his hand. Digby sniffed it then snorted a mellow greeting. "Glad to see you too, boy," he said as he stroked the creamy grey neck. The animal pranced a step or two as if to hurry the young man along.

Grabbing the reins, Macklin stepped in the stirrup and swung up into the saddle as the mustang started off. His other foot was barely in the stirrup when Digby exploded forward with a burst of speed. Chad was a little surprised but not caught off guard because it was what he had wanted Digby to do. It was almost as if at last this horse and rider were one, in perfect unison.

Leaning low over Digby's neck, Chad's heart pounded as the wind streaked past them. With his jaw squared in grim resolve, the man's dark eyes glinted with steely determination. By a strange set of circumstances, he had been given the responsibility of saving the lives of seven people: the Prestons, Hector Medina, Uncle Gib, and the Hammersmiths.

His mind raced nearly as fast as Digby was running. He knew his uncle was improving, so he prayed that the hurried move to Austin would not aggravate his condition. He thought about Sarah. What words could he possibly use to break the tragic news to her about her father? He'd almost rather go back and face the Comanche war party. He dreaded facing Luke and Mrs. Preston too, but for some strange reason, it was Sarah he dreaded telling most. It wasn't that he was afraid she would be angry with him as the bearer of bad news; in fact, he hoped she would yell at him. He would rather that than see her cry.

For the next three miles Digby's hooves fairly flew over the wagon track. Chad thought about what he would be doing at home right now if he had never come to Texas. He would be either working in the shipping company office or checking in a cargo to be loaded or unloaded from one of the Macklin ships. No danger, safe and sound, well fed, and still wondering if his only purpose in life was to carry on the family name in the business.

What if he hadn't come to Texas? Sarah would still have lost her father. The Comanches would still be on the warpath, but who would be riding to warn about them? Would there even have been a chance for them to have time to evacuate to the relative safety of Austin?

These thoughts seemed to electrify every fiber in his being. His Grandfather Macklin once told him that each of God's creatures has a purpose, but man is the only one allowed to discover what his purpose is. Could being here at this moment, given the chance to intervene for his friends, be the reason he had come to Texas?

14

"Careful now, Luke. Watch his foot there," Mariah said.

The boy and Hector Medina had just carried the patient to the front porch. It was his first time outside in nine days.

"'Tis a good thing I've lost so much weight," the Ranger commented as he was lowered into the rocking chair Sarah had brought from the bedroom.

"We'll soon have you fit, and by that time, you'll be walking on your own," Mrs. Preston vowed. She patted her son on the shoulder. "Right here. That's it." She directed the boy and Hector as they slid the chair forward a bit.

"Now you can see the trees up on the hills. They're already beginning to turn color." Mariah unfolded the blue blanket she carried. "Looks like we're going to have an early winter."

Although the afternoon of October 7 was warm, the breeze in the shade made the porch feel cool. Mariah draped the light blanket around Dunmar's shoulders. Sarah then handed him the book they had been reading. Luke and Mr. Medina returned to the cornfield where they were cutting corn stalks for fodder, and both women stepped back to see if there was anything else they could do to make their patient comfortable.

Dunmar waved them away, saying, "Stop fussing over me, ladies. You put yourselves to too much trouble. I'm fine, just fine."

"Sarah and I'll be over there under the sycamore making soap if you need anything else."

The Ranger nodded then watched her step down from the porch and follow Sarah to the large black cauldron. As Sarah poked more sticks into the fire under the pot, Mariah started stirring the bubbling lye soap mixture and Dunmar marvelled at how so much strong-willed determination could be packed into one average-sized woman.

An energetic mockingbird perched on the nearby hitching rail and trilled a jubilant song as if to remind Dunmar of what he had been missing. Still weak, the man drew in a deep breath of the fresh air. For the first time since being brought to the Preston farm, he felt like he was really on the road to recovery.

With the opened book on his lap, Dunmar was much too engrossed in the beauty of the countryside to read. Scanning the valley that stretched beyond the barn and corral, he could see the trees taking on a golden hue. Perhaps Mariah Preston was right—cooler days weren't far off.

Suddenly, his attention was drawn to the road. The man's ears picked up a distant drumming of hooves. A rider was coming fast. In a moment he recognized the familiar dun-colored mustang. Relief filled his weary bones until he sensed an urgency in the way Chad was leaning forward. *Something's wrong,* he thought. *The lad's in too big a hurry.*

The rider reined Digby to a sliding halt at the front gate and jumped to the ground before the animal had stopped. Without tying the reins, he darted through the gate toward the porch, surprised to see his uncle sitting there.

By this time, Sarah and her mother had come running. They too could see something was wrong. Everyone reached the porch at the same time.

"What is it, lad?" Dunmar asked quickly.

Chad managed to get out the word. "Comanches," he gulped.

Immediately Mariah turned to Sarah. "Go get your brother and Mr. Medina. Hurry!" she ordered.

The daughter took off running for the cornfield almost before she had heard her mother's words.

"Where are they?" Mariah's heart was in her throat, but clutching the young man's arm, she forced herself to remain calm and waited for Chad to catch his breath.

"A war party will be hitting all the farms along the river from Burnet down to Canyon Creek," Chad quickly declared, still trying to catch his breath. "We've got to get your things together and move you in to Austin by tomorrow night. I've already warned the Hammersmiths. They're probably on their way by now."

"How do ya know all this?" Dunmar leaned forward anxiously.

"It's a long story," his nephew answered. "I'll tell you about it on the way." He paused for a moment. "I'm glad to see you sitting up, Uncle Gib. I hope the ride's not gonna be too hard on you."

"I'm afraid it might be bad to move him that far that quickly," Mariah warned with a worried expression on her face. "We'd best get ready to make a stand here. Besides, the Hammersmiths might come here instead of Austin." She started for the kitchen door. "I'll get the musket."

"Mrs. Preston." The grave tone of Chad's voice caused a knot to draw up in Mariah's chest, and she came back to stand beside the Ranger's rocking chair.

Lowering his voice, Chad struggled to choose his words with care as he continued. "There's something else. While I was in Austin," the young man took a deep breath. "While I was in Austin, there was news about the expedition to Santa Fe—bad news."

As the woman listened to the account, the color drained from her face. Fearing she might faint, Dunmar reached out to her. She absently took hold of his hand and clutched it tightly as she listened. When Chad finished, she stood there and stared silently out across the valley. Finally, in a fragile voice, she asked, "Will Dolph be all right?"

"It may take time, but he should recover," Chad nodded.

Through the dogtrot, the three of them spotted Sarah, Luke, and Medina hurrying toward the house from the bluff. Mariah released Dunmar's hand. A slightly dazed expression filled her green eyes as she turned and started through the dogtrot. Just before stepping off the back porch, she stopped, straightened her shoulders, then slowly walked out to meet them.

Chad tried to swallow the lump in his throat as he watched them meet and stand about twenty yards from the house. A grave Medina removed his hat reverently and crossed himself. Sarah and her mother embraced. But Luke began shouting "No! No!" as he backed away. His mother extended her arm to her son and finally the youngster sagged against her, sobbing. Watching the scene made Chad feel like he'd been kicked in the chest. The worst part was knowing there was nothing he could do to help.

"Lad, are ya all right?" His uncle's words penetrated the heavy atmosphere on the porch. The strain in his voice indicated he was feeling the same helplessness. "Ya look like ya've had a rough time of it."

"Nothing near as rough as this," the young Macklin replied.

"Aye," his uncle agreed with a deep sigh.

Chad was concerned about his uncle. Although he was sitting up, Dunmar had lost quite a bit of weight and looked deathly pale. Chad prayed the wagon ride would not be too much for him.

Finally, the Prestons and their hired hand returned to the house. Luke ducked his head and ran inside. The stricken look in Sarah's red-rimmed, tear-filled eyes pricked Chad's heart. She quickly turned and went inside as well. Mariah and Medina came to join the two men on the front porch.

The woman still had not cried. The distant look in her eyes told Chad she was in a state of shock.

"Mrs. Preston, we really do need to be getting things together to leave," Chad urged gently. "It's still early. We can be across Canyon Creek before dark if we start right away."

"We'll be staying here, Chad," she said absently. "We have a good supply of ammunition and provisions. If the Comanche do come—"

"If," Chad declared incredulously. With great effort to remain calm, he insisted, "Believe me, ma'am, they will come. You can't stay here. You've got some time, but they will come."

It was as if he hadn't spoken, for Mariah turned toward Dunmar. With calm determination she said, "I'm very concerned that such a trip will be too hard on you, Mr. Dunmar. But if you feel like staying would present a greater danger, we can make a bed in the wagon and place a pad around your leg so it doesn't jostle too much. If Chad drives slowly, perhaps it won't be too difficult for you."

"The danger is too great for anyone to stay," Chad exclaimed. The young man briefly explained his earlier encounter. "If it hadn't been for Bobcat, my scalp would probably be hanging on a Comanche war shield right now. He's given us time to get you all to safety. You know how they've done terrible things to women and children." He looked to his uncle for help.

"We appreciate your concern, Chad," Mariah replied calmly, "but we'll stay here. This is our home. We've worked too long and too hard to give up on it now. We'll leave the horses out. Maybe that'll satisfy the raiding party. If we leave, who can say how long it'll be before we can return? There are unscrupulous land grabbers just waiting for people to abandon their places so they can swoop in and lay claim to everything. Thomas wouldn't want us to take that chance." Her voice broke slightly. "I'll not take that chance. We're staying here."

138

"They'll come in and take it anyway if you're all dead," Dunmar chimed in grimly as he closed the book on his lap.

"He said there were only eight of them." Tears began to brim in Mariah's eyes.

"That's all he saw," Dunmar challenged. "There's probably at least a dozen or more, maybe a hundred, waiting to join them."

"Even so," she swallowed hard, fighting back the tears. "I think we have enough ammunition to hold them off."

"Mariah!" Dunmar exclaimed with exasperation.

"Please, Mr. Dunmar," she interrupted, her lower lip quivering and hands clenched at her sides. "This is the only thing we can do. We have nowhere else to go. We'll stay here and pray for God's protection. Perhaps it's true about the Coronado legend. Perhaps they'll bypass us."

Dunmar grumbled, "There's never been a more stubborn woman born. You're this determined to stay?"

Mariah squared her shoulders and looked him straight in the eye. "Yes, I am."

Finally, the Ranger sighed. "May I have a word with my nephew in private, ma'am?"

Mariah nodded and went inside to her children. Hector shook his head sadly and mumbled that he would finish bringing up the last few bundles of corn stalks.

"She's the most aggravatin', most stubborn, most courageous woman I have ever seen in my life," Dunmar declared.

Chad studied his uncle curiously for a moment. He certainly hadn't put up much of an argument. Maybe he realized it was futile and he didn't have the energy to waste.

"I think that she's out of her mind with grief," the boy proclaimed.

"Aye, she's overcome by grief, lad." Dunmar sighed, then tapped his forehead. "But that woman still has her wits about her."

All of a sudden the past hour and a half caught up with Chad. He was exhausted.

"Well, lad?"

From the tone of the question, Chad realized even his uncle had no intention of leaving.

"I take it you're not in the mood for a wagon ride this afternoon, either?" the nephew queried.

"Well, it's kind of a habit I've gotten into since comin' to Texas, m'boy. Bein' a Ranger, I'm usually chasin' trouble not runnin' from it. Besides, we can't be sure your Comanche friend wasn't playin' a trick. A wagon and riders out on the road would be easy pickin's for 'em.

"But you have a family back in Boston," he went on, "who'd be beggin' ya to ride for Austin as fast as ya can. You'd have a good chance of outrunnin' 'em by yourself."

Chad shook his head then grinned slightly, "I guess I've ridden enough today myself, Uncle. We'll just not tell anyone in Boston about this. They never need to know how foolish we can be."

After removing his hat and wiping the perspiration from his forehead, the young man looked out at Digby still standing at the gate with his reins trailing in the dust. "I'd better go see to Digby," he said. "Wait till I tell you what he did, Uncle Gib. You'll never believe it. He's probably got more brains than all of us put together."

Dunmar's eyes followed his nephew out to take care of the mustang. The lad had grown up since coming to Texas. If they survived the next few days, Chad Macklin would return to his family, no longer a boy, but a man with a sense of purpose in his stride.

15

That evening, Mariah said grace before supper. As she prayed for protection from the arrows of their enemies and courage to face what may come, a somber mood hung about them like a shroud. The reality of losing their father and imminent danger left Sarah and Luke silent. Seeing her children so heartbroken only deepened Mariah's sorrow and increased her anxiety about the decision to stay.

"We'll take turns standing watch, hijo," Medina finally suggested to Chad. "I doubt they will come until tomorrow. Comanches do not like to fight at night if they can help it." Medina's words flowed with the unique rhythm of his Spanish accent. "They fear if they are killed in the dark, they will not be able to find their way to their heaven."

"Too bad your friend Bobcat couldn't make the rest of the war party stay away from here." Luke finally spoke as he poked aimlessly at the chunks of sweet potatoes on his plate. He had no appetite. "After all, you did save his life."

"Since he saved my life too, he probably figures we're even," Chad reasoned.

Although nothing more was said about it, Luke's idea kept nudging its way into Chad's thoughts. He had been so disheartened when Mrs. Preston had refused to heed his warning. Maybe, just maybe . . . The seed of an idea began to take root.

After supper, Chad followed Medina to the door. "What do you think, Mr. Medina? Would it be worth a try to find Bobcat and see?"

Hector studied the young man long and hard. Mariah and Sarah were clearing the table. When they heard the question, they stopped what they were doing.

"He did come back to warn me about the raiding." Chad hurried on. "If I explained that my uncle was too ill to be moved—"

"That's even more foolhardy than walking up to a Comanche warrior with an empty gun!" Sarah broke in as she slammed a wooden spoon on the table. "What makes you think they would even let you get close enough to say anything or that they'd listen if you did?" Tears welled in her eyes and her face flushed red. "Ask your uncle if he's ever heard of someone trying to reason with the Comanches."

"Well, I—" Chad heard himself stammer. He was at a loss for words.

"Don't expect anyone here to cry over someone foolish enough to go out and just throw their life away." With that Sarah turned and rushed out of the kitchen.

"You must forgive her, Chad," Mariah said. "The news about her father has been very difficult. If you'll excuse me, I think I'd better go see about her."

Luke pushed his chair back. "I don't care if they do come," he said as he stood up. "Just let them try to take this place. They'll be sorry." The boy hurried out the door.

"They refuse to run for safety and she thinks I'm foolish?" Chad declared hotly. He turned to Medina. "What do you think they'll do since Mr. Preston isn't coming back?"

The Mexican shrugged his shoulders. "Señor Tom thought Tejas was like what he read in a book. He worked hard, but his dream was to make enough money from this farm to buy a store and big house in town like in Virginia. It is Señora

142

Preston who knows about the land from her father. I think if the Comanche do not burn us out and kill us all, she and the children will stay."

Chad was surprised by Medina's candid comment. He pressed for an answer to his other question. "You haven't said what you think about me trying to convince Bobcat and his friends to reconsider their plans."

Chad wasn't prepared for the man's answer. "Señorita Sarah makes a very good argument but . . ." The man's leathery face was nearly as stoic as a Comanche's.

"But?"

"It would be uh, muy loco—very crazy—but some Comanches think a loco hombre has special medicine. They are half afraid of such men." The man's black eyes seemed to dance with a glint of mischief.

"You think they'd be so surprised they might give me a chance to talk to Bobcat?"

"It'd be a very crazy thing to do, Señor, very crazy, very dangerous, I could not recommend it." He turned to open the door. "I will keep the first watch until the hour past midnight. Get some sleep. You have ridden far since you left here the other day."

There was something about the way the old man clapped him on the shoulder and called him señor instead of hijo. Chad got the feeling the words carried more meaning than appeared on the surface. Was he really trying to tell Chad there was a chance it could work?

Mariah found Sarah in the bedroom, where she had flung herself across the bed and lay sobbing into the quilt covering. The mother sat down on the bed and gently stroked her daughter's soft brown hair. She let Sarah cry until the sobs slowly diminished.

"I'm sorry, Mother," Sarah finally sighed with a small shudder. "I shouldn't have spoken to Chad that way. I didn't really mean what I said."

"I know, dear," Mariah said softly.

"I'm such a horrible person, Mother. Can God ever forgive me?"

"Sarah!" her mother exclaimed with surprise and pulled her daughter up to sit beside her. "What on earth makes you say such a thing? You are not a horrible person."

"Yes, I am," the daughter replied miserably.

"Why? Because you're angry that your father was foolish enough to just throw his life away?" Mariah echoed the words Sarah had flung at Chad.

Surprised that her mother could possibly guess her conflicted feelings, Sarah nodded and confessed. "Not only that, but back home I was so angry when he just seemed to give up after the bank and everything else was taken away from him; and especially the way he spoke so harshly to you during all that time."

Seeing her mother bow her head, Sarah wished she hadn't let on that she had heard their quarrels behind closed doors and noticed the harmony that had once existed between her parents was no longer there. She hurried on. "Then, just when he was beginning to be his old self again, smiling and treating you kindly like he always used to, then he leaves us."

Mariah drew her child into her arms and held her tightly. "Oh, Sarah, dearest. Do you remember when your father caught a chill that cold spring before the bank closed? Remember how he became delirious and he didn't recognize you and yelled at you to get out of the room because he thought you were going to hurt him?"

Sarah nodded.

"When he learned what he had done, remember how bad he felt and how he apologized?"

The girl nodded her head yes.

"And you gladly forgave him because he had been so sick, didn't you?" When her daughter nodded again, Mariah continued. "Losing the bank made him terribly sick at heart, not only for himself but for us as well. It was because he was so heartsick that you may have heard him say things he didn't really mean. You must forgive him. You must forget those things and remember what a wonderful father he was. The Lord promises to forgive us as we forgive others, right?

"As for leaving us, you know he thought he was doing the right thing. Sometimes things happen that we can't understand. We only have to pray for the peace and strength to continue on, no matter what."

Sarah leaned back to look into her mother's tear-filled eyes and marvel at the wisdom shining there. Mariah stroked the side of her child's face, wiping away the tears and blinking back her own. "Now, we must make some plans for tomorrow," she said, "just in case the Coronado legend is only part of Mr. Medina's imagination."

16

That night Gibson Dunmar slept fitfully. It was still dark when he was jolted awake by a dream of hundreds of Comanches circling the cabin. He was outside holding a broken rifle in his hand, powerless to help Mariah, Sarah, Luke, and Chad who were inside. Strangely enough, it was the sound of pony hooves that woke him up. Dunmar blinked his eyes in the thick darkness while he listened to the echo of hoofbeats. A war pony was galloping away. Lying there, the Ranger cursed the snake that had robbed him of his strength and prayed for a miracle to save them from the terrible ordeal others had suffered at the hands of this merciless enemy.

Sarah had slept little too. She felt like she could hardly breathe because of the pain in her heart. The cold dread—perhaps a premonition—she had had about her father almost made the impact of the news even worse. The added weight of the possible Indian attack made the whole thing overwhelming.

She and her mother had finally fallen asleep after they had talked for a long time. Preparations to defend themselves from Indian attack were foremost in their plans. After the danger was over, then they would decide whether to remain in Texas.

Sarah was thankful for her mother's strength and courage. Even though she was brokenhearted, Mariah's concern for her family's welfare kept her from giving in to her grief at a time when they would need all their wits about them.

It was still dark outside when Sarah slipped out of bed and padded on bare feet across to the kitchen for a drink of water. Inside the door, she lit the stub of candle and reached for the gourd dipper on the hook next to the water pail.

As she did, the small light flickered a bright reflection in the silver shaving mug sitting on the shelf above the water bucket. Swirls and graceful lines etched the letters TEP, Thomas Elijah Preston, a gift from his parents on his twenty-first birthday. It was the only piece of silver her parents agreed would not be sold.

The letters blurred through tears Sarah couldn't hold back as she gingerly touched the cool shiny handle. As a little girl she had loved to watch her father shave. He would make foolish faces through the foamy lather just to hear her giggle. They had been so happy. The only dark clouds she could recall from her childhood were the unpleasant feelings she always sensed when visiting her Grandmother and Grandfather Preston's large estate. She had never understood the cool reception her mother always received there.

If only the bank hadn't closed. The strength and joy had seemed to drain away from her father during those dreadful days of financial collapse. The decision to leave Virginia brought a complete alienation from his family. For nearly three years after they had relocated to Texas, Thomas Preston had tried to keep up a bold front, but his wife and children could see through it. Then the planning began for the Santa Fe Expedition and a bit of the old excitement and joy had begun to grow as the man dreamed of regaining all he had lost and more.

Sarah took a sip of water but it was hard to swallow. Why wouldn't her father believe them when they told him it didn't matter if he couldn't buy them the beautiful clothes and gifts that he used to? If he could have believed that, perhaps he'd still be here with them.

Hot tallow dripped on her finger and she nearly dropped the candle, but the pain shook her from her sad musing. Hanging the dipper back in place, the girl touched the small candle flame to an oil lamp wick. After lowering the glass chimney, she blew out the candle stub and left the kitchen.

Then on her way back to the bedroom, Sarah heard a noise on the front porch. Thinking it was probably Chad on watch, the young woman decided to go out and see if he was keeping awake. She also wanted to apologize for her behavior earlier that evening. To her surprise, the light from her lamp fell on Luke, who was sitting on the floor with his back against the cabin wall, his head nodding forward as he dozed.

"Luke," she whispered, bending to touch his shoulder.

The boy jumped to his feet, his heart pounding with fright. "Sarah!" he gasped. "You nearly scared me to death. What're you doin' up, anyway?"

"I couldn't sleep. What are you doing out here? I thought Chad was taking the second watch."

"I'm old enough to take my turn at standing watch." The boy was indignant. "Chad stood most of his watch before he left, but he wanted to be away before daybreak."

"Away? What are you talking about?"

Luke had spoken before thinking. Now he stammered a little trying to stall. "Well, ya see . . ."

"You don't mean he actually— Even he couldn't be that— He wouldn't really go to try to find that Comanche war party. Surely not!"

When Luke stared stubbornly out into the darkness, his sister grabbed his shoulder and spun him around.

"Luke!" she demanded.

In exasperation the boy finally confessed. "He figured he had to try since we were determined to stay here. I wanted to go with him but he said I needed to stay here and keep guard while he was gone. If it didn't work, I'd be needed here more than ever."

Luke's sister waved her arm in the air exclaiming, "How can anyone be so foolish!"

"Sarah," Luke interrupted angrily. "He's not foolish. He's tryin' to save our lives. You ought to be thankful he's willin' to try. You oughta be prayin' for him."

"Shhh! You'll wake Mother," Sarah warned as she pulled him toward the end of the porch away from the bedrooms. "I'm sorry. It's just that it seems like such an impossible chance he's taking. I mean, do you really think he could possibly reason with Comanches on the warpath?"

Luke was quiet. "It's possible," he replied without much conviction. "He is part Indian himself ya know."

"Delaware, not Comanche. The Comanches are enemies with a lot of other Indians too," Sarah argued as she paced back and forth in front of the boy. "Their whole way of life is built around fighting. They don't want to reason with anybody."

Luke didn't want to listen anymore. "He's doin' it for us, Sarah. He didn't have to. He could have taken his uncle and lit out for Austin yesterday. We just gotta pray for him."

The weight of her brother's words settled heavily on Sarah, leaving her speechless. She started back toward the door then stopped.

"You're right, Luke," she said quietly. "I know he didn't have to go. I will pray for him. How long ago did he leave?"

Luke was surprised by his sister's question. The boy cocked his head as he replied, "'Bout a half hour ago. He's ridin' through the valley to the gap near where he caught that outlaw, Pruitt. He and Mr. Medina figured that the war party would be movin' toward Burnet across the Llano Prairie and he'd have a good chance catchin' up with 'em that way."

"We better pray he doesn't catch up with them. He has to turn back."

149

As she said the words, Sarah tried not to think about the gruesome tales of Comanche cruelty she had heard.

Riding through the darkness, Chad had time to consider the terrible chance he was taking. If it didn't work, there would be one less rifle at the farm to hold off the war party. On the other hand, if it didn't work, one rifle wouldn't make all that much difference anyway. From everything he had heard, the Comanche Indians were excellent war strategists. They could overpower an isolated farm with cunning and patience, riding just out of range while the settlers wasted their ammunition, then coming in for the kill. As improbable as his plan may be, it had to work.

Macklin rode the length of the valley toward the gap, close to the place he had first encountered the outlaws as well as the Comanches. His uncle had said Bobcat's warning could just be baiting a trap. Chad was convinced he'd been told the truth and followed Medina's directions to the last northern ridge branching off the eastern hills of the Prestons' valley and offering the best view over the prairie stretching northwestward toward Burnet. A person standing on that ridge should have a commanding view of the plain and might be able to spot a war party on the move. Medina felt there would be enough cover along that ridge to keep the war party from spotting him.

Chad had left a note for his uncle explaining what he was trying to accomplish and what to tell his folks if the plan failed. He didn't want to think about the fact that if this didn't work, his uncle might not be able to relay any messages to anyone either.

Digby loped along in the dark, picking out his trail with sure-footed steadiness. The eastern hills rimming the valley seemed to darken as the heavens above them began to pale. With a faint light slowly spreading in the sky, Chad could see that he and Digby were almost to the gap. There they would have to climb to reach the vantage point necessary to spot the war party; that is, if he was guessing right and they were actually out there on the plain.

By the time the shadows of night had ebbed away and the first brilliant rays of morning had ignited the horizon, Chad was standing on top of the ridge looking out over the hills and plains to the north. Digby waited on a narrow verge of grass at the base of the nearly vertical climb to the crest. The last fifty yards up the hillside had been too steep even for the agile mustang.

Scanning the vast scene before him, Chad was profoundly impressed by its dramatic beauty. The sky above was a clear cobalt blue with a line of deep blue clouds along the northern horizon. Below stretched a broad plain with rolling wooded hills clothed in rich browns, russets, deep greens, and clay reds bathed in the golden light of dawn spilling over the eastern horizon.

A sharp cry from above drew Chad's attention to a large eagle wheeling majestically in the upper currents. The regal white-feathered head and tail gleamed against the cobalt background. The powerful wings and body cloaked in dark mahogany feathers sailed with graceful ease as the bird grandly surveyed his domain.

A warm breeze swirled about Chad, setting the cedars along the ridge to whispering. Breathing deeply of the sweet clear air, the young man was suddenly filled with a sense of freedom beyond anything he had ever experienced. As he watched the eagle soaring effortlessly above, he could almost feel himself lifted up sailing alongside that royal creature. It was intoxicating.

The majesty of the view and the eagle's morning song completely distracted Chad for a moment. And, in that moment, a memory flashed before his mind's eye.

When Chad was ten years old, his Uncle Stephan had shown him a mother eagle teaching her young to fly. One eaglet was perched on the edge of a huge nest poised in a crag of a rocky ridge much like the one on which Chad now

151

stood. The young bird's new plumage of white and dark brown resembled his mother's. Standing poised with wings raised, the novice seemed eager, yet intimidated by the great empty space beneath the edge of the nest. Ruffling his feathers, he opened his pale yellow beak with anxious screeches.

The eaglet continued to refuse the encouraging calls of his mother as she circled and hovered about. Without warning, the large bird swooped down and struck the edge of the nest beneath the talons of her young. Amid the scattered nest debris falling toward rocky crags and a tangled snare of branches, the eaglet tumbled, grabbing frantically at the air with untried wings. In a split second the mother eagle swooped under her baby and steadied him before dropping out from under him again. After this had been repeated a second time, the young bird began to flap his wings, this time with more control. He finally settled in the top of a tree below the ridge.

Later that day, Chad and Uncle Stephan had watched the proud mother and her eaglet celebrating his new success by soaring gracefully together in the sapphire blue above the nest. *One day the young eagle will move on to seek out his own territory.* Uncle Stephan's words seemed to whisper to him through the sighing cedar boughs. Chad remembered those words as if it had been yesterday.

How many times over the years had that amazing aerial drama replayed in his mind? Innumerable times. And each time the desire to test his own wings had grown stronger. Chad's father had hoped his son might find the lure of trade winds and tides so appealing he would naturally assume command of the shipping business someday. Instead, the boy found the ships confining, bobbing about in a vast sea that stretched for days in mind-numbing sameness or rising up in angry billows threatening to smash any puny vessel daring to cross their trackless surface. Somehow years ago, watching the young eaglet find his balance and use his God-given abilities, the boy had known that in the same way he too would be soaring on his own one day, seeking out a whole new territory. Now he stood surveying an entirely new world, one that was vastly different from anything he had ever known yet with a magnetism he found so compelling even danger could not diminish it.

Chad's attention was suddenly drawn to the plain below. Movement caught his eye. The young man wished he had his father's eyeglass. He tried to focus. At last! There it was. An Indian camp had been set at the edge of a stand of trees some five hundred yards from the base of the ridge.

The absence of tepees told Macklin that it was a temporary camp. As the fingers of morning light touched the treetops near them, he could detect men beginning to stir. From where he stood, Chad couldn't tell whether they were a hunting party or a war party. While there didn't appear to be the hundred or more warriors Uncle Gib had anticipated, there were still more than Chad had hoped. He guessed there were around forty men. If this was the war party, this number was certainly more than enough to overrun the Preston farm.

Scanning the countryside again, Chad could not detect any other movement or signs of campfires. Deciding to take a chance, he scrambled down the steep, rocky slope toward Digby. He knew his best chance would be to reach the Indians before they broke camp. If he could confront them before they were mounted and ready to ride, he might be able to talk to them. On foot they were mere men; on horseback they became nearly invincible warriors.

Reaching the mustang, Chad noticed that Digby was standing alert with his head held high, ears twitching and nostrils flaring. The animal greeted his master with a deep, rumbly, throated grumble. Digby sidestepped nervously. Chad picked up the reins and patted the horse's muscular chest to calm him, wondering if somehow the mustang sensed the danger that awaited them.

After swinging up into the saddle, Chad skillfully tied the ends of the reins together in a knot so that if anything should happen to him, the mustang would be able to escape without the danger of stepping on the reins and tripping himself up. This accomplished, the rider set his hat purposefully up on his head and patted the mustang's neck again. "Come on, Digby, before I stop and really think about what we're doing." With that, horse and rider headed down the slope and through the gap.

17

Out of the valley, the ground levelled out across a wide grassy meadow broken by several large clusters of boulders that had tumbled down from the ridge ages ago. This formation of boulders was taller than it appeared from the top of the ridge crest and offered more cover than Chad had anticipated. By the time he had curved around the rocks in sight of the camp, he only had about one hundred yards of open ground to cover.

The rider held his horse to an easy canter until within hailing distance, then slowed him to a walk. The young man almost expected the pounding of his heart to attract the camp's attention. Swallowing hard, Chad raised his hands and yelled, "Ho, in the camp! Bobcat!"

Whoosh! At that moment an arrow sunk with a solid thud into the ground two feet in front of him. A second followed immediately. Macklin spotted an Indian standing on top of one of the boulders on the camp side of the rock formation behind him. The sentry had not been visible before this moment.

Chad tugged at the reins and Digby stopped. At the same time, he heard the scrambling of men in the camp. Within a few seconds there appeared a line of warriors, weapons in hand, shoulder to shoulder at the edge of the meadow, staring at him. He urged Digby slowly forward. "Bobcat, it's Macklin," he called out.

The warriors raised their bows. A line of arrows pointed directly at him.

Chad's pulse was pounding so loudly in his ears he almost couldn't think. The way Digby stood poised ready to bolt, he was sure the mustang was questioning his rider's sanity.

"Hold on, boy, easy now," Chad cautioned his horse.

All of a sudden a blood-curdling war whoop sounded off to his right and another to his left. Two mounted Comanches galloped toward him. Exercising every ounce of self-control he had, Chad raised his hands in the air to show he carried no weapon.

The Indian ponies dashed by within inches of Digby's nose and tail. Miraculously, the mustang stood still. More whoops followed as the warriors circled, then moved in close to the stranger. Before Chad knew what was happening, the brave on the left leaned forward to snatch Digby's rein. The mustang quickly turned his head and bit the Indian's hand. Yowling in pain, the man raised his club to strike the cantankerous horse. Chad lunged forward and grabbed the man's wrist.

For a heartstopping moment the two men glared at each other in grim defiance. Even when the brave on the right side knocked Chad's hat to the ground and grabbed a handful of his thick dark hair just above the forehead, the white man held the other's wrist firmly. He was determined that war club would not touch Digby. He felt the sharp edge of cold steel against his bare scalp.

Suddenly a lone shout erupted from the warrior line. A moment later the blade was moved away and his hair was released. The Comanche on his right backed his pony away slightly. When the other brave let his war club fall to the ground, Chad released his wrist. At once the standoff was over. As Chad took in a deep breath of air, he could feel a trickle of blood rolling down his forehead. He folded his arms across his chest and clenched his fists to prevent everyone from seeing his shaking hands.

Under his breath he muttered to Digby, "I can't believe I nearly lost my scalp and ruined everything just to save your ornery hide. Behave yourself and we just might make it out of here alive." Digby shook his mane and snorted.

"Mackl'n!"

Chad breathed a quiet "Thank you, Lord" when he heard the familiar voice. The young warrior stepped out in front of the line of bowmen.

"Bobcat!" he returned, forcing his voice to sound strong and steady in spite of his racing pulse. Chad dismounted and led his mustang forward to meet the young Comanche striding toward him.

Bobcat grasped his forearm in a firm greeting and nodded toward Digby. "Must be very great war pony if worth your scalp."

Chad only nodded in reply. Soon the two men were joined by an older man wearing a buffalo horn headdress adorned with several eagle feathers, a painted buckskin shirt, and a breechcloth with leggings and moccasins similar to those worn by Bobcat. At his signal, the bowmen lowered their weapons. Bobcat introduced his father, the war chief, Stands Before Running Buffalo. No wonder the other Comanches listened to this young warrior.

Bobcat showed Chad where to leave Digby, and the two young men followed the chief back to the center fire in the camp. When he was directed to sit down and eat some of the semi-cooked meat hanging over the fire, Chad accepted. His mission was too important to risk offending his host. Along with the meat, Chad was served slices of pemmican made from dried wild cherries and plums pounded together with dried meat and mixed with tallow to make the Comanches' version of bread. It was surprisingly tasty. They ate before they talked.

All of the Indians watched Chad closely. It was obvious they were very curious about him. Chad remembered what Hector Medina had said and assumed they probably thought he was mentally unbalanced. His Grandfather Macklin had told him stories about how many of the Indian nations back east were very superstitious. Apparently, the Comanches were as well, since they had believed the Coronado legend. However, something had changed. He wished he could speak with Bobcat alone to find out why they now dared to pass that way to attack the Prestons' farm.

"So, it was you." Stands Before Running Buffalo spoke at last, pointing at Chad. "It was you who has turned away the anger of the ancient ones."

Chad swallowed the last bit of pemmican, nearly choking. He quickly looked to Bobcat for an explanation.

"I told my father how you speak and the spirits listen. My life was given back in the valley." Bobcat wiped his knife blade clean against his right legging.

"But—" Macklin couldn't believe his ears. How could something he'd felt was so right turn around and end up so wrong? "You mean that's the reason they're not afraid to go there now?"

"That and . . ." The young Comanche nodded toward a warrior standing with two others a few feet away.

The powerfully built man was speaking in low tones with two friends, all the while keeping black eyes riveted on the white man. Chad met the man's stare without blinking. The Comanche's cocky attitude instantly irritated Macklin. Without turning his attention from those mocking eyes, he asked Bobcat, "What about him?"

"Antelope Runner want to raid Prestons' valley long time. When two of us come back alive, he goes there." The young Comanche put the cleaned knife away. "He stay there one day, one night, come back. Not hurt. Tell everyone spirits angry no more."

"Antelope Runner?" Quickly Chad turned to Bobcat to make sure he had heard right.

The chief's son gave a quick nod but before Chad could ask anything else, Stands Before Running Buffalo again spoke. "Why Macklin comes?"

Stunned to be staring eye to eye with the nemesis of his scout-friend, Senihele, Chad took a moment to answer the chief. Realizing everyone was watching him, he took a deep breath. "I come as a friend to your son, Bobcat. I come to ask you to turn away from this attack." His mouth was dry and his pulse raced faster as he watched those who understood his English begin murmuring.

Bobcat glanced at his father, whose dark eyes carefully scrutinized the young white man. "Why do you ask this?" the chief countered.

Chad was momentarily at a loss for words. He had planned to say that his uncle was too ill to move, but how would that convince these men who wanted to get rid of all of the white settlers in Texas?

Taking another approach, he began. "If you attack, the Rangers will come after you with their new weapons." One of Antelope Runner's friends whispered to the brave, and the Indian spat on the ground and folded his arms across his broad chest. Chad continued, "Many of your warriors will die, maybe even your son."

The chief said nothing. He just stared at Macklin. Out of the corner of his eye, Chad could see the Indian ponies along their picket line becoming very restless. Grasping at straws, he then declared, "And what if the spirits of the Spanish soldiers in the valley are still angry?"

A commotion along the picket line of horses drew Stands Before Running Buffalo's attention and he noticed his favorite war horse pawing the ground, then raising his head high, nostrils flaring, to search the wind. This made the chief a bit uneasy. "Antelope Runner was there and came back," he answered. "He was not harmed."

"If I were a Comanche war chief, I wouldn't risk leading my people into such a place, or even to camp this close just because one man said so."

Chad could see the chief's attention again drawn to the horses as a breath of wind swirled eddies of dust around their hooves. Several of the animals whinnied uneasily. The chief looked at Antelope Runner and Chad followed his glance. "Men have been known to tell stories of their great courage," Chad went on. "But sometimes, they are only stories."

When the big Comanche brave was told the meaning of Chad's words, Antelope Runner stepped forward, shook a huge clinched fist at Chad, and angrily rattled off several quick Comanche phrases.

Bobcat jumped to his feet and glared back at the irate Indian. Chad stood up beside his friend and waited for a translation of the obvious threat by Antelope Runner. Instead of translating for him, Bobcat spoke quickly to his father, who also stood to reply in Comanche.

Slightly exasperated, Chad finally tapped Bobcat on the shoulder. "What's going on?"

The young Comanche turned to Chad, his eyes filled with deep concern. "Antelope Runner challenges you to fight. You insult him. This not wise."

Young Macklin had known his comment would offend the cocky Comanche. Hoping to discredit Antelope Runner and the desire to raid in the Prestons' valley, Chad also felt a small sense of satisfaction on Senihele's behalf.

When Bobcat saw a slight smile on his white friend's face, he shook his head. "Antelope Runner never loses such a challenge. To accept means death."

Chad took a deep breath and squared his shoulders. "I don't think I have a choice, do I?"

Stands Before Running Buffalo was more interested in what Chad said about angry spirits than he was about Antelope Runner's bruised ego. "The ancient ones listened to you and did not harm Bobcat."

Turning from Antelope Runner, Chad answered the chief. "Yes, but wasn't Bold Calf killed and one of the white men? The white men were after the ancient ones' gold. It could be that they're stirred up even more now."

Suddenly, almost as if on cue, a strong gust of wind burst through their midst scattering live coals from the fire and sending ashes flying up in their faces. The chief and several of the braves standing close by nervously exchanged glances as they rubbed the dust and ashes from their eyes. The wind died and the air became very still. Not a bird called in the trees, but the horses continued to move about restlessly, and Chad noticed Digby shaking his head and pulling at the reins looped over a low tree branch. The calm was almost as unsettling as the sudden wind.

Antelope Runner realized his companions were on the verge of believing the white man. He was furious. Turning to the chief, he bellowed his disdain. The chief and several of the older braves stood talking a moment. Then Stands Before Running Buffalo turned and said, "This not good place to be. We cannot fight what we cannot see. We go. Fight enemy another day."

Antelope Runner and about ten other braves protested. Then everyone, except Antelope Runner, his ten followers, and Bobcat quickly gathered their belongings and began leaving the camp to head home.

Bobcat chose to remain standing beside Chad, waiting to see what would happen between him and Antelope Runner. The disgruntled Comanche stepped up to Macklin. "They run away from the wind like women," Bobcat translated for him. "But I do not run. I first take your scalp and then we burn the farms and kill all your people living along the river."

Chad directed Bobcat to translate his reply. "Tell him I don't plan on giving up my scalp today, especially to someone who doesn't have brains enough to leave this place while he still can."

Bobcat stared at the white man a moment and started to warn his new friend to reconsider this reply when one of the other braves translated Chad's words to Antelope Runner. A cruel gleam came into the big Comanche's eyes as he grunted in contempt.

The departing Comanches were barely out of sight when Bobcat shook his head and handed Chad his own tomahawk. Antelope Runner was about four inches shorter than Chad and was built like a block of granite, outweighing Macklin by at least fifty pounds.

In a surprising move, the young war leader signalled two of his followers to pull Bobcat aside. At the same time, he caught Chad off guard by sweeping the man's feet out from under him, landing him flat on his back and knocking the wind out of him. Immediately the Comanche was on top of him.

Chad gasped for breath but managed to block the tomahawk swung down at his head. As they struggled, Chad conceded it was no wonder Antelope Runner had never been defeated before. Though strong, young Macklin found that his opponent was quickly gaining the upper hand. Antelope Runner pressed all of his strength into breaking Chad's hold on his tomahawk.

Suddenly they heard hoofbeats and a shrill whinny. Antelope Runner looked up just in time to see Digby sliding to a stop next to them, his eyes wide and teeth bared. The Comanche jumped up and Chad rolled away as the mustang reared up on his back legs, striking out at the Indian. The mustang's left front hoof caught the brave's tomahawk-wielding arm and sent the weapon flying.

Chad jumped up just as two of the other Comanches ran toward the horse to try to catch his reins. The mustang wheeled around and shaking his head side to side, charged them viciously. Two warriors started toward him but the horse whipped around and kicked at them with his back feet, sending one flying and narrowly missing the other. With that, everyone scattered out of the wild creature's way.

The wind had picked up again and Digby's wild cavorting raised a cloud of dust. All movement stopped. The wind swept the blinding dust away, revealing the mustang standing protectively between Chad and the Comanches, snorting defiantly. It was obvious that Digby had decided that if they wanted to get to his master, they would have to deal with him first.

After a moment of confusion and disbelief, Antelope Runner reached for a war lance. The others stepped back and Chad grabbed Digby's reins, pulling him aside. He then stepped in front of the feisty mustang. Antelope Runner's face was a mask of fury. He intended to put an end to the white man *and* his devilish horse.

Before the warrior could take aim with the lance, however, a rifle shot rang out and a puff of dust and rock chips sprayed up at his feet. All of the Indians crouched low as another shot ricocheted off a rock to the right of Antelope Runner.

Chad whirled around to see the flash of the second shot coming from the boulders out in the meadow. Glancing back, he saw Bobcat crouching behind a tree signalling for him to make his getaway.

The increasing wind swirled the dust around them again. The Comanches dashed for their horses. Chad swung up on Digby and spurred him toward the boulders. Another shot rang out as the mustang flew across the meadow.

Galloping toward the rock formation, Chad was stunned to see Sarah seated on his uncle's bay, frantically reloading a rifle. He pulled Digby up short beside her. "What are you doing here?" he demanded.

The color had drained from her face. Her eyes were wide with fear. She tossed the percussion rifle to him and picked up the other one lying across her lap. As she dropped the cartridge envelope containing powder and a ball down the muzzle and jammed it in place with the ramrod, she asked, "Do we really have time to discuss this?" She pointed toward the fast approaching Indians.

"Let's head for that hidden canyon we found the other day when we were looking for Luke," Chad shouted above the rising wind. "If we can reach the entrance and duck in there before they close in, we might lose them."

The girl nodded and the two of them spurred their horses toward the gap. Thankfully, the strong wind at their back almost pushed them along. Chad glanced over his shoulder. The Indians were still coming. Then he noticed an amazing sight. Although the sun was still shining directly above them, an ominous dark blue bank of clouds was rolling in behind the Indians. Chad now understood what had been disturbing the Indian ponies. They had sensed the approaching storm before the humans were even aware of it. Behind the leading edge of the clouds the sky was dark grey. Thick curtains of rain stretched across the landscape.

"What kind of storm is that?" Chad called to Sarah over the wind.

"It's a blue-norther. We're really in for it now!" she warned in a loud voice.

The riders passed through the gap and were nearing the partially concealed entrance to the narrow canyon. Suddenly the wind turned very cold. Looking back, Chad spotted the Comanches just inside the gap. If his eyes weren't deceiving him, he thought they were slowing down. Perhaps they feared Antelope Runner was wrong about the spirits of the Coronado legend.

The Indians were only a short way past the gap when an ice-laden wind hit them like a frozen fist. The weather phenomenon convinced the Comanches that their chief had been right. Instantly the warriors circled their horses and stampeded back the way they had come.

Chad reined in. "Look, they're turning back," he called to Sarah. "Can you believe that?"

164

The girl shouted over the wind, "Yes! They're heading for shelter! We'd better too! I've seen northers since we've been here, but I've never seen a blue-norther like this one! If we don't find shelter soon, we could freeze to death!"

"Freeze to death? But a few minutes ago it was almost hot!" Chad declared.

"It's getting colder by the minute! You're used to northern winters. I've heard people talk about an ice and snow storm that came in here so fast the livestock froze to death before they could be brought into the barns."

Sarah had to yell even louder now. "Some people who were caught outside without coats got lost in the blinding snow and died a few feet from their door. We're an hour away from the house; if we can find some place to stay dry until the worst of it passes, that might help!"

"What about the caves?" Chad asked, shielding his eyes from the blowing debris.

"There's one down by the old creek bed," she called. "We can get the horses inside along with us. Come on, we don't have much time!"

18

Within a few minutes, the wind was blowing so hard the wildly waving cedar bushes almost obscured the cave entrance. Finally Sarah spotted it and Chad followed her, stopping near the opening. They dismounted just as tiny wind-driven pellets of sleet started pelting them like little frozen needles.

"Take Digby," Chad shouted over the wind. "I'll gather up some driftwood for a fire."

Sarah grabbed the mustang's reins and led him with Dunmar's big bay toward the gaping entrance in the hillside. She had brought the Ranger's horse because he was younger, with more stamina for a long, fast run trying to catch up with Chad. The bay halted at the cave entrance, reluctant to enter a dark hole. Spooked by the wind, Digby shied sideways.

Chad began snatching up chunks of old dried wood when he suddenly remembered Sarah's aversion to Digby's temperament. He looked up to see her gently rub the side of the mustang's face and coax him easily into the cave. The big bay followed closely.

By now, the sleet was being driven by the wind so hard it stung even through Chad's shirt. With an armload of wood, he finally joined Sarah and the two horses inside the shelter of the cave.

The cave was cold and damp, but out of the wind, it felt a few degrees warmer than the weather outside. Chad dropped the armload of wood and joined Sarah at the entrance.

She stood there catching her breath and looking out at the fury of the storm sweeping in over the valley. Trees were being whipped and twisted so that branches snapped and sailed away. The sleet, mixed with rain, was getting heavier and beginning to glaze every surface it touched. Chad realized that Sarah was shivering. Going over to Digby, he removed the buckskin jacket he'd tied down on top of the Mexican blanket and gum coat his uncle had provided as part of a Ranger's standard gear.

"Here, this'll help block most of the chill," he offered, holding it open for her.

The young woman hesitated only a moment before slipping into the soft leather coat. Though it nearly swallowed her up, she pulled it close. "Thank you," she said. "It's a beautiful jacket. I've never felt such soft leather."

"My Aunt Marianne made it for me," he smiled proudly.

"The first winter we spent here, it seemed so mild, we hardly ever wore our jackets." Sarah's teeth chattered slightly as she spoke. "Now, I guess we've gotten used to the summer heat. The winters seem a lot colder."

"Uncle Gib said the same thing." Chad looked out at the storm. The clouds seemed darker and the ice rain was now driving in sheets. The temperature was still dropping. "How long do these things usually last?" he asked uneasily.

"I don't know," she replied. "We've had regular northers blow through in one or two days. But—" She looked up at him and noticed the trickle of dried blood from the small cut on his forehead. "Oh, my!" she gasped as suddenly the whole incredible drama she'd witnessed flashed before her.

Hearing her gasp, he glanced down at her and she pointed at the slight wound. Chad reached up and gingerly touched it, causing it to bleed a little bit more. He started to say it was nothing when he saw that she was still shivering and growing very pale.

"Are you all right?"

"I never actually shot at a man before. I'd better sit down."

Slightly dismayed, Chad realized Sarah might faint. Before he could help her over to a large rock just inside the entrance, her knees buckled and she started to sink to the ground. He quickly grabbed her arm to catch her and pick her up. The last thing Sarah saw before blacking out was the look of concern in Chad's dark eyes as he reached for her.

When she awoke, a small fire burned brightly just a few feet away. The Mexican blanket from Chad's saddle covered her and she could feel the gum coat between her and the cold stony cave floor.

"Sarah?" She glanced up to see him kneeling beside her. His brow was furrowed with concern. "Are you all right?"

Nodding yes, she put her hand over her eyes and murmured in embarrassment, "I can't believe I fainted. I just saw that cut on your head and . . ."

Chad grinned. "My sister Abigail faints at the sight of blood too. My first bloody nose, she fainted twice before they could get me cleaned up."

"I've never fainted at the sight of blood before," Sarah countered. "For some reason it just hit me when I realized how close you'd come to being scalped and that I'd nearly killed a man. I guess it's pretty silly to faint after everything's over."

Chad's warm smile put Sarah at ease. "Don't worry about it. I've seen strong sailors survive a narrow escape and pass out after the danger is completely passed. Which reminds me," he declared as he reached for the canteen, "what in the world are you doing here in the first place? You should be back at the farm with your mother."

"If I were, that big Comanche might have killed you," she returned defensively as he helped her sit up to take a drink from the canteen.

He stared at her a long moment as she took a swallow of water. "You may be right," he chuckled. When she'd finished, he replaced the cork in the canteen. "You didn't answer my question. What are you doing out here?"

Sarah sat up straighter and pulled her knees up, tucking the blanket and hem of her long skirt and petticoats around her feet. "I was trying to stop you from getting yourself killed but didn't catch sight of you until you started through the gap. You were too far ahead to hear me calling when you started across the meadow." She rubbed her hands together trying to warm them as she continued. "When you slowed down to ride around the boulder formation, I thought I'd be able to catch up with you. By the time I came around the boulders, there you were, flanked by those two Comanches and in front of a line of arrows pointed at you."

"How come the fella standing watch out there didn't see you?" Chad asked as he placed a stick on the fire.

"Thankfully, the rocks blocked me from his view while he climbed down to join the rest of them. He must've been watching you so closely he didn't see me before I saw him, so I had time to duck back in the rocks until he was gone. I had one of those Comanches beside you in my sights in case you needed a chance to escape."

Chad grinned at her. "I probably wouldn't have been so scared if I'd known that."

"You didn't look that scared," she declared with amazement. Wrapping her arms around her knees, she huddled deeper in the jacket. "What in the world ever possessed you to grab that brave's arm like that?"

"He was going to smash Digby's skull with his war club." Smiling sheepishly, he glanced over at the mustang and admitted, "I may have felt like doing it myself sometimes, but I wasn't about to let that Comanche do it."

"I just about pulled the trigger when that other one grabbed you ready to scalp you," Sarah exclaimed as she pointed to his head again. "But then I didn't have a clear shot at the Indian without hitting you."

"I guess it's a good thing you waited," he remarked, holding his hands out to the small fire.

"Well, I was amazed when everything calmed down and you still had your hair."

"So was I," he agreed as he settled back, sitting cross-legged, Indian style.

"Anyway, I stayed in the rocks waiting to see what would happen next and praying you'd get out of there in one piece. It looked like you were eating, then there was some arguing, but pretty soon most of the Comanches rode away. I was about to breathe a sigh of relief when it looked like you had actually accomplished the impossible. But then that big Indian attacked you and Digby charged and all of them scattered." She took a deep breath recalling the sight of a Comanche war lance aimed at Chad.

"You'll never guess who that big Indian was!" Chad interjected. "Remember that scar on Senihele's forehead?"

Sarah nodded.

"That's the Comanche who put it there. He also killed Senihele's brother. His name's Antelope Runner and he's the meanest man I've ever had the displeasure to meet."

"It looked like he was about to kill you with that lance." Sarah shivered thinking about how she had fired the rifle almost before realizing she had even raised it to her shoulder. "That's when I shot."

"And a good shot it was," he remarked.

She blushed slightly at the compliment then scolded, "That Antelope fellow is just the kind of Comanche I feared you'd run into. There was no reasoning with him, was there?"

He shook his head and chuckled. "Nope; no reasoning with him at all." He continued with a sly grin, "Tell me, if you thought I was foolish for trying to reason with the Comanches, don't you think it was just a little foolish for you to follow after me?"

"Luke wanted to follow you," she said as she fingered the fringe along the buckskin sleeve and avoided his glance, "but I told him he'd already worried Mother enough as it was and he needed to stay there."

"So, it's your turn to worry your mother?"

"No." She glanced at him, finding his teasing grin hard to resist. "It's just, well, someone needed to try to stop you before you got into serious trouble. Why are you shaking your head like that?"

"I've just never seen anyone like you before in my life, except for my Aunt Christa. Of course, my Grandfather Macklin still teases Grandmother Macklin about how headstrong she was when they first met."

"I'm sure I don't know what you're talking about," the young woman declared indignantly as she pulled the buckskin jacket closer against the increasing chill. Traces of her smile lingered.

Chad placed another piece of driftwood on the fire. "Well, it's just that you look. . . ." Chad studied Sarah's upturned face. The wind had tousled her hair wildly. She had a smudge of dirt on her chin, but there in that firelight, he was suddenly struck by a beauty he had not seen in any other girl ever before. Her blue-green eyes looked almost black in the flickering light and they returned his searching gaze with an open, almost vulnerable quality.

At that moment, Sarah found herself mesmerized by the look in Chad's brown eyes. Trying to convince herself that the quickening of her pulse was a result of her fainting spell and had nothing to do with being so close to him or the warm depths of his dark eyes, she asked softly, "I look what?"

By now Chad was totally distracted and thinking about how much he'd like to take her in his arms and kiss her.

"You started to say I look like something," she explained. When he still didn't respond, she added, "I'm sure I look like a mess."

"No," he argued, clearing his throat. Then changing the subject quickly, he hopped to his feet and walked over to the cave entrance. "Boy, listen to that wind howling out there. It's started snowing now," he reported, arms folded tightly across his chest.

Taking in a deep breath, Chad hoped the cold air would clear his reeling senses. The only result of breathing in the frozen air was a sudden wave of goose bumps. He might be used to cold, snowy winters back east, but he usually had a warm, heavy coat. The cold was beginning to cut sharply through his homespun shirt now.

Sarah's knees were still weak, so she remained sitting. "Do you want your jacket back or this blanket to wrap around you?"

"Thanks, I'm all right," he answered, returning to the fire.

The dried wood was burning up quickly. It was nearly time to place another piece on the small blaze. Chad could see they would need more fuel if they had to stay here for much longer.

"Let's hope this thing moves out as quickly as it moved in," he said as he walked over to loosen the cinch on Digby's saddle. After doing the same to his uncle's bay, he pulled a packet of sweetened parched corn out of Digby's saddlebag. He held it out to pour into Sarah's hand. "Here, you probably didn't have breakfast, did ya?"

"At least you got to eat breakfast with the Comanches," she teased.

"Yeah, it was great, if you like raw meat. Pemmican wasn't bad. I've got some coffee beans here, too, but I think the coffeepot bounced out of my saddlebags on the way back from Austin. But then I don't think we have quite enough water for coffee anyway."

At the mention of Chad's return from Austin, Sarah remembered the news. With the impact of her father's death, she hadn't even thought to ask about Dolph Hammersmith.

"Mother said you saw Dolph Hammersmith when you were in Austin. Was he badly wounded?" she asked soberly.

172

"Yes, I saw him," he replied, nodding. "I didn't talk to him directly though. It looked like he'd had a pretty rough time, but I don't think he had any serious wounds."

"Good," she responded with a feeling of relief.

"Luke said you really like Dolph," Chad casually ventured as he broke up a few of the longer pieces of driftwood.

"Of course I like Dolph," she agreed. "He was very kind to help build our cabin, and he's been a very good friend since we came to this valley."

"Courting friend?" Chad pushed a few more stones toward the fire as he asked the question.

Sarah studied him for a moment, trying to guess what he was really thinking. "Maybe, someday," she finally replied with thoughts of Luke's teasing comments in the back of her mind.

The sound of the horses shifting about distracted them for a moment and to her relief, Chad changed the subject. "Did you see the way he went after those Comanches?" He still marvelled at Digby's actions.

"Yes, I did," she replied. "Maybe that Comanche looked like the evil horse trader who was cruel to him."

Chad caught the hint of teasing in her voice. "I'd kinda like to think he was protecting me," he confessed.

"As strange as it seems, that's what it looked like from where I was sitting." Sarah stretched her hands toward the fire. "Apparently you've won him over."

"Sometimes it's hard to tell, but I guess if it weren't for him—and you—I might not be here now."

Sarah glanced over at him and their eyes met once more. He quickly crouched down to busy himself for a moment by emptying the contents of the saddlebags on the ground beside him. Laying one side bag on the ground next to the rocks surrounding the fire, the young man began pushing several of the heated stones into the bag with a stick. He repeated the process with the other side, closed the flaps, and sat down beside Sarah on the gum coat. Then he handed her one side bag while he held the other as makeshift warmers.

The leather bag was already warm from the rocks inside. "That's very clever. Thank you," Sarah said. She hugged it to her, thankful for the warmth and surprised that someone who had probably never been without would come up with such a clever innovation.

"Here, take this blanket and wrap it around you since I have your jacket," she offered.

"We'd probably stay warmer if we sat closer and shared the blanket," he suggested. "That'd keep these saddlebags warmer a little longer too."

"I suppose you're right," she agreed. "Let's just hope the storm stops before this wood is all gone."

The young man scooted closer. In order to overlap the blanket in front, they had to huddle very close. Chad placed his arm around her shoulders and before too long they both stopped shivering. Nothing more was said for a while, and the silence in the cave was punctuated only by the whistling of the cold wind outside.

Finally Chad spoke. "I guess it's true what they say."

"What's that?" Sarah asked softly, on the verge of nodding off to sleep.

"I guess something good can come out of any bad situation."

Turning to look up at him, she waited curiously for him to continue with his observation.

"Well, we've been talking together for nearly an hour without snapping at each other," he smiled.

"We've talked before without snapping at each other," she replied drowsily.

"For a few minutes maybe," he granted. "But anything more than a few sentences and we've been like flint against steel. I still don't know what I did to make you dislike me so much from the start."

This statement brought her wide awake. "I don't dislike you," she declared emphatically. "Where did you get that idea?"

174

As Chad cocked his head and raised an eyebrow, color rose in Sarah's cheeks. She was having to face the reality that her harsh words had really bothered him.

"Perhaps I did snap a bit sometimes," she admitted. "But when I offered even the slightest suggestion, you seemed almost insulted."

"No, I didn't," he protested, pulling the blanket tighter around his shoulder and turning to look at her.

"Yes, you did," she insisted as she met his gaze.

For a long moment, the two stared at each other and inexplicably, in that exchange of glances, there emerged a silent understanding between them. An almost magical connection seemed to let each of them see the barriers they had raised against the other.

Chad broke the spell. "Maybe I was a little too quick to take offense," he admitted reluctantly. "Guess I was just set on getting away from my sisters telling me what to do all the time. It seemed like you were trying to do the same thing. I'm sorry if I seemed contrary."

Sarah enjoyed the unexpected rapport of the moment. "As long as we're confessing, I'm afraid I've been a bit resentful. Luke seemed to hang on your every word and I'm the one who's always looked after him. Knowing you'd only be here a short time before going back to Boston, I was afraid he'd be like a lost pup after you left." She swallowed hard. "I'm sorry I was so sharp."

Suddenly the sound of her voice and the look on her face made returning to Boston seem like the very last thing Chad wanted to think about right now. "What makes you think I'll be returning to Boston?"

Sarah forced a small laugh. "Of course you'll be returning. That's your home. Your family is there, and I'm sure there are a dozen girls just dying for you to get back."

When Chad didn't reply, her curiosity got the best of her. "There is someone special waiting back in Boston, isn't there?"

He shrugged his shoulders. "Maybe. I haven't exactly found that someone special yet." Wanting to steer the conversation away from himself, he added, "If you could go back to Virginia, would you?"

His question caught her off guard. The young woman stared at him as she searched her own mind and heart for the answer. There used to be no question about it; she would have returned to Virginia at a moment's notice. Now, the realization that such a choice was no longer an easy one surprised her, especially considering her current predicament and the events earlier that day.

"Well?" Chad asked again, his dark eyes studying her so closely she felt he must be able to read her thoughts himself.

"I used to know the answer to that," she finally admitted.

"And now?"

"Now I'm not so sure. It's hard to describe just how Texas begins to take hold of you. Blue northers, Comanches, and rattlesnakes aside, there's something about it here that feels right. It's so wild and free, it'll probably never be completely tamed, and it can be very hard and unforgiving. Mother says it's almost like the Lord has given us this testing ground to show us what we can accomplish if we use the strengths and talents He's given us. There's plenty of game and fish and good soil, and the people—most of the people—you can depend on to be there when you need 'em."

"Like you were today," he reflected out loud, "saving me from that Comanche war lance."

Sarah's mouth turned up in a smile. "Like *you* were today," she said softly. "You risked your life for us, trying to stop a Comanche war party. I've never in my life known anyone like you, including uncles and grandfathers."

Chad's ears turned a light red. Somehow, no matter how foolish and dangerous his mission might have been, Sarah's words to him now made it well worth the risk.

19

The wind continued to howl outside the farmhouse as the hours dragged by. Mariah paced the floor clutching her shawl about her shoulders. The snow stopped for a while, only to be replaced by more sleet and rain, then snow again.

"I should have gone instead of Sarah," Luke mumbled miserably as he stared out the frosted window.

Mariah stood beside him and put her arm around his shoulders. "You're not to blame. If only I'd listened and packed us up for Austin, Sarah and Chad would be with us right now."

Luke looked at the worry lines across his mother's forehead. She bit her lip to fight back the tears.

"You know what I bet, Mother," Luke tried to cheer her. "I bet Sarah caught up with him before he ever got out of the valley, and they're probably riding out this storm in one of the caves."

Mariah hugged her son. "I wouldn't be at all surprised."

"The boy may be right, Mrs. Preston," Dunmar encouraged from the rocking chair beside the fireplace. "Chad grew up in the city, but he's not a complete tenderfoot. He's spent a lot of time in Kentucky with his aunt and uncle. That uncle, I might add, was raised in a Shawnee village."

Luke left the window and walked over toward the rocker. "Chad told me about him, that he thought Tecumseh was a better man than some of his officers in the war."

"That's what I understand." Dunmar shifted his injured leg slightly on the footstool. "Did Chad tell you he has sailed across the Atlantic twice and to the West Indies several times?"

Luke shook his head. "No. He only said he'd sailed on his father's ships before. He's talked more about an Indian mission in the Virginia mountains and his aunt and uncle in Kentucky than anything else."

Dunmar's glance met Luke's worried look. With an encouraging wink, he directed his next comment to the woman standing at the window. "My point bein', Mrs. Preston, Chad can take care of himself and Sarah too. I'm sure Luke's right. They've found shelter and are stayin' out of the storm. As soon as there's a break in the weather, they'll make their way home. And no self-respectin' Comanche is goin' to be out on a raid now. Those lads have hurried back to their village and a nice cozy tepee. You can mark my words."

Mariah turned to look out the window again. She knew the Ranger was trying to cheer her up, yet he seemed to believe what he was saying. This realization encouraged her heart tremendously and helped her push aside some of the mind-numbing worry.

"I pray you're right, sir," she breathed hopefully. Focusing on this thought, she turned with a determined air and declared confidently, "They'll be starvin' hungry when they get home. Luke, climb up there and hand down that jar of wild plum preserves and a jar of those persimmons from the top shelf. I'll bake a pie and some biscuits to go with our venison stew."

Luke smiled gratefully at Dunmar. Even though the patient was not fully recovered, the boy could tell by his voice that he was getting better. Over the past few days, as Dunmar's health improved, Luke had discovered that the Ranger possessed a surprisingly droll sense of humor. It was a comfort to see how the man's words truly encouraged his mother.

The lingering storm forced Chad and Sarah to get up and walk around from time to time to keep their circulation going. During the first of these exercise jaunts the stranded pair used a lighted stick from the fire to explore their shelter. As the flickering flame of their torch cast eerie shadows about them, they discovered that a cave-in had blocked off the passage less than seventy-five feet from the entrance. An icy draft sifted around the tumble of rocky debris indicating that the cave continued past the blockage.

"At least we know we're not sharing this place with any bears or mountain lions," Sarah said through chattering teeth.

"I'm sure the horses would never have come in if there'd been anything like that in here," Chad replied as he studied the seven-foot-high wall of debris that blocked the tunnel.

Sarah was ready to return to the brighter light of their small fire, but Chad kept studying the stone floor and walls as closely as the dim light permitted.

"What are you looking for?" she wondered.

"Nothing probably. Just curious," he mumbled as he bent down and brushed his hand across the thick dust collected in the recesses of the chilled stone floor.

"Curious?" Sarah watched him move the small torch across the swept places wondering if he was growing delirious. "Perhaps we ought to go back by the fire and warm up a little."

He stood up and the pale light moved across the obstructing debris again. "How long has Mr. Medina worked for you?"

The question was so unexpected, she grew uneasy about her companion's mental state. She had to think a moment before answering. "He was here when we came and started working for us from the first. Come on, Chad, let's go sit down, please."

Hearing the concern in her voice, he held the torch so the light fell on her face. "Are you all right?" he asked.

She stared at his dimly lit face. "Other than freezing cold, I'm fine. What about you?"

"I'm all right," he nodded as they turned to walk back to their fire.

"Are you sure?" she asked.

Glancing down at her, Chad held her arm to steady her along the uneven floor. "I'm fine, why?"

"It just seemed a little odd to be poking around in the dust and then out of the blue asking about Mr. Medina, that's all."

"You know that map we found on Pruitt?" he began to explain.

"The supposed treasure map?" she asked as they passed the horses and sat down again to share the blanket.

"When I showed it to Medina, his reaction was very strange, almost mysterious. He said, 'It is the one,' then walked off in kind of a daze."

"The one what?" Sarah asked, resting her head against his shoulder and watching the small flames of the fire dancing in bright orange and yellow tongues along the pieces of wood.

"I'm not sure," Chad shrugged. "At first I thought he meant the map itself. Luke told me some distant grandparent of Medina's was supposedly given the original map of the place Coronado's men hid their gold and that Medina had seen it when he was a boy. I thought maybe he believed that the old prospector's map was really the one that belonged to his ancestor."

"That sounds logical," she agreed. She wasn't shivering as much now. "You said you thought that at first?"

"Yeah." Chad scooted one of the few remaining pieces of wood toward the fire with his foot. "I was just thinking about that map a little bit ago and maybe Medina was talking about a *cave* being the one. Maybe he recognized a certain cave on that map."

Sarah found it difficult to take any of this discussion seriously, but it did help get her mind off of the penetrating cold. "And you were looking back there for some clue because you thought this might be the cave he was talking about?"

He chuckled. "Sounds pretty far-fetched, doesn't it? But there were some markings on the map that could have been those caves in the cliffs where Pruitt and his partner camped. Then farther along one of the lines was another circle connected to a smaller one above it. It might have been a single, larger cave with a second entrance."

"Was it marked with an *X?*"

He could tell by the sound of her voice that she was teasing and he smiled too. "No, no 'X marks the spot' or anything. But there were some Spanish words written in a very fancy script that you don't see anymore."

"Well, if this cave is the one Mr. Medina referred to, he'll be very disappointed to find the treasure is buried under a mountain of debris. Did you ever ask him about it?"

Chad noticed Sarah's voice sounded like she was getting sleepy again so he answered her question in hopes of keeping her talking. "No, I haven't had the chance. A few other things have kinda kept me too busy to even think about it."

"I guess that's true." Her voice grew softer.

"Sarah, you said Medina's been here since before your family came. What if he came to this valley looking for the right cave?"

"Well," she sighed wearily, "the legend of Coronado's gold has always been his favorite story. It's possible, I s'pose."

"The day he showed me the creek where he found that piece of coffee pouch, I got the feeling that he pretty much knew every inch of this place."

"Ummhmm," was her only reply.

"So, he's probably already explored this cave and knows it's blocked. That draft coming through there probably means there's another entrance somewhere. Do you think he's found it?"

Sarah was silent.

Chad decided to let her doze a little while. He would wake her before long so they could take another walk around the cave. Looking toward the entrance, he saw that the wind and sleet hadn't let up. When he had started out before dawn that morning, he had considered the possibility of death at the hands of the Comanches. He certainly never dreamed of becoming a victim of a Texas blue norther. As the storm raged outside and their fuel supply dwindled, that possibility began to loom before him.

The rest of the day was spent moving, then huddling, sometimes dozing, sometimes talking about their homes back east. They learned about one another. Sarah's home had been just outside Culpepper, Virginia, and within twenty miles of the Cherry Hills Horse Farms owned by Chad's Uncle Robert. She knew of the reputation of the fine stock produced there. The two even speculated that they might have passed on the streets of Culpepper when Chad had traveled through there on his way to Cherry Hills for a visit.

By late afternoon, the wind still continued to send swirling clouds of snow by the cave entrance. From inside, it was hard to know if it was still snowing or if the wind was just scattering what had already fallen. Either way, the two captives decided that it would be even more dangerous to try to make their way home through the blinding gale.

It was hard to guess what time it was when the coals of the fire finally dimmed to the last few sparks. Chad had tried to conserve each piece of wood as long as possible, letting it burn down to mere coals just big enough to ignite the next piece. Finally, only a gnarled piece of knotted cedar with beads of resin oozing from the twisted grain remained. He had saved this piece as the last. Now he laid it on the coals so the beads of resin would catch. The knot burned slowly,

182

giving them light for a while longer, but the shadows of the shallow cave slowly closed in around them.

As darkness fell the temperature dropped. Puddles of water just inside the cave entrance were already frozen. It promised to be a long, miserably cold night. Chad prayed that the temperature wouldn't drop any lower.

"Come on, Sarah, let's take another stroll," he said as he watched the cedar knot turn to embers.

"I'll let you walk this one by yourself," she mumbled sleepily. "I can't feel my toes anyway."

"Come on." Chad stood up and pulled her to her feet. "Just a couple of turns around the floor."

Sarah obliged. "Are you asking me to dance, Mr. Macklin?" she joked wearily.

In the growing darkness she could just make out the features of his face.

"Yes, Miss Preston, if you'd do me the honor."

Despite the fact she was very tired and could hardly feel her feet or hands, Sarah placed her left hand on Chad's shoulder. Her companion took her right hand in his as if they were about to waltz around a ballroom floor. When he found that she could hardly shuffle her feet, the young man drew her close and held her up as they moved about the cave floor.

"You've probably danced at all kinds of balls, haven't you, Chad?" She had to force her numb feet to move.

"A few," he answered.

"I was only thirteen when we left Culpepper. Before that, my friends and I could hardly wait until we turned sixteen and could be presented at our first summer cotillion, our first real ball."

"I remember my sister Amanda's first cotillion." Chad wanted to prolong the dance. He was growing more and more worried about her. "She was excited for weeks. But that day, she was so nervous she got sick and couldn't even go."

"Poor thing," Sarah sighed as she sagged against him. He tightened his arm about her holding her up. With all of her remaining strength, she tried to hold on to his shoulder. "What color was her dress?" she mumbled.

"Her dress?" Chad chuckled. "I have no idea."

"I always thought my first ball gown would be pink satin, the color of Mother's roses." Sarah's sentence trailed off into a whisper.

Shaking her slightly, he said, "Sarah, the dance isn't over yet. Come on now, just a little longer. We need to keep moving. Then we'll sit down and rest."

Even though his own feet felt like blocks of ice and his fingers were numb, Chad feared that once they sat down, they wouldn't be able to get up and move again.

"It's been a lovely evening, Mr. Macklin. I do hope you'll call again." Sarah's knees gave way.

"Yes, it has," he replied, still holding her close. "I'd be very happy to call again."

Seeing it was no use, Chad helped her over to the spot at which he had propped the saddles as back rests beside the gum coat. He settled his companion on one saddle blanket covering the gum coat, and stiffly lowered himself down next to her. Wrapping the other saddle blanket around their feet, he cuddled the Mexican blanket around Sarah and held her close, settling back with her against the saddles.

"Don't you think the moon shines brighter in Texas?" Sarah's words trailed off as she fell sound asleep with her head resting against his chest.

"Sarah, please don't give up," he whispered. "We never finished our dance."

The tiny glow of the cedar knot faded and soon the couple was enveloped by the cold, clammy darkness.

As he too dozed, Chad's dreams were filled with the memory of the last time he had danced at a ball. His Aunt Christiana had given a ball in Boston honoring his parents' thirtieth wedding anniversary.

Chad and his aunt were dancing a waltz when she mentioned his eldest sister, Amanda. "I don't think Amanda realizes you are old enough to be considered one of the most eligible young bachelors in Boston," he had heard her say. "On the other hand, I think she almost wishes you'd settle down with one of these debutantes. There are so many pretty girls here tonight," his aunt had laughed, "and I think you've danced with just about all of them. But I take it you haven't found that special young lady yet?"

Chad shook his head. "Yeah, there are a few pretty ones, some a little more interesting than others, but none of them hold a candle to you, Aunt Christa. That's what I'm looking for, someone just like you."

She smiled. "No wonder you're so popular, such a gift for saying just the right thing."

"I'm serious," he assured her. "There's just something . . . Well, look at that cake over there on the table, all that delicious icing and beautiful decorations. It's great for dessert, but if that's all you ever ate, you'd get sick after a while."

His aunt laughed with glee at his example. "So what you're saying is you can enjoy a party or dancing or the theater with these girls, but you haven't found one that has something more than surface decoration?"

"Exactly." Chad whirled his partner to the music's gentle rhythm. "Don't get me wrong; I enjoy looking at a pretty girl, but I want to find somebody I can enjoy being with even if I'm blind, someone who's interested in more than just the latest social gossip or some new fashion thing. Most of them haven't even heard of Texas and can't imagine why I'd ever want to go there. Am I as crazy as they think I am?"

"I think you're wise beyond your years, dear," his aunt replied. "I'm sure the right young lady is out there somewhere just waiting for you."

"Aunt Christa, how did Uncle Stephan ever convince you to leave the comforts of home in Virginia to live out on the frontier?"

"Well, to be honest, I loved your uncle so, there really wasn't any convincing to be done. With Stephan, the frontier was more of a daily adventure than something to be feared."

"That's what I mean. You're a beautiful lady, but you're also brave and spirited."

At that moment, his uncle had cut in. As they circled away, the couple exchanged looks filled with affection and admiration. After nearly thirty years, Chad could see in their eyes a special connecting bond that time and circumstances had only strengthened. This was what he was determined to find someday.

Then the scene in his thoughts faded, leaving him standing by himself. He could still hear the music playing. A hand touched his arm. He turned to see a beautiful young lady dressed in a pink satin ball gown. Her wavy, light-brown hair was pulled back from her smiling face. A joyful gleam lit up her blue-green eyes. The two of them didn't speak as he took her in his arms and they moved out onto the dance floor. Slowly, the ballroom ceiling and walls faded away, leaving only the polished floor perched high on a ridge, now bathed in brilliant moonlight and surrounded by fragrant cedars. The music floated on a soft breeze as the couple swept across the floor, gliding in such sweeping turns Chad felt like he was soaring like an eagle.

20

"There we are, lad. Mariah, I think the lad's comin' 'round."

Chad didn't want to open his eyes. He was sure he must still be dreaming. The voice sounded like his uncle.

"Thank goodness."

Hearing Mrs. Preston's voice this time, the young man opened his eyes and blinked at the brightly lit room.

"Here's some chamomile tea. Let's get some down him to warm the inside too."

Sure enough, there bending over him was Mariah Preston! Chad blinked again only to discover Uncle Gib sitting in a cane-bottom chair next to the bed and Luke standing on the other side.

"Hello, lad." Dunmar smiled.

Chad's head cleared a bit. Then he remembered. "Sarah?" he managed to say.

Mariah took the cup of tea from Dunmar and laid a hand on Chad's shoulder. "She's fine. Just settle back there and keep covered up. You were nearly frozen to death. Here, drink some of this."

His mind was a whirl of questions as he sipped the hot tea. The liquid slipping down his throat filled him with a wave of life-giving warmth. "You're sure she's all right?"

"Yes, she's all bundled up and thawing out in the other bedroom," Mrs. Preston assured him. "Would you like some venison stew?"

He was so hungry, he quickly nodded. "How did we get here?"

"You'll never guess," Dunmar chuckled as Mrs. Preston left the room. "The weather finally broke before dawn. This mornin' at first light, we heard a whinny outside. There's old Digby standin' there, my bay trailin' after him, demandin' his breakfast! All we had to do was follow their trail through the snow to find you. I must say, you gave us quite a scare, lad."

"*You* followed the trail?" Chad still blinked from the brightness of the morning sun streaming in through the bedroom windows.

Dunmar held up a rough carved cane. "I've been layin' about long enough. I wasn't about to stay here while the rest of 'em rode out to find ya."

"He's not going to be up and dancing a jig right away," Mariah countered as she returned with a bowl of steaming venison stew. "He's still got a ways to go before he can be up and about too much."

"Sarah musta caught up with you before you found the Comanches," Luke chimed in as soon as he had a chance.

Chad reached up to touch the tender cut on his forehead. "Not exactly."

"What happened?" Luke's eyes widened.

"It's a long story." Chad grinned wearily.

"And he's going to eat this stew before he starts telling it," Mariah intervened. "Now, you scoot on out and help Mr. Medina bring in some more wood for this fire."

Luke frowned but quickly obeyed his mother, knowing the sooner he finished the chore, the sooner he'd get to hear Chad's story.

After Chad had finished a second helping of wild plum pie, he gave a brief account of his encounter with Bobcat and his war party. When everyone had gone, the young man found he couldn't rest. He finally climbed out of the warm bed, wrapped the down-filled quilt around himself, and headed for the bedroom next door.

The morning air was still brisk as he stepped into the dogtrot. He was just going to knock when the door suddenly opened and there stood Sarah, wrapped in a quilt from her bed.

Startled, she gasped, "I was just coming to see if you were all right!"

"I am," he said grinning. "What about you?"

"Still can't quite get warm, but otherwise, I'm fine."

The two of them stood there smiling until Mariah called from the kitchen, "If you two aren't going to rest in bed, come and sit by the fire in here. You'll never get warm standing out there."

Sarah wasn't sure she agreed, for she had a decidedly warm feeling in her heart at the moment. However, the couple followed her mother's advice and joined the rest of them in the kitchen.

The cold spell lasted two more days. Then true to the changeable Texas climate, temperatures warmed to the pleasantly mild fall weather of mid-October.

One afternoon, about a week after the freakish blue-norther, Chad and Hector were repairing the barn roof. Medina had refused to discuss his reaction to the map, so although still curious, Chad had dropped the subject.

It was nearly dusk when Pepper began barking excitedly, announcing an approaching rider. Chad was pleasantly surprised to recognize Senihele.

"Hey, *kpaihakwinakwsi!*" Chad called the Delaware greeting.

"Hey, Macklin. I see you still have your hair. I told you. It is good to have a swift horse!"

"You have no idea," Chad said with a smile as he climbed down the ladder.

189

"What brings you out this way?"

"When I got back from San Antonio, Captain Anderson said the Hammersmiths had arrived. They said you came by to warn them about Comanche raiders. He sent me out to check on you. Hasn't had anyone else to spare."

The tall scout knelt down on one knee and picked up a stick. Drawing two intersecting lines and two circles along the shorter line, he said, "When the weather cleared, a small band of probably ten Comanches wiped out the Kelly homestead on Canyon Creek just west of here. They also took all of the Bennetts' horses from their place just the other side of the Kellys'."

Chad studied the scout's dirt map. "Antelope Runner," he guessed aloud.

"Antelope Runner?" Senihele's head jerked up to stare at Chad.

"I wouldn't be at all surprised," Chad replied. "That's the way he was supposed to be heading the last I saw of him."

Sparrow Hawk stood up, his face hardened in a grim stony mask. A faraway look filled his dark eyes.

Chad clapped him on the shoulder and suggested, "Why don't you bring your roan into the corral and I'll tell you about my run-in with that Comanche."

He led the Delaware scout over to the corral. While Senihele unsaddled the horse before releasing him in the enclosure, Chad began to explain about both of his encounters with the Comanches. Senihele listened to Chad's account without a word.

While they stood leaning against the corral fence, Chad finished. "I've never seen anyone that mean or that strong. If it hadn't been for my mustang and Sarah Preston, I'd most likely be dead now."

Absently the Indian ran his forefinger along the scar on his forehead in silent reflection. Finally, he stood straight and glanced at Chad. "Does your uncle feel up to visitors yet?"

190

"He's almost as good as new," Chad replied, wondering what the scout would plan to do. "Come on; he's on the back porch shelling pecans with Mrs. Preston."

Dunmar and Mrs. Preston were sitting at a small table with a large bowl of pecans on the table between them. "Are you feeling all right?" she asked as she discarded an empty shell. "You look a little pale this afternoon."

"Feeling fit as can be, thank ya very much, ma'am," the man replied with a smile and popped a pecan half in his mouth. "I feel stronger every day, and my leg is healin' nicely. I even thought about takin' a ride this afternoon to test it out in the saddle."

"Uncle Gib, look who's here!" Chad's voice echoed across the porch.

The men shook hands warmly and Mariah invited Sparrow Hawk to sit down.

"Sarah just made some fresh coffee. I'll go get some for you gentlemen," the woman offered.

The men thanked her, and she left the table as the scout began to report his news to Dunmar. Returning to the porch carrying three cups of steaming coffee, Mariah heard Senihele talking.

"The captain was wondering how much longer you're going to be laid up. He's already sent half the company against the Comanche village we've located about twenty miles west of here."

Mariah quickly set the cups down in front of the three men and declared, "Mr. Dunmar is hardly ready to be riding after a war party. His leg hasn't healed properly and—"

"Mrs. Preston," the Ranger exclaimed, "what have I just been tellin' ya? I'm feelin' quite fit, just a little tired."

"Exactly. You're asking for trouble if you try dashing off after Comanches. But, if you're determined to do it, well, go on and see if your leg continues to heal as well. I've done all the worrying over you I intend to do." With that, the woman stormed off the porch and headed toward the bluff.

All three men exchanged puzzled looks. Finally, Dunmar stood up and leaned on his cane. "Excuse me, lads. I need to have a word with Mrs. Preston if you don't mind. You lads enjoy your coffee."

Mariah had stopped at the edge of the bluff overlooking the cornfield and was gazing out over the Colorado. She was a handsome woman with a nice figure. As he walked toward her, Dunmar thought about the many nights he had been so deathly ill. He would awaken to discover Mariah sitting beside his bed. Her delicate features and perceptive eyes, that lovely bright smile, had filled many of his dreams. This seemed only natural since she had been so kind to him. Then he thought about her stubborn, hard-headed streak that could make a body fit to be tied with aggravation.

Coming to stand beside her, the man looked out over the wide river meandering its course to the Gulf. The cliffs across the river and the wide expanse of wooded hills were clothed in splashy autumn splendor and basked in the late October sun.

"I must ask your forgiveness, Gibson Dunmar," she began without looking at him. "I'm afraid I was about to make the same mistake twice."

"I beg your pardon," he said, surprised by this statement.

Mariah continued. "When Tom's bank went under in Virginia, I was the one who talked him into coming to Texas. It's my fault. He was a hard worker and very bright, but he wasn't cut out to work on the land. After I convinced him this was the place to start over, he had dreams of creating a new financial empire here. If we'd stayed back east, he probably would still be alive."

She swallowed hard and blinked back sudden tears. It took a moment for her to continue. "Instead, he began dreaming about being a part of President Lamar's expanding republic. Making this farm a success was only a step in his overall plan to rebuild. He never believed me when I told him that I was happy here with what we had."

"I'm not one to speak ill of the dead, ma'am," Dunmar interjected, "but the man was a fool to go chasin' off after riches when he had somethin' so precious here."

She shook her head, unwilling to be held blameless for her husband's fate. "I almost did it again, just now. I almost interfered with your decision to return to your duties. Please forgive me."

"Well, you're a fine nurse, and one can understand why ya'd want your patient to take care of himself after all you've done a pullin' him through." He shifted his weight, leaning on his cane. "I'm only surprised that you would be willin' to delay bein' rid of a cantankerous chap like me."

"You are cantankerous. There's no question about that," she agreed with a smile. "But I fear I was being selfish. I've rather gotten used to you being around. I'll miss our little confrontations 'cause I know you're not afraid to speak the truth. I've come to think of you as a good friend, Mr. Dunmar, and I'll miss you. Please forgive me."

"There's not a thing to forgive, m'lady," he declared sincerely. "You pay me a great compliment. I've come to think of you as a good friend as well." His smiling eyes twinkled with good humor as he looked at her.

Suddenly, he cleared his throat and gazed out over the river. "Now that you mention it, I am feelin' a little more weary than I thought. If you'd kindly take my arm, I think I'll have to postpone my plans for an afternoon ride."

Still watching his face, Mariah realized the true meaning of his words. "Now, Gibson," she began, "you mustn't . . ."

"Indeed, you're right, lass," he broke in with his brisk Scottish brogue. "I mustn't try to hurry this recovery too quickly. Senihele will be able to move faster without me holdin' him up anyway."

"That's probably true," she agreed as she took his arm.

Chad and Senihele had been watching the couple from the porch.

"Suppose the captain's going to have to recruit another Ranger," the Indian scout surmised. "Looks like Ranger Dunmar will be retiring."

Chad took the last swallow of coffee and nodded. He could see Sparrow Hawk was right.

That same afternoon in Austin, Captain Anderson was laboring over a letter relaying the tragic news of the Kelly family to relatives back in the States. The skill of letter writing was something he hadn't had much use for before his duties with the Rangers became more administrative than anything else. He had no family to speak of and most of the few friends he had wouldn't be able to read a letter if he did write.

He had crumpled six sheets of paper from false starts and was not in a good mood when two rough looking men entered his office. The taller of the two was a big burly man with a bushy beard and matted hair topped off by a tall crowned hat with a narrow brim. The bear claw necklace and buckskin clothes reminded Anderson of the men from Kentucky he had seen back in '36 on their way to the Alamo at San Antonio.

The younger man was dressed in an ill-fitting suit, white shirt yellowed with age, the collar of which was held closed by a string tie. He was about the same height and build as the captain, five-foot-eleven and slender. His reddish brown hair was slicked down like a young man out to impress the ladies. While he had rather ordinary features, the young man's grey eyes held a dangerous glint of someone with a volatile personality.

"What can I do for you boys?" Anderson asked after a quick appraisal.

The younger one spoke first. "Captain, m' friend here says he saw one a' yer pris'ners out hoein' in the garden behind the jail this mornin'. Said he thought it was someone we been lookin' fer."

"An' who you been lookin' for?" The captain leaned back in his chair.

"Name's Clifton Pruitt," the younger man replied as he hooked both thumbs in his belt. "His brother sent us to find 'im. We'd surely like to know if'n it's him."

"Well, sir," Anderson nodded, "you found him. You can tell his brother that as soon as the judge gets back from San Antonio next week, Mr. Pruitt will be tried for murder and no doubt sentenced to hang shortly thereafter." Leaning forward again and smoothing out a new sheet of paper, the Ranger was ready to return to his letter writing. "If there's nothin' else, I've got work to do."

"See there, Yarnell, I told ya it was him," the big man boasted.

"If ya don't mind, Captain, we'd like to speak t' Pruitt," Yarnell requested.

Anderson studied the two men. "Only one of you," he replied. "Turn out your pockets and leave whatever you're carryin' on the desk here. Tell the deputy back there I said it was all right to speak with the prisoner for five minutes."

Yarnell eyed the Ranger sullenly but did as he was told, turning his pockets inside out and depositing a small derringer on the desk along with a plug of tobacco and a few coins. Turning to his companion, the younger man ordered, "Go settle up with the livery and bring the horses over here. Soon as I talk with Pruitt, we'll ride out."

As the two men left the office, the captain appeared busy with his paper work. However, he watched the two men through the window as the big fellow headed toward the livery stable and the other turned the corner to go back to the jail. By the time Yarnell reached the jail, Anderson was standing at the back door of his office with his six-shooter in hand, casually checking the ammunition in the revolving barrel.

Yarnell told the deputy guarding the jail door he had permission to see the prisoner. Receiving a confirming nod from Captain Anderson, the armed officer stood aside and called Pruitt to the window.

"Hey, Clifton!" Yarnell greeted when Pruitt looked through the bars. "Yer brother's none too happy with ya. Sent me and Paxton to find ya and bring ya back. You shouldn't a never took the boss's money like that." The young man shook his head. "He's real mad. He wants his money back too."

Pruitt was surprised to see the young tough who worked for his brother. Not surprised that his brother was angry, he nevertheless saw a chance for getting out of his predicament. "Deputy, would ya mind steppin' away a mite? I'd like to give this here fella a message to take to m' brother."

The bored deputy shrugged his shoulders and stepped a few paces away but kept his rifle ready.

"Yarnell," Pruitt whispered excitedly. "You gotta get me outta here. They're fixin' to stretch my neck fer sure."

"Sorry, Pruitt, but that don't look like too easy a job," the younger man drawled as he nodded toward the armed deputy and the Ranger captain in the nearby doorway. "Besides, as mad as the boss is, he prob'ly wouldn't care if they did."

"Aw, half that money was rightfully mine anyway," Pruitt whined. "But you go back and tell Rayburn that I've got a way to give him that money back and a lot more besides. Ya just gotta git me outta here."

Yarnell smiled skeptically. "You do beat all, Pruitt. Ya think I'm as dim-witted as ol' Paxton? If you had such a deal, you wouldn't be coolin' yer heels in there."

Pruitt clutched at the bars desperately and declared, "But I do, an' I'll even give you a share. Just git me out."

When the young man stared back at him unconvinced, he lowered his voice and said, "It's a treasure, a gold treasure. I nearly had my hands on it when ol' Brandy Jacobs 'n' me was jumped by Comanches."

"How's that?" Pruitt had Yarnell's attention.

"A map. I had a map leadin' to Coronado's gold," the prisoner rushed to say.

"Had?"

Sensing Yarnell's pessimism, Pruitt quickly tried to brush it aside. "It don't matter none that I don't have it no more. I know what it shows. I remember where the treasure is. So you hurry on back to Rayburn and tell him I need a good horse and some provisions and I'll go back out there and git that gold and split it with him."

"What about my share?" Yarnell asked.

"Course you'll get a share. I need a gun too. I got a score to settle with someone."

21

"You sure you don't want to take the bay?" Gibson Dunmar leaned heavily against his walking cane at the hitching rail while Chad saddled the mustang.

"Thanks anyway, Uncle Gib, but Digby'll be just fine." Chad gave the cinch one last tug and Digby snorted. Turning aside, Chad added quietly, "I rode the bay the other day and Digby was really put out. He wouldn't even take the carrot I offered him."

"Maybe he was off his feed," Dunmar suggested.

Chad shook his head. "Nope, because Luke was standin' right next to me. Digby took one from him. Besides, to be quite honest, I think Digby's twice the horse the bay is."

The mustang raised his head proudly as Chad patted his chest.

Dunmar chuckled. "Aye, as I told ya to begin with, he's the more interestin' of the two."

The two men fell silent as Chad finished packing his saddlebags and situating the rest of his gear. Gibson watched his nephew, and his heart filled with as much pride as if he were watching his own son.

The uncle blinked back a sudden blur in his eyes and cleared his throat. "Now, don't forget to go by the mercantile and get ya another hat first thing. And don't let ol' man Leggett charge ya more than's reasonable."

"Yes, sir. I've missed my hat since that Comanche grabbed my hair," Chad agreed as he tied down his buckskin jacket behind the saddle.

"Well, I guess that's about it." Young Macklin looked around the farm. "Since Mr. Medina and I finished the barn roof this morning, most of the major repairs after the storm have been finished. With that doe Senihele and Luke brought in, there should be enough meat to last until you feel like ridin' out to hunt again."

Dunmar nodded. "Aye, we'll be fine." Squaring his shoulders, the older man laid his hand on his nephew's shoulder and looked him in the eye. "Chad, ya are a credit to the Macklin name. Your Grandfather Macklin would be very proud of you, not to mention your Uncle Stephan and myself."

"Thank you, sir," Chad replied.

"Take care of yourself, lad. I'd rather face the entire Comanche nation myself than have to tell your mother and sisters that somethin' happened to ya."

Chad grinned.

"There's someone else I wouldn't want to tell either," Dunmar added, glancing toward the porch where Sarah was standing with her mother.

Chad countered, "I don't know that she'd care, Uncle Gib. She hasn't spoken to me since I told her I was riding back to Austin to join the Rangers."

"Well now, I doubt she would've gotten upset if she didn't care," his uncle observed with a smile. "Go on now. Tell her a proper good-bye."

"Are we ready?" Senihele was leading his horse toward the hitching rail.

"I think so," Chad answered. "Just give me a minute."

Sarah watched Chad as he walked toward her. No matter how mad she wanted to be, his handsome young face only made her heart pound as he drew near.

"All set?" Mariah asked when Chad stepped up on the porch.

"Yes, ma'am. Thanks for making us supper for the trail."

"Just take good care of yourself," Mariah cautioned. "I'll see that your uncle behaves himself and gives that leg time to heal."

Chad gazed at Sarah as he said, "Thanks." Mariah discreetly excused herself. The two young people stood there alone.

"Sarah," Chad began as the girl walked around toward the back porch. He followed, stopping beside her. Looking out at the river, he remembered that first morning the two of them had stood here. It was the morning he and his uncle had been brought to the farm. Could that have been just over two weeks ago? So much had happened.

"Sarah, I thought we had gotten past this fussing at each other."

"Who's fussing?" she replied icily.

"Granted, you're not fussing because you're not even speaking to me and I don't know why."

Casting an incredulous eye his way, she declared, "You're marching off to join the Rangers and get yourself killed chasing Comanches just to prove to your family that you don't want to be coddled anymore, and you wonder why I don't feel like talking?"

"I'm not doing this to prove anything to anybody," he insisted.

"You're not?" she declared skeptically. Avoiding his stare, she went on. "If you aren't trying to prove something to somebody, then why don't you just go home to Boston where you won't be riding around inviting some Indian to lift your scalp."

"I don't want to go home to Boston." He was growing exasperated. "I know you think I'm just a crazy easterner come here to Texas for some exciting adventure and don't know what's what, but—"

"No, I don't anymore."

200

This unexpected response surprised Chad, and the head of steam he was building up suddenly cooled. "You don't?"

As she shook her head no again, her blue-green eyes met his.

"Then try to understand that I'm doing this because it's a job that has to be done. They need men unencumbered with responsibilities who're willing to do it. You heard what happened to the Kelly family. What if things had turned out differently when I went to the Comanche camp? What if Bobcat hadn't been there and it'd just been Antelope Runner? What happened to the Kellys could've happened here, Sarah. If Antelope Runner isn't stopped, it still could."

Sarah didn't want to think about what could have happened, nor the fact that Chad was leaving, and she turned away.

Macklin stepped up from behind and put his hand on her shoulder. "Sarah, please don't be angry with me."

"I'm not angry," she responded, this time more softly.

He turned her around to face him and saw tears welling up in her eyes. "But I'll be furious if you go and get yourself killed," she warned. "I've already lost someone dear to me; I'm not ready to lose another."

A twinkle lit his dark eyes. "I don't plan on gettin' myself killed, Sarah. We still have a dance to finish, remember?"

With that he drew her toward him and their lips met in a long, sweet caress.

Dear Sarah,
    I wanted to write to you before we head out since I'm not sure when I'll get back. Tell Uncle Gib that Captain Anderson regretfully accepts his resignation and wishes him the best.
    I was sworn in this morning, October 19, 1841. Today is my eighteenth birthday. Captain Anderson said the year-long enlistment passes quickly and he'd like to lengthen it. But at

just $1.25 a day for rations, clothing, and supplies for a horse, not many are willing to sign up for more than a year at a time.

Will be riding out in a few minutes with Senihele and twelve other Rangers to meet up with the advance scouting party searching for the Comanche raiders responsible for the recent deaths along Canyon Creek.

Tell everyone hello for me. I miss you.

Sincerely, Private Chad Macklin,

Texas Ranger

The new Ranger sealed his hastily written letter and gulped down a last swallow of coffee. Paying for breakfast, the young man grabbed his new hat and left the hotel dining room to post the letter. As he stepped out onto the boardwalk, however, he nearly collided with two people walking by.

"Excuse me," he apologized.

"Slow down, son," the man warned before hesitating. "Chad? Chad Macklin?"

Instantly, Chad recognized the Hammersmiths. "Hello," he greeted, tipping his hat to the missus.

"Hello there," the gentleman returned. "Where're you off to in such a rush?"

"I was on my way to post this letter to the Prestons and my uncle," he replied.

"We're headed back home, Chad. We'd be happy to carry it to them for you," Mr. Hammersmith offered. "If you wait for the postal rider, it may be another month before they get it."

"That'd be very nice," Chad said, handing the envelope to him. "Thank you."

"Yes, Dolph is planning on going by there tomorrow to see Sarah. You'll be happy to deliver this for Chad, won't you, dear," Mrs. Hammersmith added.

Chad turned around to see a tall, broad-shouldered man with blonde hair and blue eyes step up onto the walk. Flashing a big smile, he thrust out his hand to Chad.

"You're Chad Macklin? I have to thank you for warning my folks about the Comanches. I'd be happy to do whatever I can for you."

If he hadn't known better, Chad would not have believed this was the same young soldier he'd seen in Captain Anderson's office two weeks ago. The way his clothes still bagged on his large frame, it was clear he had not regained all the weight he'd lost on his torturous journey back to Austin. Yet, the grip of his handshake proved he was on the road to recovery.

Chad returned the good-natured smile, all the while wishing he could personally deliver the letter instead of Dolph.

"Private Macklin, do you plan on joining us today?" The Ranger sergeant's voice boomed from the street.

Chad turned to see him seated on his horse with eleven other Rangers and Senihele leading Digby.

"Yes, sir," Chad responded, tipping his hat again before hurrying out to swing up into the saddle.

As the party moved down the street, Chad glanced back at the three Hammersmiths. "Senihele, can you believe that's Dolph Hammersmith?"

The scout riding beside him nodded. "Looks like we'd better find those Comanches quick. Might not do for you to be gone too long without checking on things at the Prestons."

As the Ranger company rode by, two men walked out of the mercantile, the larger one grumbling at the younger one.

"Stop complainin', Paxton, that's the plan. We'll go ahead and bust Pruitt out, just in case he's tellin' the truth about that gold treasure. You 'n' him can lay low at my cousin's place upriver while I go git the boss. He's sure to want to be in on this."

"I think we shoulda both left yesterday like you said," Paxton grumbled, his bushy beard waggling with his angry words. "I don't wanta sit out there for a month at yer cousin's, especially with that little weasel, Pruitt."

Yarnell punched his arm to make him lower his voice. "You heard what that Ranger captain said. The judge will be here next week. Pruitt will be swingin' in the breeze long before both of us could get over to New Orleans, get the boss, and be back here."

They entered the livery and Yarnell looked about to be sure no one could hear them. "We can't have that if he's right about that gold now, can we?"

The big man finally shook his head no. Yarnell continued. "Wait here while I go over to let Pruitt know we'll be back after dark. We'll come up behind the jail; you jump the guard and do it quietly. I'll get Pruitt and then we light out. You head upriver with Pruitt. I'll head over through Nacogdoches to New Orleans."

They stuffed the provisions just purchased into their saddlebags, and Yarnell grinned wickedly at his partner. "Cheer up, Paxton. Just think, if Pruitt really knows what he's talkin' about, we'll all be so rich we can do anythin' we please for the rest of our lives."

Paxton had been along on enough of Yarnell's get-rich-quick schemes that he wasn't holding his breath, but he couldn't pass up the chance just in case he might be right this time. He watched the young tough scurry across the street to the jail.

The town was spread out enough that there were wide gaps between some of the buildings. Although the jail was behind the Rangers' office, it could easily be seen from the street. Likewise, anyone standing at the jail window could see a wide portion of the street in front of the hotel and the activity going on there. So it had been only a few minutes earlier when two hate-filled eyes watched through the jail bars as young Ranger Macklin had a friendly discussion with three people. Listening to Yarnell unfold his plan, the prisoner began making additional plans of his own. Some day, some way, the new Ranger would pay dearly for bringing in the great Clifton Pruitt.

22

A brisk wind of late November stirred through the dry leaves scattered across the yard. Sarah pulled her grey wool coat tighter as she hurried out to the wagon stopping in front of the hitching rail.

"Hey, Sarah, here's another letter for ya from Chad," Luke called from the wagon seat.

Her heart jumped with excitement as she tried to appear nonchalant while waiting for her brother to hop down.

"Aye, had a long talk with Captain Anderson and it looks like he'll be back in Austin soon," Dunmar announced as he lowered himself down, still careful of his recently healed leg. "Captain says his company has been picked as honor guard for the President's inauguration next month on the thirteenth."

"He's doing well, then?" she asked.

"Apparently," Dunmar nodded.

Luke pulled the envelope from his jacket and handed it to her. "Well, come on, let's see what he says."

"The letter is addressed to me," Sarah said, staring down at the bold handwriting. She had read Chad's first letter over so many times she could have recognized his writing anywhere.

"Yeah, but you'll read it to us anyway," Luke replied impatiently. "Won't ya?"

"Luke," Dunmar advised. "Let your sister read her letter in peace. Here, help me carry in these supplies for your mother."

"But—" the boy protested.

Sarah didn't hear the man's next comment to her brother, for she was already halfway back to the house to read in the privacy of her room.

Since Dunmar's decision to stay on and help the Prestons, he had felt it was not proper for him to remain in the house any longer. With Luke and Hector's help the ex-Ranger had built another bunk and had slightly enlarged the hired hand's quarters attached to the barn. Now Sarah had her room back. At this moment, she was glad to be able to escape there and read Chad's letter by herself.

Dear Sarah,

I hope this letter finds you and everyone there well. It's been only two weeks since riding away from the farm, but it seems much longer. Have been told the postal delivery takes quite some time, so hope this reaches you before too long.

It's taken nearly a month, she thought, *and it feels like an eternity.* The letter continued.

Am sitting in the shade of a live oak not far from the broken walls of the Alamo. Hearing the stories of what happened here five years ago moves even a newcomer like myself to respect the courage and honor shown by those hundred and eighty-seven men who held off Santa Anna's army of three thousand for two weeks before falling. I have finally gotten to meet Captain Jack Hays and the other Rangers who often stand outnumbered against Indian and Mexican forces in order to protect the citizens of this republic, and I've become even more convinced that I've made the right decision to join their ranks.

Nearly eighty miles away in San Antonio a month ago. No telling where he might be right now, Sarah thought. She frowned and kept on reading.

Tell Uncle Gib that our search for the Comanches responsible for the raid on the Kelly and Bennett homesteads led us to the main village that Senihele's fellow scouts spotted. They folded up silently in the night and disappeared before we could move in the next day. When we ran into Antelope Runner and the band that hung back to engage us, I realized it must have been Bobcat and Stands Before Running Buffalo's village. I have to admit, I'm glad they were gone.

Antelope Runner and his men led us on quite a chase. When we caught up with them Senihele met his old enemy in a ferocious hand-to-hand combat. Although our Delaware friend was injured, he managed to overcome Antelope Runner, which I know from experience was a tremendous feat. I don't suppose I will ever see a more savage fight.

Senihele is back in Austin recovering. His injuries will take a while to heal, but he has peace of mind. He has at last avenged his brother's death.

At least he doesn't mention being wounded himself, she reasoned hopefully. *Then again, he probably wouldn't.* Hurrying on, she read:

Digby continues to serve well. I think he enjoys the chase and battle skirmishes we've been in. Seeing him charging after them seemed to unnerve some of Antelope Runner's band. They hadn't forgotten our earlier confrontation, I guess.

They weren't the only ones. She would never forget the heart-stopping sight of Chad's struggle against the Comanche warriors and the mustang's savage intervention.

Did Dolph Hammersmith deliver my last letter? He seems to be recovering from his ordeal very quickly. I suppose he has asked to escort you to the inauguration ball next month on the thirteenth.

How did he guess that? she wondered.

There is hope among our company that we will be in attendance. If so, remember we still have a dance to finish.

How could she forget? She often awoke from a dream of being in his arms and gliding in sweeping turns around a ballroom floor.

I find myself thinking about you much of the time, Sarah, and wonder if you occasionally think of me (without losing your temper).

Well, I must close. There's the sergeant calling for us to get ready to move out. Give my best to everyone there.

Sincerely yours, Chad

Sarah lightly touched the ink lines of his name and closed her eyes. The image of Chad's face, his wonderful smile, and that good-humored twinkle in his eyes filled her mind.

"Sarah!" Luke pounded on her door interrupting her thoughts. "Sarah, come on, let's hear what Chad has to say."

Aggravated, the young woman opened the door. "You'll have to wait until I can read it to everyone tonight at the dinner table," she said irritably. "I intend to read it aloud only once." Luke grumbled but followed her to the kitchen without much of a fuss.

After grace, the group filled their plates and everyone eagerly listened to the young Ranger's letter.

"Well, I'm relieved for Senihele," Dunmar reflected. "He's been bedeviled by the memory of what that Comanche did to his brother too long. Now maybe he can put it behind him."

"Thank goodness Chad doesn't mention anything about being wounded," Mariah commented as she spooned more Irish stew on her son's plate.

"Hmm, I'm not sure he would," Gibson mused. "Still, he was healthy enough to write a nice newsy letter, heh?"

"Maybe when he returns to Austin for the ball, if Sparrow Hawk is recovered, they'll both come out to visit for a few days," added Mariah.

Luke had been listening intently to Chad's written words and his mother's comment brought an interesting thought to mind. "Boy, I wish I could go to the ball," he broke in. "I'd love to see whether Chad or Dolph would win the fight."

"Fight?" Sarah exclaimed. "What fight? Don't be ridiculous."

"Luke," his mother admonished. "Sarah's right; don't be ridiculous. They're two civilized young men and I'm sure if Chad's able to attend, there'll be no fighting."

Dunmar quickly changed the subject. "By the way, Luke, tell everyone what Captain Anderson told us about that outlaw, Clifton Pruitt."

"Oh yeah." The boy sat up straight. "He broke out the night Chad's company left Austin. Captain said two fellas broke him out and killed the deputy. With all the Rangers out looking for the Comanches, a posse of men from town tried to pick up their trail along the river to where those two men cuttin' cedar posts were killed this summer. They turned back figurin' the Indian danger was such that no one with a lick of sense would stay out there waitin' to be scalped by Comanches."

Dunmar raised an eyebrow at this statement and looked at Mariah, who blushed slightly as she realized he was thinking about her refusal to run to Austin in the face of an Indian attack.

"More corn bread, anyone?" she offered.

The rest of November passed uneventfully with cold rainy weather restricting the activities of nearly everyone. With December came clear skies and Chad's return to Austin.

"Whatcha got in the package, Macklin?" Captain Anderson asked as Chad emerged from the mercantile.

"A birthday present," he replied as he fell in step with the Ranger captain on the way back to headquarters.

"For your Uncle Gib, heh?" the captain guessed absently as he moved along at a brisk pace.

"No, sir," Chad grinned, prepared to take the ribbing. "It's for Sarah Preston."

The young Ranger's answer caught his full attention. "Is it, now?" The captain stroked his handsome black mustache thoughtfully.

Chad nodded as they stepped down to cross the dusty street. "If I remember correctly, Luke told me her seventeenth birthday was December fourth, just last week. When we were in Houston last month, I bought it and had it shipped over here."

"Well, I heard that she's goin' to the inaugural ball with Dolph Hammersmith."

"If he has any brains, he'd ask her," Chad replied soberly, "but I plan on dancing a couple of dances with her myself anyway."

"Well, now, this may be as interestin' a rivalry as the one we've had between Sam Houston and David Burnet during this last presidential election. Good luck to you, son. You headin' out that way then?"

"Yes, sir," Chad said, glad the topic of conversation had changed as they stopped beside the hitching rail where Digby was tethered.

"You wouldn't mind stoppin' by the Hammersmiths' place on the way, would ya?" Anderson held up a folded piece of paper. "I got some news Dolph would be interested in, about the expedition."

"I don't mind," Chad replied as he tied the package behind his saddle.

"Your uncle and the Prestons might be interested too."

The Ranger unfolded the paper, then pushed his broad-brimmed hat up so it sat on the back of his head. Since becoming a Ranger, Chad had learned that this gesture meant the captain, who was very reserved in expressing any emotional reactions, was irritated about something. His subordinates had to rely on this sort of clue to know what his feelings on a matter were.

"Just came from talkin' to President Lamar. You knew I sent Senihele down to San Antonio with the news about Dolph?"

Chad nodded and leaned back against the hitching rail next to Digby's head as he listened.

"Well, what with Mexican forces practically campin' on Hays' doorstep and with our Injun trouble over here, the President decided us Rangers had enough to say grace over. He wanted just to wait for word from Santa Fe instead of sendin' a company to search for the expedition."

"Made sense," Chad agreed.

Anderson nodded once then grimly announced, "Word from Santa Fe seems to be that what was left of the expedition was surrounded and taken prisoner by Mexican soldiers and is being marched all the way back to Mexico City."

The Ranger refolded the paper. "The list of prisoners includes John Brookes, Thomas Preston's business partner, and several of Dolph's soldier friends. President Lamar is sendin' out dispatches requestin' diplomatic intervention from the United States, England, France, and just about anybody else he can think of."

Chad groaned inwardly. He didn't want to hear any more about the ill-fated expedition because he wasn't sure he could bring himself to carry the news about it to the Prestons. He was still haunted by the devastated look in Sarah's eyes that day he had to tell them about her father.

Digby nudged Chad's hand, breaking in on the young man's thoughts and making him reach up to scratch the mustang's forehead.

The captain folded his arms across his chest and sighed bitterly. "As long as all that diplomatic folderol could take, those poor souls will have to march every step of that twelve hundred miles. By that time, there may not be anyone left to negotiate for."

At least Sarah won't have to be worrying about what her father might be enduring along a brutal forced march, Chad thought.

Their conversation was interrupted by a man dressed in a dark suit stopping on the walk and addressing the captain. "Captain Anderson," he began, "I have a few questions about the expedition being captured. I need a quote or two from you for the *Gazette.*"

Chad and the captain looked at each other. "Well now," the captain said, "I do have a quote or two about that, but you couldn't print 'em in your newspaper."

"Aw, come on, Captain, surely there's some comment you can make," the reporter begged.

Anderson offered his hand to Chad. "Reckon I'd better see about comin' up with somethin' printable."

The two men shook hands and the captain continued, "You take care, Private Macklin. We'll see everyone back in town day after tomorrow all slicked up for the inauguration festivities."

Digby seemed almost as anxious to make the ride to the Preston farm as Chad did and they rode at a steady pace, stopping for only brief rests. For the past six weeks, both horse and rider had developed an increased endurance. Therefore Chad found that this ride from Austin seemed much easier than the last one.

Just past noon Chad directed Digby up the wagon track to the Hammersmith farm. The December sun was warm on the young Ranger's back, but a chilly breeze nipped at his face.

Riding close to the farmhouse, Digby's ears began twitching nervously testing the wind for sounds. Chad felt a strange prickling on the back of his neck as well. Something was not right. Reining to a stop, the man drew his Colt and checked the ammunition. Scanning the field behind the barn, the yard, and the house, he could detect no sign of life.

Chad dismounted and looked around. The front door of the Hammersmiths' cabin stood ajar. Tracks from at least four horses criss-crossed the yard. From their distance and depth, the hoof prints showed horses had been racing back and forth. A large smear of blood stained the barn door. The trail of four horses cut cross-country in a northwesterly direction from the farm. The angle indicated to Chad that the trail probably intersected the road to the Prestons about a mile away. Tracks of a wagon and team also appeared along the lane heading back to the road.

Putting all of the signs together, Chad had a fairly good picture of what had occurred. It appeared that three or four riders had approached the farm, two stopping at the cabin and two more walking to the barn. It was easy to see that the hoofprints were made by shod horses not Indian ponies.

From the looks of things, either Mr. Hammersmith or Dolph had walked out from the barn and been shot. Another man's prints and a rounded indention made by a knee suggested that the other man had knelt down and picked up the wounded man and walked over to the wagon. A smaller footprint nearby showed where a woman had climbed onto the wagon and driven it away.

Swinging back up into the saddle, Chad spurred Digby to a gallop. The tracks were less than an hour old and there had been no fresh tracks along the trail from Austin. The riders had either come cross-country or along the road from Burnet. The wagon had to have turned toward the Prestons. With a tightening knot of dread, Chad realized that trouble lay ahead.

23

Martha Hammersmith received the cup of tea with a trembling hand.

Sarah gently patted the woman's shoulder. "Try not to worry. Mother and Mr. Dunmar will be out in a few minutes. They've removed the bullet and nearly stopped the bleeding. Mother could almost have been a doctor, I think."

The woman clutched the girl's hand. "Thank you, Sarah. You're such a dear. My little Jane Marie would have been just your age, but the yellow fever took her from us in '39. Now, my Randolph—" The woman began to sob. "I still can't believe this has happened. All along we've been afraid of the Indians, not some worthless horse thieves."

"Just rest there, Mrs. Hammersmith. Try not to think about it right now."

Suddenly Luke shouted from the front porch, "Rider comin'! Hey! Hey, Sarah, come quick. It's Chad!"

Sarah's heart leapt for joy as she hurried outside. Luke was already racing down to the hitching rail when his sister reached the porch. Even the grave emergency arising in the past few minutes couldn't diminish the excitement stirring inside her as she watched Chad slow the mustang from a gallop to an easy loping approach.

A wave of relief swept over Chad. He spotted Sarah and Luke standing there waiting for him, apparently safe and sound. Luke had grown, and Sarah had just gotten prettier. The breeze played gently in her long hair, and the look of glee dancing in her eyes answered the question he'd been asking himself all the way from Austin. She was glad to see him.

Stepping down, the Ranger shook Luke's hand. "You've stretched up a bit, lad." But he couldn't keep his eyes off Sarah. He drank in the very sight of her.

"Hello, Sarah."

"Hello, Chad," she said softly.

Standing there Macklin didn't notice the tall figure walking up from behind. Suddenly Dolph Hammersmith pushed in between them.

Gritting his teeth in a sneer, the man declared, "This is all your fault, Macklin."

Without another word the man swung a wicked uppercut catching Chad under the chin and nearly taking his head off. Reeling back against Digby, Chad tried to catch himself, but the horse scooted out of the way before he regained his balance. He ended up on the ground.

"Dolph!" Sarah shouted. "Have you lost your mind?"

The furious man reached down to yank Chad by the jacket lapel and pull him to his feet for another blow. Chad quickly recovered and raised his arm to block the punch and grab Dolph's arm. Instantly, Luke rushed forward and seized Dolph's other arm, but the powerful man shook him loose and swung again at Chad.

Using a move he had learned from Senihele, in one quick motion Chad ducked and twisted Dolph's arm behind him; he then wheeled around to strike a sharp blow to the back of the knees, sending the six-foot-four-inch Hammersmith crashing to the ground. Chad coiled the man's arm behind him, almost up to his shoulder blade and knelt with one knee in the middle of his back, thus ending the surprise attack.

"Now, hold on!" Chad shouted impatiently. "Just hold on."

"Dolph," Sarah cried in disbelief. "What's wrong with you?"

Dolph struggled, but Chad had him firmly under control. He had no choice but to calm down.

"Wow, where'd ya learn that?" Luke exclaimed.

Chad caught his breath and glanced up at the awestruck boy with a satisfied grin. "The Delaware scouts love to wrestle. I made the mistake of getting in on it one time and Senihele showed it to me firsthand, but I was on the ground that time." Chad winked at Luke when he spoke.

"Get up; you're breaking my back!" Dolph shouted angrily and continued to struggle.

"I'll let you get up when you've calmed down and promised to tell me what all this is about," Chad declared firmly. "And when you promise to stop fighting."

Sarah was impressed by Chad's self-control. When he had every right to be furious for being attacked so viciously, he seemed only interested in restraining Dolph, not in fighting it out.

After a few more futile efforts, Dolph finally gave in. His voice was flat. "All right, just get up."

"Are you through fighting?" Chad wanted to be sure. The way his jaw ached, he wasn't ready to take another such blow.

"I'm through," Dolph surrendered. "Just get up."

Chad got to his feet, then offered Dolph a hand and pulled him up. Luke dusted off Chad's hat and handed it back to the young Ranger.

Stepping back, the boy remarked under his breath, "I knew Chad could beat him in a fight."

Sarah ignored her brother's comment and rushed to Chad's side. A large welt on his chin was already turning black and blue. "Are you all right?" she asked.

Chad carefully tested the movement of his jaw side to side and nodded. "Now, what exactly happened, and why do you think it's my fault?" he demanded.

"Four men stopped and stole our saddle horse 'cause one of theirs was lame," Dolph began to explain sullenly as he rubbed his sore arm. "Then one of those bushwhackers remembered seein' us talkin' to you in town the day you left with the Rangers. Thought we were good friends. He asked my pa where he could find you. Course Pa told 'im he didn't know.

"That wasn't good enough, and the dirty coward just up and shot Pa. Then he laughed and said next time we run into you to let you know what he's savin' for you. Then this other fella, younger than the others, whips up his horse and goes tearin' around the yard like a mad man, tickled to death to see a man shot."

"How's your father?" Chad asked in concern.

"Bad. Mrs. Preston doesn't know if he's going to make it or not," Dolph responded dismally.

"Did you recognize any of them?" the Ranger questioned, trying to think who could possibly have that kind of a grudge against him. Only one name came to mind.

"It was that murderer you brought in, that Clifton Pruitt," Dolph echoed Chad's thought. "As soon as I know about my pa, I'm goin' after 'em. They headed off toward Burnet. I figure they plan to cut northeast to Nacogdoches."

"Am I right in figuring they have about an hour's headstart?" Chad asked, looking up at the position of the sun and estimating about three hours of daylight left.

"That's probably right," Dolph agreed.

"Okay, I'm going to let Digby rest up a bit here and talk to Uncle Gib, then I'll head out after them." Chad turned toward his saddle and untied the large package strapped to the back.

"You?" Sarah asked with dismay. "By yourself?"

"I'll be taking Digby," he replied playfully. Then seeing her worried frown, he assured her, "It's my job, Sarah."

"Not to go after four men by yourself," she declared emphatically.

"Chad?"

At the sound of his uncle's voice, Chad turned. Uncle Gib was hobbling down the steps, still using the cane but moving much better than he had when Chad left. They greeted each other with a bear hug, and Dunmar slapped him on the back.

"Look at ya, solid as a rock, fit as a fiddle."

"You're lookin' fit yourself," Chad said with a smile.

Luke nudged Dunmar's arm. "They didn't even get to the dance before they started fightin'." Glancing at Dolph, who was brushing the dirt and grass from his shirt, the boy grinned from ear to ear. "And Chad beat him just like I knew he would."

"Chad's planning on going after the men that shot Mr. Hammersmith all by himself," Sarah announced, stepping in front of Dunmar. "Maybe you can talk some sense into him."

"Well, you really shouldn't try to go up against four men by yourself until you've been a Ranger a bit longer, lad," his uncle cautioned. "I'd better ride along just in case you could use a hand. Dolph can stay here and help Mr. Medina and Luke keep an eye on things."

Ranger Macklin wasn't so sure he liked the idea of the junior Hammersmith keeping an eye on Sarah, but he knew that Uncle Gib was right. Sarah seemed relieved with the plan, so he agreed.

"Dolph," Dunmar said. "I came out t' tell ya that you can go in to see your father now. We got the bleedin' stopped. He's beginnin' to wake up."

Chad stepped forward. "I'm sorry about your father. We'll catch those men and bring them back to Austin to stand trial."

"We'll see," Dolph said glumly as he turned to go to the house.

"What's the problem?" Dunmar asked as he watched young Hammersmith walk away.

"Dolph actually blames Chad for this trouble," Luke began.

"The lad must be daft," Dunmar exclaimed, shaking his head.

"Aye," Luke replied, absently mimicking the Scotsman. "That's what I told Mother when he was here visitin' last time. He seemed okay until he started talkin' about the expedition and bein' out there all by himself tryin' to get back; then he sounded unhinged to me. Mother said he's probably still recoverin' from that ordeal."

"She's probably right, lad." Dunmar clapped the boy on the shoulder.

"Sarah," Dolph called from the porch. "Would you mind comin' too? Ma was wantin' to talk to you a minute."

The look in Sarah's eyes told Chad she would rather stay there with him, but she excused herself. "She was very upset. I'd better go see about her," Sarah acknowledged.

The Ranger watched her walk away. "Is it just me or has she gotten even prettier while I've been away?" he finally asked his uncle.

Before Dunmar could reply, Luke asked, "What's in the package, Chad?"

The Ranger hesitated before responding. "Didn't you say Sarah's birthday was last week—the fourth of December?"

"Aye," Luke answered, imitating the familiar Scottish reply again.

"It's a birthday present for her. I bought it in Houston and had it shipped to Austin. I hope she likes it."

"What is it?" Luke persisted.

"You'll see when she opens it," was Chad's evasive answer.

"Why don't you give it to her now?"

"Now doesn't seem to be a very good time, lad," Dunmar intervened. "How about bringing Digby some oats?"

"All right," the boy grumbled as he went off to do the bidding.

Loosening Digby's cinch, Chad had noticed something missing since his arrival. "Where's Mr. Medina and Pepper?" he finally asked.

His uncle glanced around and scratched his temple. "Can't say for sure, lad. Mrs. Preston and I've been busy doin' a bit o' surgery. That is, Mariah was doin' the surgery and I was standin' by to help, but mostly just admirin' what a talented lady she is."

Scanning the ordinary places the hired hand was usually working around the farm, Dunmar was puzzled. "Come to think of it, haven't seen either one of 'em since breakfast."

Back in the house, Martha Hammersmith had become quite distraught when she went in to see her husband. He appeared deathly pale. Mariah asked her daughter to take Mrs. Hammersmith into her bedroom and have her lie down for a rest. Sarah helped the sobbing woman into the bedroom and made her comfortable. When she turned to leave the room, the woman clutched at her hand and begged her to stay and talk.

For nearly an hour, Sarah sat in the bedside chair listening to the story of how Randolph Sr. had come to Texas in 1835 and served with Sam Houston, fighting at the Battle of San Jacinto. After Independence, he claimed his land and sent for his family who had arrived in Galveston in October of 1839. Unfortunately they were in Houston during the last days of a yellow fever epidemic when their thirteen-year-old daughter fell victim to the disease and died. Sarah could tell that the mother still grieved the loss.

Finally, the woman fell asleep. Sarah quietly left the room and found her mother in the kitchen adding carrots to the stewpot.

"Where is everyone?"

"Dolph's sitting with his father. Luke's splitting firewood," her mother answered as she stirred the simmering stew. "I'm not sure where Mr. Medina is."

"What about Chad?" Sarah asked, a chill of dread gripping her.

"He and Mr. Dunmar have gone after those men," Mariah answered. "Chad thought it best to go without saying anything to you first. He didn't want you getting upset. He did leave this for you, however. It's your birthday present."

Sarah took the large package from her mother. "Birthday present?"

"Apparently Luke told him the date of your birthday. He saw this in Houston and said it looked like something you'd like. He had it shipped to Austin."

Sarah was stunned.

At last her mother asked, "Well, aren't you going to open it? I'm dying to see what it is, even if you aren't."

Holding her breath, Sarah carefully pulled back the wrapping paper. She could hardly believe her eyes. Tucked in the box was a beautiful pink satin ball gown.

The afternoon shadows were beginning to lengthen before Chad and his uncle picked up the trail of the four men. The December air was brisk and grew cooler as daylight waned. As they followed the tracks, Dunmar signaled for Chad to hold up a minute.

"Does this seem a little familiar to you?"

"This is the trail we followed when we were trackin' Pruitt and his partner the first time," the nephew exclaimed after a few minutes. "Does this bring us out on the plain that lies just outside the gap at the north end of the Prestons' valley?"

"Aye. Dolph must be right. They're headed for Burnet," Dunmar replied.

Spurring their horses on, the two men rode out on the plain where the Comanche war party had camped. They traveled at a steady pace, pressing to close the distance between them and the bushwhackers. The sun was setting on the rim of the western hills as they galloped past the gap leading back into the valley. Chad pointed to where the Indian camp had been, and they slowed down to give the horses a breather.

"Where do you think Bobcat's people will go, Uncle Gib?" Chad asked, thinking about his strange encounters with the Comanches.

"Farther west, I imagine, lad. It's all they can do. Of course, with Sam Houston president, I look for the Indian policy to change some. Maybe things will cool down."

As they began to discuss Antelope Runner, Uncle Gib suddenly stopped.

"Where'd the trail go?" Chad asked, pulling back on Digby's reins.

Circling back, they at last picked it up only to become deeply disturbed to discover that the riders had doubled back and headed toward the gap. With a growing sense of dread, the men slowed down and followed the trail through the deep cut in the northern ridges of the valley.

It was a perfect place for an ambush. Did the four men know someone was on their trail? The tracks proved they did not. The two Rangers passed through the gap and headed straight down through the valley back toward the Preston farm.

24

"Sarah, call your brother and Mr. Medina in for supper," Mariah directed as she turned out a fresh baked batch of corn muffins into a napkin-lined bowl.

The light had nearly faded from the sky and two lanterns burned brightly in the kitchen where Sarah had just finished setting the table.

"All right, and I'll check to see if Mrs. Hammersmith feels like coming in to eat."

"Thank you, dear."

Sarah's hand was on the door latch when she was startled by a pistol shot and a scream in the dogtrot. Throwing the door open wide, she found the passageway full of people: Luke, Mrs. Hammersmith, three rough-looking men, and a man in a suit.

Mrs. Hammersmith screamed again when she saw her son sitting on the floor holding his head. The youngest looking ruffian grabbed her. "Be quiet," he ordered, "or I'll slap you quiet."

Strangely, one of the four intruders looked vaguely familiar to Sarah. With a start she recognized Pruitt, the outlaw Chad had shot in the leg and taken to Austin. Stunned, she barely had time to think before two of the men pushed her brother and Mrs. Hammersmith into the kitchen. A third one pulled Dolph to his feet and shoved him forward to join the others. Dolph staggered and Sarah helped him into a chair. A red streak rippled along his temple where he'd been grazed by Pruitt's shot.

When Luke regained his footing, he went to stand protectively beside his mother. Martha Hammersmith clutched frantically at Mariah's arm, and the Preston woman patted her hand. Although Mariah's own heart was racing, she stepped in front of the terrified woman and put her arm around Luke's shoulders.

"I think they musta killed Mr. Medina," Luke blurted out. "I was lookin' for him out in the barn, but he's not there. He should be back by now."

"What is the meaning of this outrage?" Mariah demanded boldly of the man in the suit.

"Please forgive the intrusion, lady," the man said in a deep voice, bowing his head slightly. "If I may introduce myself. My name is Rayburn Pruitt, and these two men, Yarnell and Paxton, work for me. I understand you may have already met my brother, Clifton Pruitt."

The well-dressed Pruitt was middle-aged, slightly paunchy with dark brown hair and a thin mustache. He pulled out a chair at the table and sat down. "It seems my brother has been fed from your table once before. Since we were passing by, he thought we all would enjoy your cooking. Being on the trail all day without eating makes you hungry.

"Now if everyone behaves himself—or herself—no one else needs to be hurt. We'll just have our supper, avail ourselves of your warm fire and sheltering roof on this cold night; then in the morning we shall be on our way and you can go back to your normal activities."

For all his high-toned speaking, Sarah had a feeling Rayburn Pruitt was no better than his contemptible brother.

Mariah looked at Dolph and remarked icily, "Yes, I can see you mean no harm to anyone."

"Ma'am, the young man lost his temper. Clifton simply had to defend himself. He's lucky it only grazed his head. Next time, he might not be so lucky. I'm afraid my brother was badly spoiled as a child and if he doesn't get his way or is crossed, he seems to strike out in the most unpleasant ways."

"Do you mind if I at least tend to the wound?" Sarah asked, feeling nearly as bold as her mother.

"By all means, pretty little lady." Rayburn Pruitt smiled thinly.

After Sarah had poured some water in a basin, she set about to cleanse Dolph's wound and then wrap a bandage around it. Hammersmith was still slightly dazed and said nothing as she worked. When she had finished, she stepped over beside her mother.

Luke's shoulders were so tense he seemed ready to lunge at any moment. His mother squeezed his arm tightly and whispered, "Luke, please. Now's not the time. Stay calm.

"I was just about to serve our supper," Mariah said aloud to the men.

"Good, we're just in time. Sit down boys," directed Rayburn. "These two pretty ladies are going to serve us right now."

The three men scurried over to sit down as Mariah began ladling out the rich beef stew. Sarah carried the bowls to the table. Yarnell, the youngest of the four, eyed Sarah almost as hungrily as he did the bowl of stew she carried. As she placed it in front of him he caught her wrist and smiled. "Pull up a chair, and join me why don't ya, pretty thing."

Sarah let the bowl tip, spilling hot liquid on his hand. He quickly released her wrist and yelled. "Why you little . . ."

Luke jumped in front of Sarah and glared. "Touch her again and you'll have a Texas Ranger to deal with!"

Yarnell raised his hand to strike the boy, but Rayburn stopped him. "Enough! Where are your manners, you lout."

Slowly the man slunk back down, wiping the stew from his hand and glaring back at them.

"Texas Ranger, you say?" Rayburn's eyebrows went up. "You wouldn't just be trying to worry us with a little bluff, would you, boy?"

"Just ask your brother . . ."

"Luke, that's enough," Sarah warned.

Clifton looked up from his stew and a wicked gleam came into his eyes. "Now, there's one Ranger I'd like to get in my sights. My leg still hurts from where he shot me. Where is he anyway?"

Luke looked up at Sarah, squaring his jaw to tell them further how much trouble they would be in if Ranger Chad Macklin was on their trail.

"We have no idea," Mariah responded for her son. "Would you like some milk to drink?"

Rayburn had been watching this exchange with interest. Smoothing his mustache thoughtfully he asked, "You haven't seen him recently, by any chance?"

"I told you, we have no idea where he is," Mariah said coolly. "Now, do you want something to drink or not?"

"You got to have something stronger than milk," Clifton complained.

"The only thing stronger is coffee," Mariah returned.

"Paxton," Rayburn ordered, "take your supper out to the porch and keep watch. We wouldn't want any other guests poppin' in without an invitation."

Paxton, the largest of the three, was fully absorbed with gobbling up his stew. Sarah noticed the bear claw necklace hanging around his neck and wondered if he had killed the bear himself or taken it from an Indian.

"Paxton!" Rayburn repeated his demand.

"Ahh, Pruitt, you don't believe that kid's story about no Ranger, do ya?" Paxton protested.

"Well now, if it was just him, maybe not," Pruitt admitted as he studied Sarah's face. "The pretty little miss there would rather we didn't believe it. Just look at her face. Oh, there is indeed a Ranger and he's someone very dear to her, it appears."

"Okay, so maybe there is," Yarnell interrupted gruffly, still eyeing Sarah. "He could be anywhere in the Republic of Texas. Don't mean he's gonna come in here botherin' us."

"I doubt she would be so anxious to keep her brother quiet if there was no chance that he might drop by. So do as I say, Paxton."

The burly man drew his large bulk up out of the chair. Before leaving the table, he picked up three corn muffins, which fit easily in his large fist, and carried his bowl of stew out to the porch.

Sarah's heart sank. She began praying that Chad and his uncle would be expecting a lookout to be in place watching for anyone approaching the house. Knowing the two would be able to follow the trail back to the farm, Sarah was confident that it was only a matter of time before they returned. She would have preferred the ruffians had never become aware of that possibility. Now it would be difficult to catch them off guard.

If Pruitt was true to his word that they simply wanted a place to stay the night and would be gone in the morning, then the four scoundrels would become some other lawman's problem to handle. Such men could not travel far without crossing swords with the law.

As the time slipped away, Sarah became more apprehensive. She didn't want Chad to be the lawman going up against four such men. However, knowing the young man's determination to set things right, now that he was on their trail, she knew he would do whatever was necessary to try to bring them to justice, even to the point of putting his own life on the line.

As darkness enveloped the valley, the two Rangers pushed their already tired horses. The farther they penetrated the valley, the straighter the trail toward the Prestons' farm and the more anxious the two men became. Even Digby sensed the extreme urgency with which his rider directed him and

227

somehow tapped into a reserve of strength, responding with a longer stride and moving them along faster.

Chad and Dunmar were confident that if the men had stopped to make a camp, they would be able to see the light from their fire in time to approach without being detected. The closer to the farm they came, however, the more apparent it became that the men were not stopping to make camp.

Sarah and her mother stood together beside the fireplace with Luke right in front of them. The Prestons watched the intruders finish their meal.

"Mother, we must do something to warn Chad and Mr. Dunmar," Sarah whispered.

"It's not polite to whisper, ladies," Rayburn Pruitt commented as he took out a white handkerchief and wiped a bit of stew from his mustache. "If you have something to say, let's all hear it."

"We were just wondering about our hired hand, Mr. Medina," Mariah said.

"What about him?" Rayburn Pruitt asked.

"What have you done to him?" she asked.

"Please, madam, take my word for it, we have not seen this Mr. Medina," Rayburn assured. "However, if he makes an appearance and behaves himself, nothing will happen to him."

Puzzled by this, Mariah tried to remember if she had seen their farmhand since breakfast. She had not, but then the Hammersmiths had arrived just before noon and she had been too busy caring for Mr. Hammersmith to notice if Hector Medina was around or not.

Suddenly she noticed her son shaking his head trying to tell her something.

When Rayburn turned back to his meal, Luke mouthed the words, "He was going to the caves this morning."

"Heh, what's that, boy?" It was Clifton Pruitt who had caught Luke's words. "What was that about caves?"

"Nothin'," Luke replied tensely.

"Rayburn!" Clifton jumped up. "He's talkin' about the caves. The kid saw the map too. He and the girl were both there at the caves. They know all about the treasure. I bet they even know where the right cave is."

The well-dressed Pruitt shook his head and lamented, "Is it any wonder why I've always felt that some low-minded gypsies left you on our doorstep when you were a baby? We simply cannot be real blood kin."

"Why? What'd I say?" Clifton glared at his brother. He hated it when Rayburn talked down to him like that.

Rayburn forced his voice to remain calm. "If they knew about the treasure and which cave it was in, don't you think they'd already have it?"

Clifton sputtered. "Maybe, maybe not."

"Can't you see how much you've complicated things, you dolt?" The outlaw leader's eyes were ablaze with anger but his voice sounded ominously cold and emotionless. "We could have ridden out in the morning, and no one else would have had a clue what we are really after. They'd have just thought we were drifting through and probably let it go at that. But you've let them know what it is we've come all this way for, and now we'll have to make sure that they can't tell anyone else."

Mrs. Hammersmith gave a sharp little cry of terror and inched closer to her son. Dolph still paid little attention to the scene before him.

"But what if we do know which cave it is?" Sarah spoke up.

Her mother clutched her arm. "Sarah."

"If you do, why are you still living here?" Rayburn questioned snidely.

"Because of the ghosts of the Spanish soldiers," Sarah suggested. "They've kept the Indians away and we didn't want to make them mad."

"Ghosts?" Yarnell nearly choked on his stew and stared at Rayburn to see what he would say.

"Oh, come now, Miss Preston. You don't really expect me to believe that," Rayburn scoffed.

"I guess not." She forced a thin smile. Taking a deep breath, she improvised. "Actually, the tunnel's blocked and Luke and I aren't strong enough to move the rocks by ourselves," she replied.

"And this Mr. Medina, what about him going to these caves?" Rayburn pushed his chair back from the table, stood up, and began to pace back and forth, studying Sarah. "Was he going to try to figure out how to move the rocks for you?"

"I wouldn't be surprised." The young woman shrugged her shoulders.

"Somehow, Miss Preston, I'm having a little trouble believing you," the leading Pruitt confessed as he rubbed his chin.

"Ask her 'bout the map. She'll tell you she saw the map and musta figured out which of the three caves it is." Clifton riveted eager eyes on Sarah and came to stand beside his brother.

Sarah was stalling for time trying to think of something that would convince them they didn't really want to do away with their hostages. Remembering her discussion with Chad in the cave, she said, "Your brother and his partner were looking in the wrong place. It wasn't one of the three caves. It was the other cave shown on the map. The big one with the second entrance."

Rayburn nodded, able to accept the fact that his brother would very likely be looking in the wrong place. "And how do you know that's the right cave?"

"Well—"

"Does your brother speak or read Spanish?" Luke jumped into the conversation. Sarah had been stalling, but seeing the gleam in her brother's eye she realized he was delighted to see her leading these men down a rabbit trail. He was going to help.

Rayburn Pruitt looked at his brother and laughed derisively, shaking his head no.

"Well, Mr. Medina does," Luke declared confidently. "He could read those Spanish words on the map. He told us what they meant."

Now Sarah watched in fascination as her brother was weaving this fabrication. Or was it? Their hired hand had always appreciated Luke's interest in his stories about the Coronado legend. It was possible that Mr. Medina had translated the words on the parchment for Luke after Chad let the man see it. Chad even told her that Medina had acted mysteriously after he looked at the map.

Be that as it may, she hoped her brother was not getting so carried away with his story that he might go too far. She wasn't sure he understood how cold-blooded this Clifton Pruitt was. She had seen him in action. Watching Rayburn Pruitt and the look in his eyes as he listened to Luke's story, she somehow felt that the characteristic ran in the family.

Please, Lord, hurry Chad along, she prayed silently.

25

The two Rangers approached the farm through the black shadows beneath a line of trees behind the barn. Tying their horses to the back corral fence, they slipped silently around the enclosure and crouched at the corner post to look across the yard between the barn and cabin. Lights still burned in the kitchen window, but they could see no movement at all.

Six-shooters in hand, Uncle Gib motioned for Chad to skirt quickly around to the back porch while he checked the barn. Then Dunmar would sneak up to the front porch and they'd meet in the dogtrot. Chad nodded in agreement.

His knee-high moccasins made no sound as he moved like a shadow, keeping low and darting across the yard to the corner of the cabin. Passing under the front bedroom window, he heard no sounds from inside. His heart was pounding as he finally reached the back porch. With still no sign of movement, he could hear a muffled sound coming from the kitchen.

Peeking around the corner into the dogtrot, Chad spotted a dark shape limping quickly up the front path. He leaned back against the wall and took several deep breaths, trying to slow his racing pulse as he waited for his uncle to reach the other side of the dogtrot. Finally, hearing the low coo of a dove, he looked around the corner and saw the shadow motion to him.

As the two men crept toward the center of the dogtrot, Dunmar paused to open Mariah's bedroom door carefully and peek in while Chad did the same at Sarah's bedroom. Mr. Hammersmith lay sleeping in Sarah's bed, but otherwise her room was empty. Mariah's room was empty as well.

Almost in unison, the two turned toward the kitchen door and slipped to either side of it without a sound. Closer now, Chad could detect that the muffled sound was a woman sobbing. The noise gripped his heart like a vise and he was tempted to smash the door down. However, his uncle was two steps away and shook his head in warning, so Chad reached for the latch.

When Dunmar paused, Chad glanced at the door and was surprised to see a piece of rope securing the latch handle to the wooden peg above the washstand just to the side of the door frame. The younger man quickly unfastened the rope and moved the latch to push the door carefully open. The sobbing grew louder as he peeked through the widening crack. He could see Dolph sitting in a chair with his mother crumpled on the floor beside him sobbing into her hands.

A slight scraping noise behind the door warned Chad that someone was hiding there. He motioned to his uncle who was a step behind him. Dunmar nodded. They mouthed a count of one, two, and Chad slipped into the room as his uncle suddenly pulled the door and stepped around it, his gun ready to fire.

At the same instant, Chad whirled around to see Mariah Preston poised with a crockery pitcher held high. Just as she swung the makeshift weapon down toward his head, she recognized him. As she gasped in surprise, he dodged just as the pitcher crashed to the floor.

"Chad!" she cried, reaching for him as she took a weaving step forward.

The man grasped her arm and she started to sag to the floor.

"Mariah!" Gibson called in dismay as he encircled his arm around her to keep her from falling. The two men helped her over to a chair beside the table.

"Gibson," she whimpered and clutched his hand as he pulled a chair close to sit down beside her. "They took the children. I tried to stop them but . . ."

Through a haze of fury, Dunmar could see a trickle of blood coming from a cut on her lower lip surrounded by a dark bruise. He tenderly touched her chin but was unable to speak for a moment.

"Mrs. Preston." Chad knelt beside her chair, his hand on her shoulder. "Are you all right?"

The woman reached up to touch the side of her head and choking back tears, she forced herself to explain what had happened.

"They think Sarah and Luke can tell them which cave has Coronado's gold in it. Rayburn Pruitt told them that if they showed him where it was, we would be left here and nothing would happen to us." She shook her head wearily. "But I think they plan to come back and do away with all of us."

From the side, Mrs. Hammersmith's sobbing let up a little. "We thought you were those horrid men coming back to kill us," she relayed. "I thought they'd killed Mariah when she grabbed that wretched young monster's gun to try and stop them. He struck her so hard, she fell and hit her head on the table."

Mariah could see Gibson's knuckles turning white as he gripped the edge of the table in front of her. She lay her hand on his and gently touched his face. "Gibson," she assured softly, "I'm all right. Please just find them before they hurt the children."

He laid his other hand on top of hers and squeezed it gently, nodding his promise to her. Taking a deep breath, he struggled to bring the rage inside under control. "I don't

234

understand why we didn't run into them if they're headin' for the caves."

Chad was fighting down his own anger and anxiety. "Sarah knew we'd be able to follow their trail back here. She's probably leading them along the dry creek that runs along the base of the eastern hills." Shaking his head in wonder he grinned. "What a girl! That way takes nearly twice as long as the trail we just followed from the gap."

"I hope you're right, lad," his uncle said. Then he noticed Dolph, who hadn't moved from the chair or said a word. "What happened to him?"

"One of the Pruitt brothers shot him," Mariah explained. "It just creased his temple, but he's been in a daze ever since."

Chad stood up and squeezed her shoulder. "We'll find them," he pledged. "If Sarah's doing what I think she is, we can reach the caves about the same time they do."

The woman started to stand up. She wanted to go with them, but Gibson shook his head. "No. You must stay here and rest yourself. Ya've had your share of excitement. Now, let the young Ranger do his job. I'll tag along in case he needs a hand.

"Mrs. Hammersmith," Dunmar commanded impatiently. "Please pull yourself together, ma'am, and tend to Mrs. Preston. This brave lass could use a stout cup o' coffee."

Turning back to Mariah, he placed his Colt pistol on the table in front of her. The admiration in his eyes as he looked down at her nearly made her blush. "I trust that, with this in your capable hands, if any of those blackguards slip by us and come back this way, they'll be sorry they did."

Chad was already at the door when his uncle asked, "What's happened to Mr. Medina?"

"Luke thought he'd gone to the caves this mornin' and was supposed to be back," Mariah replied, "but we haven't seen him. You know how strangely he's been acting lately. I hope nothing's happened to him."

"Uncle Gib," Chad called from the doorway.

"Aye, lad, let's go." Gibson squeezed Mariah's shoulder as he whispered emphatically to her. "We'll find 'em, lass. I promise. We'll find 'em."

26

Chad hated to have to press Digby into further service that cold night, but there was little choice. Only the Hammersmiths' old mare remained in the barn.

"We'll keep the pace easy," his uncle said as they reached his bay and the mustang. "They're both young and strong and in good shape. Besides, there's naught else we can do."

Digby snorted and moved restlessly, waiting for Chad to swing into the saddle. "Ahh, so you know we're ridin' to battle, heh, boy?" The young Ranger patted the mustang's deep chest and added, "This is the most important one yet."

They rode north following the trail Digby had taken from the cave to the farm the morning after the bad storm. The air was crisp and so clear the myriad of stars glittering in the black expanse above them cast a whisper of light across the valley. Chad knew that within an hour or so a bright three-quarter moon would be rising over the black eastern hills. In the cloudless atmosphere it would illuminate the valley and surrounding hills like frosted daylight. They must reach the cave before that or they would have very little chance of catching the four outlaws off guard, and that could be deadly for their hostages.

The crisp December air was hard to breathe and stung their ears and faces as they rode. Chad hoped Sarah had a thick coat to keep her warm this night.

"How much farther, miss?" Rayburn Pruitt demanded. He was glad that they were no longer stumbling along in the dark and could easily see the trail laid before them in the moonlight. However, he was weary of the saddle.

"We're almost there," Sarah replied, trying to flex her hands stiff both from the cold and from being tied together. At least her hands were in front of her so she could hold on to the saddle horn, and at least Rayburn Pruitt was holding the other end of the rope instead of Yarnell.

She was still furious with Clifton Pruitt for insisting that poor Luke's hands be tied behind his back just because the boy had laughed at the outlaw when he had to ride the pack burro. That anger, however, was pale compared to the fury she felt toward the repugnant Yarnell for striking her mother and then refusing to let Sarah make sure she was all right.

"Hey, Boss, I think I see somethin' up ahead," Paxton called back from his point position on the trail.

"Miss Preston?" Rayburn asked, wanting her confirmation.

Recognizing the cave she and Chad had taken shelter in, Sarah nodded. "Yes, that should be it."

The men spurred their horses to trot the last few yards and eagerly dismounted. Rayburn allowed Sarah to step down from the saddle then yanked on the rope tied around her wrists to hurry her along.

Paxton struck a match and lit the coal oil lamp they had brought from the farm and handed it to his boss. Rayburn pulled Sarah up beside him only to push her a step ahead of him as they entered the yawning dark hole. With Luke shoved next to her, the Pruitt brothers walked a pace behind them with Paxton and Yarnell bringing up the rear.

As they passed the charcoal remains of the small fire that had helped keep Chad and Sarah from freezing, she thought about the young Ranger. No doubt he and his uncle had returned to the cabin by now and had discovered what had happened. She prayed they had found her mother not badly hurt. When the two men learned that she and Luke were being forced to guide these outlaws to the treasure cave, Sarah could only hope that Chad would guess to which cave they were going.

The air inside the cave was as chilly and damp as it had been that day she and Chad had found shelter there. At least this time she wore her heavy grey woolen coat. As the group slowly moved along the passage, their shuffling steps echoed around them.

"How far do we have to go in here?" The plaintive voice from behind them was Yarnell.

"It's not much farther," Sarah returned, her voice edged with contempt. "The last time I was in here, we heard some strange noises."

"Noises?" came Yarnell's voice again. The blustering tone could not disguise his nervousness. "What kind of noises?"

"A sort of moaning sound coming through the rocks blocking the tunnel." Sarah spoke up and looked down at Luke who grinned as she added, "It was probably just the wind."

"Or the Spanish soldier ghosts." Luke's voice wavered dramatically as he winked at his sister.

"That's enough, boy," Rayburn Pruitt commanded. "They're just trying to scare you, Yarnell. There are no ghosts."

He then yanked the rope attached to Sarah's wrists, spinning her around to face him. "Perhaps you don't understand, young lady. I'm not in the mood to play any silly games. I don't like the frontier. I detest Texas and its primitive conditions. The only reason I'm here is to find this gold and go back to my riverboat in Louisiana."

"Our riverboat," Clifton interjected lamely. "Pa left half of it to me."

In the lantern light Sarah could see the anger burning in Rayburn's eyes as he turned on his brother, spitting his words venomously. "You ignorant cretin. When you took that money from the safe, you jeopardized everything. If I don't get back to Louisiana with this gold, there'll be no riverboat."

Luke and Sarah glanced at each other, a bit startled by this outburst. Then Luke grinned. But Sarah could see Rayburn's mood was no laughing matter. She frowned at her brother, hoping he would temper his boldness with caution.

Her concern was justified when the angry Pruitt turned on Luke and threatened, "You'll not think it so funny if you find yourself left tied up in here with no one knowing where you are. I'm sure the bears or other hungry beasts would find you before anyone else did."

Luke took a step back.

"Now," Pruitt regained his composure and addressed Sarah, "young lady, if you please, continue on."

They moved on through the cave until they reached the wall of tumbled rocks blocking the way. Rayburn gave Paxton the lantern and the big man held it high, allowing them to see the entire seven-foot barricade. As they stood there studying the obstacle, an eerie moan came floating along the cold draft that seeped through the rock crevices. The sound made the hair stand up on Sarah's neck. Luke turned a frightened stare her way.

"What was that?" Yarnell demanded in a frantic whisper.

It took a moment for Rayburn to answer, "It's . . . it's just the wind. Calm down."

When the moaning came to them again, it sounded like a human voice blurred together with an unearthly howling. The group stood silent, straining their ears to hear.

"Help . . . me. . . ." The low moaning words were unmistakable but immediately followed by a long wavering howl.

The moan came a second time followed by, "Dios mio, salvame. Save me."

Yarnell whispered, "Hey, that's Spanish."

The next sound they heard was the scrambling of the young outlaw's feet as he turned and ran.

"Yarnell!" Clifton shouted, his voice reverberating off the stone walls. Paxton began edging away from the barricade. Sarah and Luke stared at each other as they both recognized the voice. But where was it coming from?

"Mr. Medina?" Sarah called anxiously. "Mr. Medina? Where are you?"

"Medina?" Rayburn asked.

"Yes. It sounds like he's hurt." She called out again, "Mr. Medina!"

When they heard the sound again, it was obviously coming from the other side of the jumbled stones blocking the tunnel.

"You sure?" Clifton asked nervously. "It could be them ghosts tryin' to trick us."

Sarah only shook her head in disbelief at the outlaw's stupidity.

"Do you see what I've had to put up with?" Rayburn grimaced, turning to the Preston pair.

Sarah had little pity for the other Pruitt brother and was more concerned about Hector Medina. "Mr. Medina," she called next to the stones, "how did you get in there?"

It took a long moment and they had to listen very carefully to hear, "Fell . . . hole."

Sarah and Luke spoke at the same time. "The second entrance! He must have fallen through." Sarah said as she turned to Rayburn. "We have to find the other entrance. We have to get him out of there."

"Yes," the man agreed. "Yes, we'll look for the other entrance. It makes sense that Coronado's men would seal up this way and have a secret way in."

"What?" Sarah couldn't believe her ears.

"Hey, that's smart, Brother," Clifton admitted. "I bet yer right. I bet that gold is right behind this wall just waitin' fer us."

It was clear that these men could care less about rescuing Mr. Medina. All they wanted was to find the gold.

Clifton looked about nervously and added, "But what's that awful howling?"

"Now *that* might be the ghosts," Luke suggested dramatically.

As Clifton turned to address Luke, Paxton finally spoke. "Boss, I don't think we can move these rocks."

"Idiots. I'm surrounded by idiots," Rayburn declared, grabbing the lantern from the big man's hand. "Come on, Paxton, let's get out of here. We don't have to move the rocks."

Pulling on the ropes to make Sarah and Luke follow along, the Pruitt brothers headed back toward the entrance. The rope cut into Sarah's wrists as Rayburn pulled her up next to him. "Where did the map show the second entrance was?" he demanded.

"I'm not sure, but it has to be up on top of this hill somewhere," she guessed. "Mr. Medina has always said these hills were honeycombed with caves and hidden holes."

Once outside, Sarah took a deep breath of the cold fresh air. Glad to be out of the cave, she scanned the moon-bathed valley stretching before them. In the silver light she could see nearly as far across the valley as if it were day. It would be next to impossible for anyone to approach the cave entrance from the valley floor without being seen.

"Yarnell!" Rayburn called. "Now where did that fool kid go?"

"Pssst, Boss."

The young outlaw crouched beside a tree stump holding his rifle ready to fire. "I heard it out here, too. They followed me!"

"Heard what?" Clifton asked nervously.

"The howling, and I think I saw somethin' white movin' over there."

At that moment they all heard the mournful howl again.

"Pepper!" Luke exclaimed.

"What?" the outlaws chorused.

"Yes," Sarah agreed excitedly. "He must be up there close to where Mr. Medina fell through."

"What are you talking about?" Rayburn demanded, keeping Sarah in front of him as a shield.

"Mr. Medina's dog," Sarah answered, filled with sudden hope. If their captors were busy climbing and searching for the other entrance, they would be too busy to notice Chad and his uncle when they came. As certain as the young woman was that the sun would rise in the morning, with her whole heart she knew Chad would come.

"See, Yarnell," Rayburn smiled with relief. "There's a very good explanation. I told you there were no ghosts."

"Maybe, maybe not," Clifton put in warily.

Ignoring his brother, Rayburn ordered, "Come on, let's get up there and find that dog."

It took a minute to convince Yarnell to give up his hiding place and begin climbing the steep hill. However, he finally joined the rest preparing to make the climb.

"Paxton," the outlaw boss directed, "we may need a rope to get down into the cave from up there. Bring the one from your saddle."

The bushy-faced man grumbled but turned back to get his rope while the Pruitt brothers began pushing their hostages to ascend the rocky incline.

Unable to help pull himself along, Luke stumbled forward. Looking up at Clifton he said, "Untie my hands or you're gonna have to carry me up there."

Grudgingly, Clifton Pruitt saw the truth in what the boy said and untied him. "Give me any trouble, kid, and you'll find yourself down in that hole with yer friend," the bully Clifton threatened, and he pushed Luke in behind Yarnell who followed Rayburn and Sarah. Paxton brought up the rear.

Although the footing was treacherous, the moonlight illumined their way as they scrambled up the slope. Sarah had a difficult time not tripping over the hem of her long skirt and petticoats and was hindered by the rope binding her wrists. They were nearly to the top of the one-hundred-foot climb when Paxton's foot caught on something and Clifton heard him scrambling frantically to regain his footing.

Luke slowed down to look around, but Clifton ordered him to keep going. Watching his own footing, Luke's guard finally crawled up to the top of the hill and glanced back down to see where the big man was. With the curve of the climb and the deceptive lighting, it took a minute before Clifton caught sight of the crown of the man's tall hat and could tell that the burly figure was moving up the incline once more.

"What's wrong?" Yarnell asked as he came to stand by Clifton and look down the slope.

"Just that clumsy oaf havin' trouble gettin' up the hill," Clifton chuckled derisively. He then noticed Luke was edging away and reached out to grab the boy's arm. "Where ya goin', kid?"

"Goin' to find Pepper," Luke replied.

"All right, let's go," Pruitt snarled, yanking the boy's arm and following his brother and Sarah.

The hilltop terrain was uneven with scattered boulders, short clumps of cedar and sage, and shocks of tall dried grass. The scene was a colorless array of shapes shaded in black and grey and highlighted in silver light. A cold biting wind picked up, rustling with a ghostly whisper through the lifeless grass. One last howl wavered on the wind then stopped.

Even though Sarah and Luke were certain that the moaning voice was Mr. Medina and the howling was really Pepper, the eerie atmosphere was unsettling. To Yarnell, who was already on the verge of bolting, everywhere he looked his imagination found ominous shapes and unearthly wisps of light moved by the wind.

The Pruitts were not quite as skittish as Yarnell, but when Luke suddenly began calling Pepper's name, it made Clifton jump. The third time the name sounded, they heard an excited yelping. It was close by, but they couldn't see the animal even though the moonlight was bright. They moved closer to the barking.

Yarnell kept turning in circles to be sure nothing was creeping up from behind. Suddenly the earth seemed to dissolve beneath his feet and he disappeared from sight, his terrified wail stopping short a moment later. Just a step away Sarah jumped back from the edge of the gaping hole that now lay in plain sight after the eroded edge covered by a thick mat of grass broke under Yarnell's feet.

"Yarnell!" Rayburn called down into the blackness. The only reply was another yelp from Pepper.

Rayburn carefully knelt at the edge of the hole and lowered the lantern to reveal a large opening with a drop straight down from the place Yarnell had stood moments before. Across the gaping chasm they could see the other side sloped steeply inward.

There on a narrow rock ledge about four feet below the top sat the forlorn looking Pepper, his white furry face reflecting the lantern light. Seeing them made him wiggle excitedly on his haunches yet cast an anxious eye down into the space below. Whining, he tried to stand up, but his back foot began to slip, which made him lie down quickly, digging his claws into his perch.

Luke started over to the side above the dog, but Clifton held his arm. "I'm just going to pull him up," Luke explained. "I'm not gonna run off."

Rayburn nodded his assent and Clifton released the boy's arm. They watched as Luke made his way around the rim of the hole to the other side. There he eased himself down the slanted wall and stepped on the ledge beside the dog. Pepper sat still; only his tail wagged nervously. Then Luke reached down, grabbed the dog's scruff, and pulled him up the incline until Pepper could reach the top with his forelegs. The boy supported the dog's rear legs, giving him a push as the animal dug into the earth and rock then scurried over the edge. Once out of his trap, Pepper barked happily and ran around in circles.

The younger Preston pulled himself back up from the ledge and knelt on the ground while the grateful pup licked his face. The dog then darted over to Sarah and happily greeted her, only to dash back to the edge of the hole and begin barking into the darkness.

"I knew it; Mr. Medina has to be down in there." Sarah called, "Mr. Medina! We're up here. We'll get you out."

"Ya s'pose Yarnell's still alive?" Clifton asked as he peered over the edge.

"If the fall didn't kill him and he didn't scare himself to death," Rayburn said coldly, pulling Sarah around with him to the place Luke had descended. Holding the lantern down and crouching slightly, he added, "There they are. I believe the old man must be your Mr. Medina. Yarnell is there beside him, but he doesn't look good."

Clifton moved over beside him. "How far down is it, ya think?"

"Maybe fifty to sixty feet," Rayburn estimated. "Looks like the old man slipped down this side and that's why he's still alive. It's steep, but with a rope, I think we can ease down there and find our treasure."

He turned to hurry Paxton along with the rope. "Paxton, don't take all—" For a moment Rayburn thought his eyes were playing tricks on him in the moonlight, for the outlaw seemed to have shrunk in size. Then the man stepped closer and raised his hand holding a Colt pistol.

"Paxton couldn't seem to make the climb." The man's Scottish brogue was clipped with anger as he stepped closer. "Mr. Dunmar!" Sarah exclaimed. "Thank goodness. Where's Chad?"

"Right here," came the young Ranger's voice as he stood up behind a low cedar bush about fifteen feet away.

It was apparent that while Dunmar had assumed Paxton's place climbing the hill, Chad had made his way up the slope keeping behind the low cover of rocks and bushes. Having given his pistol to his uncle, he had his rifle trained on Clifton Pruitt as he walked briskly toward them. "Are you all right, Sarah?"

"Yes," she choked with relief and started toward him. Just then, Rayburn suddenly yanked on the rope still tied to her wrists, jerking her back. The outlaw clutched her tightly in front of him as a shield against Dunmar's six-shooter.

"Now, gentlemen," the man said coolly. "I suggest you move back and put your guns down."

When Chad and his uncle did not do as he said, Rayburn stepped back closer to the edge of the chasm and turned Sarah so she was standing on the very brink. "Drop your guns or I'll drop her."

"Sarah!" Luke yelled out and turned to Chad. "Do something! Shoot him!"

"He won't take that chance, boy." Rayburn grinned cruelly as he wrapped the end of the rope he had been holding around his own wrist. "If I fall, this pretty little lady falls with me. Now, put the guns down."

"Better do as he says, lad," Dunmar sighed.

Clifton cackled when he saw Chad's face etched with anxiety for Sarah. Chad slowly lowered his rifle to the ground in front of him.

"Now, step back," Clifton Pruitt growled.

When Chad stepped back, the outlaw grabbed up the rifle and aimed it at the young Ranger's head.

His brother shouted at him. "Get the other gun first! There'll be time for that in a minute."

"No!" Clifton yelled through gritted teeth. "I've been waitin' fer a moment like this!" Stepping closer to Chad, Clifton snarled, "Down on yer knees, boy. I want you down on yer knees."

Chad glared back at the man without flinching. "I'll not get down on my knees to the likes of you," he declared evenly.

The enraged Pruitt swung the rifle barrel striking the taller man across the jaw. Chad's knees swayed slightly but he remained standing.

"Chad!" Dunmar commanded. "Kneel down, lad!"

Chad looked at his uncle, his vision blurred slightly from being dazed by the blow. He couldn't believe what his uncle was asking him to do.

"Kneel down, I say," Dunmar repeated emphatically. "It's what your grandfather would want you to do."

"That's right, kid, listen to the old man and kneel down to the great Clifton Pruitt."

"We don't have time for this foolishness," Rayburn exclaimed angrily. "Get the other gun."

Still watching his uncle closely, Chad finally realized what he was trying to tell him. Slowly, he knelt down on one knee.

Sarah's feet were so close to the edge, she could feel small stones slipping out from under her. She was afraid to move a muscle. Then she noticed Chad's hand going down beside the top of his knee-high moccasin. His eyes met hers.

"Now he's kneeling," Rayburn growled. "Get the other gun and bring it to me!"

Clifton was relishing the moment so much he ignored his brother's angry command. This so infuriated Rayburn he moved toward Dunmar's gun still holding Sarah tightly as a shield. When he did, the young woman's feet were again on solid ground.

Dunmar took a step toward Rayburn, which caught Clifton's attention for a split second. Still grinning, the outlaw swung the rifle barrel toward Uncle Gib to warn him back. It was the chance the young Ranger was waiting for.

Springing like a cat, Chad threw his shoulder into Clifton's midsection, knocking him flat and sending the gun flying out of his hand. Dunmar moved as swiftly as a man half his age and scooped up his Colt before Rayburn could reach it. Having drawn his knife from the scabbard at the top of his moccasin, Chad landed a bone-jarring punch to Clifton's jaw with knuckles hardened in a tight grip around the knife handle.

Pruitt sank back unconscious at the same moment that Chad spotted Rayburn moving back to the brink of the chasm carrying Sarah with him. But this time Chad was only a foot away and instantly on his feet. Chad and Dunmar both reached out for the young woman as Rayburn tried to tear her away from their grasp. In doing so, his foot slipped, and for a heart-stopping moment the man teetered on the edge with Sarah. In a flash, Dunmar grabbed enough of her coat sleeve to pull her back and separate her from Rayburn's clutches.

For a split second, Chad caught sight of the rope between them. With one swift slash his sharp knife severed the rope and Sarah fell back against him. Pruitt's momentum carried the outlaw out over the edge and he careened out of sight, too startled to cry out.

Sarah turned into Chad's arms and he held her tightly, pulling her back from the edge. The couple stood for a long moment trying to catch their breath. Then she held up her hands, and he carefully cut the rope from her wrists. With that, the girl threw her arms around him and held on to him for dear life.

Luke scrambled over a rock, found Chad's rifle, and standing next to Dunmar, grinned down at the unconscious Clifton. In a moment, when Sarah's racing pulse began to calm, she remembered Mr. Medina.

27

Clifton Pruitt and Paxton were trussed up so tightly they couldn't move. Chad and his uncle brought Rayburn up out of the cave. He had suffered a broken leg and arm but managed to survive the fall. Yarnell had not fared as well, breaking his neck and dying instantly. They buried him in the cave.

The next half-hour all efforts were centered around getting down to their injured friend and bringing him back up out of the cave. The farmhand had broken his leg, suffered a lot of bruises, was very hungry and thirsty, but otherwise was all right.

Luke and Sarah sat beside Mr. Medina, who was propped up against a rock, two pieces of driftwood splinting his leg. Pepper lay close to his master with his head on the man's lap.

Hector told them he had fallen through on the sloped side and ended up sliding down the rough sixty-foot rock surface. He seemed thankful to have been saved from the cave that had occupied so many of his thoughts since seeing the parchment map.

Thinking about the map now, the man motioned for Luke to lean closer. He then pulled a large gold coin out of his pocket and placed it in the boy's hand.

"What's this?" Luke gasped. "Did you find the treasure?"

Medina smiled. "Es possible. That coin and this was passed down to me from my grandfather."

Pulling a piece of parchment from the inside of his shirt, he handed it to Luke. The boy opened it quickly to discover that it looked like the other parchment Pruitt had stolen.

Medina placed a wrinkled brown hand on Luke's and said, "The map Señor Macklin showed me was torn from this many, many years ago. At the bottom here, what do you see?"

Luke looked closely. "It looks like the letters *NAND BEXAR.*"

Medina nodded. "Do you remember seeing the letters at the bottom of the other piece of parchment?"

"Let me think," Luke puzzled. "Oh yeah, *FERDI.*"

"Si." Medina smiled. "Ferdinand Bexar, un conquistador con Coronado, one of Coronado's soldiers and my ancestor."

"What?" Luke and Sarah chorused. Luke continued, "But you said you saw the map once as a boy and that a relative of a scout for Coronado gave the map to an old Indian who gave it to your great-grandmother's grandfather."

Medina nodded wearily. "Lo siento, hijo. I'm sorry I didn't tell you the truth, but I have been searching for many, many years for this place. That's why I was here when I met your family. I never let anyone know that I had half of the map or that it was my ancestor who drew it. You saw what happened to the old prospector who let people know he had a treasure map.

"I had told the story so many years I almost forgot the truth until Señor Macklin showed me that map. Now I know."

"Know?" Luke asked in an awed whisper.

"Si."

Everyone was listening intently as Medina went on. "As I lay on the floor of the cave, I found this in the dirt nearby."

Luke took a piece of metal from the man and held it up so the moonlight could strike the image stamped on it. He held up the first coin next to it and realized they were identical.

"You did find it!" the boy exclaimed.

"I believe in my heart that this is the place, but everything except this coin is buried under fallen rock. This coin tells me I am right. My search is over. The legend of my ancestors is true. Even though I will never see anything more than these two coins, they have led me to discover something more important."

"What's that?" Luke's question lay in everyone's mind.

"That I have wasted many years searching. I have no family, no children to pass my inheritance to. In the end, I could have died holding this cold lifeless coin but having true riches right close by. When I was in the cave, my greatest sorrow was not that the gold was buried forever. My greatest sorrow was that I was not dying in my room with my friends the Prestons close by."

Even the night sky couldn't hide Hector's tear-filled eyes. "The last three years with your family have been happy for me," the man went on. "This cursed gold almost ended it all. I am happy God has given me another chance. He has made me see that the real treasure is this life in this land and its people. If the Prestons will stay, I will stay. I believe it is where we belong."

Epilogue

The night of December 13, 1841, was crisp and clear. An air of excitement filled the streets of Austin. In honor of the new administration taking office, both Texas and American flags adorned the Senate chamber. Also prominently displayed was the Mexican flag captured at the Battle of San Jacinto on April 21, 1836, when Santa Anna surrendered to Sam Houston and Texas became a free republic.

Earlier in the day, Sam Houston had taken the oath of office as President of the Republic and Edward Burleson had been sworn in as Vice President. With the formal business out of the way, everyone was prepared to celebrate heartily. The capitol building was crowded with citizens dressed in their finest.

Dunmar had helped Chad bring the three outlaws in to Austin. With the judge in town for the festivities, a trial and judgment would take place before the week was out.

Regardless of the stressful events of the past day and night, the Prestons decided to carry on with their plans to attend the inaugural ball.

Mr. Medina preferred to stay on the farm with Pepper, claiming that he would be glad for the peace and quiet. After all, he wouldn't be able to do much dancing for a while with his broken leg anyway.

With the prisoners secured in the jail, Chad and his uncle had dressed in new suits to escort Sarah and her mother to the capitol. Luke was allowed to join them. With a few slight alterations, he was able to wear one of his father's good suits. He proudly tugged at his lapels as he walked along, now the man of the Preston family. Sarah looked like a vision in her pink satin ball gown, and Chad stood tall and very handsome in his new suit. They made a stunning couple.

While music filled the air and couples took their places on the floor, Mariah and Gibson sat along the side to watch. Observing her daughter and the handsome young Texas Ranger glide past them circling to the strains of a waltz, Mariah put her hand on Dunmar's arm. He looked at her to see tears welling in her eyes.

"What is it?" he asked in concern, covering her hand with his own.

"They're no longer children, are they?" she asked with a wistful smile.

"No. No, they're not," he agreed with a sigh. "They're the future of this Texas, m'lady. And with the likes of them—and you—it's going to be the grandest place in this whole world."